Praise for *The Cartography of Others,* Fin.

'McNamara's work has a fierce, vital beat, her stories robust yet finely worked, her voice striking in its confidence and originality. She writes with sensuous precision and a craft that is equally precise. This is fiction that can stand up in any company.'

Hilary Mantel

'Catherine McNamara's writing is superb, this latest collection presents a unique way to talk about displacement and sensuality.'

Eric Akoto, Editor-in-Chief *Litro*

'Catherine McNamara's haunting stories map landmarks of psychological encounter. Hers is an international canvas, marking the points where contemporary lives cross with sensuality and finesse. Beautiful work.'

Cathy Galvin, Director Word Factory

'An enchanting smorgasbord of addictive stories. These beautifully sensual tales linger. Catherine McNamara's writing is vital and insightful.'

Irenosen Okojie

Praise for *Love Stories for Hectic People,*
Best Short Story Collection Saboteur Awards 2021

'I rarely receive a review copy, sit right down and read most of it in one sitting. Catherine McNamara's *Love Stories for Hectic People* had me doing that. It's a beguiling collection of flash fiction that's as briskly inventive and various as the form demands, embracing sensuality and ugliness in equal measure, and darting from one international encounter to another… Love lies at the heart of the matter, each time round, but grief and brutality are there too. "The quixotic animals and wise elders with spectacularly gnarled toes…"'

Michael Caines, Editor *Brixton Review of Books*

Praise for *Pelt and Other Stories*

'Every story in this collection is a delightful surprise. McNamara's lucid prose shines on every page, creating stories that are both difficult to put down, and unforgettable.'

Chika Unigwe, New York Times Editor's Choice *On Black Sisters' Street*

'I opened the book and found myself lost within an in-depth exploration of humankind that didn't sweeten the reality of the world, but instead showed the true nature of humans.'

Sabotage Reviews

The Carnal Fugues

Selected Stories

Catherine McNamara

PUNCHER & WATTMANN

First published in 2023
Published by Puncher and Wattmann
PO Box 279
Waratah NSW 2298

https://www.puncherandwattmann.com
web@puncherandwattmann.com

ISBN   9781922571748

Cover image © rawpixel (ID: 3820426)
    www.rawpixel.com/image/3820426/illustration-psd-sticker-flower-abstract
Cover design by Miranda Douglas
Edited by Ed Wright
Typesetting by Morgan Arnett
Printed by Lightning Source International

A catalogue record for this book is available from the National Library of Australia *for my father*

Contents

Ah, only the leaves! But in the west,
In the west I see a redness come
Over the evening's burning breast —
— 'Tis the wound of love goes home!

D.H. Lawrence 'Cruelty and Love'

Adieu, Mon Doux Rivage

There are four of us on the boat. Jean-Luc and myself, and the Belgian music manager Raoul Vidal with his Japanese soprano wife Mieko Inoue. Raoul, big as a cupboard, stands on the deck with arms folded, squinting back at the coast. After a few days he's discarded his shirt. When Mieko comes on deck he bends over her like a poised wave and whatever they say is soundless. Jean-Luc has read that she sang at Covent Garden twice, but he is pretty sure her career has flatlined. Jean-Luc has a nose for these things. He was the drummer in my old band in Marseilles.

They've booked a week-long cruise around Corsica, emailed me strict diet instructions (no gluten, no sugar or cheese, preferably grilled fish). Looking at Raoul, I'd say he was brought up on *moules frites* and tank-ards of beer. I once toured in Belgium with an all-female group and this is the truth: they fry pig's blood sausages in butter. This is something that requires an explanation.

Raoul has sought me out a couple of times when I am having a quick puff at the stern. He has a range of slight criticisms and needs. Do you have sanitary napkins? Could you chop the cabbage in the salad a little finer for Mieko's digestion? All over his body, his skin has surrendered to the sharp summer sun and explodes in blisters wishing to be pricked. His nose is peeling and he doesn't care, which in turn means that Mieko doesn't either.

He asks, 'Do you have any copies of *The New Yorker*?'

I shake my head. I imagine he is used to long lunches.

Their suite at the bow of the boat must be agreeable to Mieko. She stays there a lot. On my way to the laundry cupboard I think I hear a sound – a voice ascending – but this ceases on its path. The boat moves ahead with a steady rolling. When I back into her with clean linen in the galley, I hear a word that is released almost inaudibly, at great cost: 'Sorry.' She looks at me at with my pile of clean towels and fresh sheets. It seems as though she wants to take this word back. I should ask if she wants anything, or remind her that I have seasickness tablets if she feels unwell. She is carrying a big hat and a Japanese novel, wearing loose ivory trousers and a cotton shirt. Most probably because my ragged blue-painted nails are on show, and Jean-Luc says I have feet like a platypus, I have made it my mission to see the opera singer's toes. Mieko wears a pair of closed black espadrilles and her feet are pressed into their jute spirals.

Jean-Luc has given Raoul a Michel Houellebecq novel in French, the one where they massacre the tourists. Raoul sits on a bench and reads it through like a man on a train, his back in burning shreds. Mieko drapes herself on a deckchair, fully clothed. For a long while she does not read. They sit far from each other, uninvolved. Before it's time to prepare lunch I sit with Jean-Luc at the stern. We've just come through a rough patch. Jean-Luc misses the band life. He's come to sailing late and has doubts on the water. He doesn't like me questioning him and stresses out when we anchor or come into port. Jean-Luc puts his hand on my thigh. As his fingers dig in, I watch the fuzzy-edged scorpion inked into his skin. His nails are broken and black. The wind is high, higher than he'd like, and he has trimmed both sails as we cut as close as possible to the coast. We can see the point of Nonza now, the village stranded high above the pebbled grey beach as though washed up in a storm. Once we are anchored in the bay I will set up lunch on deck, the *sole meunière* Mieko just tolerates, with an avocado salad that perhaps she will not. Though initially she said she would eat prawns, her face dropped yesterday when I grilled a dozen scampi. Raoul removed the platter.

'There has been a misunderstanding,' he said, after tilting the plate in the boat's wash. 'Mieko does not eat prawns.'

If the couple nap after lunch, and perhaps swim at the beach through the afternoon, I will have time to borrow Manon's scooter in the village and do a quick shop at the bigger town of Saint-Florent. Our supplies are dwindling. Jean-Luc removes his hand, eases off the sheets, prepares to tack the vessel and veer in towards the coast. I watch his tattoos, some of them are busty women who seem to be feasting upon his physique. We don't speak much when we are at work, not even when we are anchored for the night in a star-swept bay. If his heavy arm reaches around me it feels almost inanimate, like a stranger's cool skin.

Though Jean-Luc hasn't entered me in a month we have laid bets on who will hear Mieko and Raoul at it first. People get frisky on boats, in confined spaces. I see it happen always. We have had a man and woman groaning and growling on deck for hours. In the morning they were sedate, reading books and newspapers. The woman had a dental issue and had to be taken ashore.

Mieko stretches up an arm and unfurls a hand against the glare of the sail. Raoul looks over to her, watching the boom move across as the vessel turns. Jean-Luc's orchestration is gentle. The sails rattle like stage curtains above the small soprano, then the wind throws them into shape. Mieko's hat falls back as she stares up into the grandeur of the mast. We are no longer shouldering against the open sea but are propelled to the land in the bellies of long emerald waves without crests. These make a lulling wash-ing sound. Mieko's hand falls away and she raises her book in the glossy light. Raoul resumes rifling through his novel.

Jean-Luc tramps across the deck to see to the jib and I hold the tiller while watching his body. He was with another woman in his prime. I have seen the photographs of his thick hair and bright teeth and leather jackets. Jean-Luc came down to the south from Le Havre on a motorbike.

—

After lunch Jean-Luc untethers the dinghy and rows me ashore. Mieko and Raoul retire below deck – the meal has gone smoothly. There are two other boats at anchor but the vast beach is empty. It is the hottest hour of the day and the island looks wrought and faded, pressed against the distance even as it begins to loom. Bushfires will roar down these hills again. Beneath us, the sea floor of black-green pebbles inks the water with cold tones and the waves are dark and sharp. It is an awkward, remote place that Jean-Luc likes. Guests enjoy viewing the dramatic ascension of the land, but few make the climb to Nonza to have a gelato or see the sea stretching in a gauzy endless slate. Most want to move on to l'Île-Rousse or Calvi where there is a marina and nightclubs. Our guests like to get dressed up at night.

Jean-Luc pitches the dinghy onto the stones and when we kiss good-bye my tongue flicks into his mouth. The water withdraws, fizzing over wet black knuckles. I step out barefoot and push the boat off, holding up my sandals and shopping bag. There are a few sunbathers in the strip of shadow under the gouged cliff thrusting the village into the air. The pebbles shimmer all the way to the scrub where the path begins. Some are oily gems, others are lozenges the size of children's feet. I drop my things. With Jean-Luc staring at me, rowing solidly, I strip down and wade into the water, diving under the bucking waves.

Two hours later I am back on the beach with my full shopping bag, grateful that Manon's brother Pietro took me all the way to Saint-Florent in his van. We've had two beers at the summit – Corsican red beer brewed with chestnuts – that spill through my head. I've hiked down the path at breakneck speed to save the groceries from spoiling, and torn across the hot stones to the shore. I see Jean-Luc on deck and wave for him to row out. There is a man's head in the water which I recognize as Raoul's. The seabed carves away quickly and Raoul thrashes through the waves, letting them belt over his head which pushes out of the foam, his fair hair whipped around his cranium. His red face splutters and he spews water from his mouth, paddling as more waves crash upon him. For a minute, I worry he is in trouble and I will have to set down my bag and rescue him. But then his body scrambles out of the surf. He is naked. He throws himself face down in the shallows as water streams over his glowing back. His white bottom has a surprisingly round shape.

I look back out to the boat to see if Jean-Luc has registered me waving. He is speaking to Mieko, which hardly seems possible. Mieko, dressed in baggy black trousers and a long-sleeved cream top, stands watching her husband in the water. Soon enough, Jean-Luc is metres away from me in

12

the dinghy and I hand over the shopping. There is wine to chill for this evening. I am certain Raoul will succumb to chilled Sancerre. I toss my sundress and sandals into the bag and push Jean-Luc off. He looks at my body as though it is an outline on the landscape.

Mieko appears for dinner in a floral dress that is not becoming. It is as though she is indulging Raoul, who may have Belgian floral leanings. Watching him in the surf may have invited her hands to hover over this dress. I prefer her in dramatic blacks and whites that denude her features. Mieko totters across the deck in a pair of low gold heels, an expensive mesh covering her toes and the fretwork of both feet. There are contrasting copper and white threads woven through the sheer substance. I see the glint of nail varnish, but there is no sense of shape or proportion. Before the week is up, I will see Mieko's toes.

Mieko refuses a glass of wine and walks the length of the deck. I wonder when she will get cabin fever. After a few days they all do, they have to set foot on the ground. Today, she had no wish to go ashore. I suspect she'll come back on board with shopping bags when we sail on to Calvi. The soprano likes to shop.

Jean-Luc has anchored a little further from the shore for the night and has gone below to take a shower. The lights of Nonza sway high above us. I wish I were up there with Pietro and Manon in the piazza drinking beer. Strains of folk music cascade towards us, from the bar a guy from Ajaccio has built on the cliffs. Waves barely stir. The forecast is for more of this. Jean-Luc joins me after his shower and I know he is not relaxed. He, too, would like to go ashore, but he would sleep alone in the dunes. He kisses my cheek, takes a glass of wine over to Mieko. She accepts it from him and they clink glasses. I watch them, the man I love and the tiny floral soprano. I haven't asked Jean-Luc what roles she played at Covent Garden, whether she was allowed to stray from the confines of her race. I imagine Mieko in a kimono with a powdered visage. I see her collapsed in fabrics on the stage with a trickle of fake blood.

Raoul climbs the steps. He wears a loud shirt and is redder and more blistered than yesterday, his washed hair feathery. He is exhausted. His face droops and he snatches up a glass of wine. Raoul asks me what is for dinner but doesn't listen to my reply. He tells me he has just finished his book. He says, 'Did I already ask you if you had copies of *The New Yorker*?'

I tell him he has, and I'm sorry I don't. I ask him if he liked Houellebecq's novel.

'Not much,' he says.

He puts out his glass for a refill, looks across the deck and notices Mieko's dress. For a moment, his eyes dampen.

I ask him what he usually reads.

'I don't have time to read,' he says.

At the table this evening I see Mieko's face close up once again. We have passed the three-day marker, where people's barriers soften and they remember our names. Raoul is satisfied my cooking is delicate enough for Mieko's tricky digestion and Mieko no longer looks aghast at her plate. I watch food entering Mieko's mouth. The crêpe has just started around her eyes though she has a young woman's taut plump skin, well-hydrated and radiant. Her face is a broad palette which I can see would transform in light, with song. Her eyes are exquisite marbles that reveal kindness in their spheres. When Mieko smiles at Raoul, he looks a better man. A third bottle of wine is opened, this one a local rosé from the burnished hills. Raoul raises a glass and makes a toast to his wife. Jean-Luc's hand smooths my thigh. I try to remember my bet with Jean-Luc and who wagered whether Day Three would be the night. I see Raoul's eyes slide over Mieko, over her lifted breasts, into the folds of flowers. Dishevelled, they spill with veneration.

I go below deck for our desserts, a crème caramel made with almond milk. I arrange my tray, putting a bottle of Muscat under my arm. I stand there, smelling wood varnish and the bleach in the cupboards, the whiff of diesel at this end of the boat. I listen to their voices above. I wonder if

14

what Mieko and Raoul will rediscover tonight is any different from the clumsy relishing we have seen many times over, each couple so mortal under the night skies, so afflicted by the feigned simplicity of sleeping on a powerful boat. When I reach the deck they are dancing. The folk music drifts on the air and Mieko is pressed into Raoul's oversized embrace. Jean-Luc holds his glass. I distribute the desserts and slip beneath his shoulder. The geography of his body is weary. I worry that this life will make him ill one day. I nuzzle his rough cheek, his neck.

Raoul sways back to the table with his wife tucked beside him. Mieko's face is bright, new dimples have appeared in her cheeks. She takes a few spoonfuls of her dessert then dabs her lips. Clearly, her doubts about my cooking have come home. Raoul empties his dish, goes to the stern where he pisses into the motionless water and Mieko can't contain her laughs. Raoul brings up a bottle of Calvados from their suite and fills everybody's tumblers. His wife lies down along the seat, nestles into his lap with her eyes open. I see it is a very long time since they have made love.

—

Our band had quite a following. There was a year that my voice was good and we'd taken a string of Cassandra Wilson songs and transposed them into higher keys. Jean-Luc and I were the only ones who had any music theory, so we worked on the songs together. He could play classical piano as well as drum like a god. He could also dance. After the gig we'd go to nightclubs in Marseilles, the darkest, meanest ones with Algerian bouncers who would push a guy in the chest, knock him down in the street. There were absinthe cocktails in dirty glasses and Jean-Luc unrolled our magic pills from his trouser hem. We would dance until we were raw and dawn spat on the harbour.

The boat cruises, they were my idea. I thought we were getting washed out. I thought that one day Jean-Luc would wake up and walk out the door, he already had left a wife and kids in the north. I thought the band was fading and we were seeping into the crowd. There was a fuzz in between songs and you knew they were waiting for something bigger. I started to get scared. In the end Sonia and Beaté brought in a half-Tunisian girl and it fed them.

I know Jean-Luc will want to sell up at the end of the season. And I'll say yes, just to stop his soul from getting any harder, anything to the change the flavour of his eyes.

I wake on the cusp of dawn. Jean-Luc has pulled over the bed sheet and I am stiff from lying for hours in the damp. I lift the sheet and trace a finger across his shoulder, down along the fold of his back, the crevice of his arse, his hairy thighs. He doesn't feel a thing. I tuck him in and rise. I won't make noise now, but I still have the dishes to do from last night. I didn't hear Raoul and Mieko come downstairs beyond their murmuring on the sofa after dinner, so I'm pretty sure Jean-Luc has won our bet.

I go up on deck. This is the time when the water is a silken mass you could glide into, never needing oxygen again. I have always known I would end my life in water. Of course they are here, under a blanket that doesn't come from the boat. I can't see how their bodies are entwined, whether Raoul simply cradles her from behind, or if their faces are mirrored together, sharing breath. In a band, you see the way people sleep. I light a cigarette and I guess the smoke travels over to them. There is not an odour, not a sound written on the morning. Mieko pulls away the cover and her eyes flutter, she pulls it up again. I sit down and inhale. Sleeping out here can't be good for a soprano's voice.

I head to the galley to start the dishes. Above, I hear moving limbs, speech. There's not much you can't hear on a boat. She speaks so quietly to him that I still don't know what language they use to communicate in intimacy. I hear them step down to their cabin and the door clicks shut. I hope we can make it to l'Île-Rousse today. There are friends I'd like to see in town. Jérome, who runs a bar now; Mélanie, who sells second-hand books in the square. I doubt that Mieko and Raoul are browsing types but there is a sophisticated food market under an open-air structure just off the piazza. It has thick chalky columns and the grace of a temple.

I think of going back to stir Jean-Luc but instead I spray down the surfaces. A boat is always grimy, so even this doesn't help much. All metal develops green encrustations, all wood swells beneath its thick varnish. I bring a pot of coffee upstairs, the flan I bought at Saint-Florent and a basket of yesterday's croissants. There is a splash from one of the other anchored boats. A man has dived in. I drink a coffee, remove my shirt and ease off the ladder, paddling softly. The dry mountains are purple, while Nonza sits on her outcrop. I hear cars in the village taking the tight turn before the rust-coloured church dedicated to Sainte Julie, the patron saint of the island. It is so beautiful that one of my deepest wishes has always been to have that name, but I do not. Perhaps my life would not be so different if I did. Inside the church there is a painted, beckoning statue of the young woman whose short life ended in torture on these shores. I backstroke to the beach and lie stretched out on tiny pebbles, a carpet of beads. I see Mieko on deck wearing a beige shift, then Jean-Luc, who sits down to speak with her.

By the time I join them on board Raoul has surfaced. He is wearing a crushed business shirt. He looks cranky. His hand shakes before it lifts a glass. He dunks a croissant into his *café au lait* and eats more slowly than he did yesterday. Mieko sips the tea she brought herself. Neither of them wears sunglasses. Her kneecaps are just visible and they are finer than I had thought, encouraging me to imagine that her feet are sinuous sculptures. I see short strands on her almost hair-free legs. On her feet are the same espadrilles as before.

As he stares at a piece of flan on his plate, Raoul announces that he and Mieko would like to go ashore. In fact, he says, this area pleases them a lot. Jean-Luc and I look at each other. The sun, bound to her course, already makes a blazing sweep of the bay. The sea here is windless and there is no shade on deck. Raoul says they'd like to spend less time at the other ports along the way and relax here, along the unending grey beach he now points to while Mieko nods. They'd like to investigate the bottom of the cliffs. They're keen to hike up to the village. Raoul says he has heard about this place. Perhaps he read something in a newspaper supplement.

I am already thinking of the long trips to Saint-Florent for supplies rather than the easy walk to the supermarkets at l'Île-Rousse and Calvi. But Jean-Luc seems mesmerised by the idea. I see him unlocking. He is pleased to anchor here because the pressure is off for him.

Mieko reappears in trousers and a navy long-sleeved top, wearing a hat and carrying a large bag woven of the finest straw. Jean-Luc helps her into the dinghy. Raoul, wearing his open business shirt and a pair of baggy shorts, has trouble transferring his weight to the smaller vessel and Mieko grasps the gunwales as the boat rocks. They set off. I light a cigarette watching them, watching as seagulls swoop for crumbs I have thrown into the sea. Raoul carries her ashore, sets her down and rights her. Gingerly, she takes a few steps like a cat out of a cage, then advances to the cliffs, Raoul following. I turn away to take the breakfast things below deck. When I come up I see Jean-Luc has overturned the dinghy on the beach and walked a few hundred metres in the other direction. I see Mieko and Raoul as figures beneath the earthen mass of the cliff face, treading over rocks to the beach that lies further on. They look like a pair of runaways.

When Jean-Luc returns I am dozing under the canopy I have set up under the boom. His hand runs along my thigh but then stops as I awake. He climbs over me, naked, turning me face-up so our bodies fit together. He is aroused. He slides across my bikini pants and pumps hard, gripping my body. He kneels back, his genitals in a dark, wet cleft. He leans over and kisses one of my platypus feet.

—

Mieko told Jean-Luc she lost her voice while performing in Paris a year ago. She was onstage singing when her vocal chords became two arrow shafts in her throat. She was taken away in an ambulance. She thinks the video is on YouTube. She asked Jean-Luc not to watch. We have no signal here, but I know that Jean-Luc never would. Mieko said that she and Raoul had been married for eight years. Normally, they went to Osaka in the summer, but her parents had recently died. Raoul had no family left in Leuven, except a sister he didn't get along with. They were childless. They lived in Paris in the 14ᵗʰ arrondissement. Mieko was a singing teacher for Japanese students at the international school and the children of diplomats. She hoped to get her voice back, but the process had been lengthy and disappointing so far. Doctors had been unable to diagnose a specific problem apart from the strain of major performances. Mieko herself said she suffered from nerves, and a Japanese doctor in Paris had been treating her. They were here because he had advised a week on a boat in the Mediterranean.

Jean-Luc tells me that they won't be coming back until late. He showed them the steep path to Nonza and told them to order pizza at the bar, to get a cool table by the fountain. He said Raoul should tell them they were from one of the sailing boats anchored offshore. They'd get treated better that way.

The morning passes and we do not see them cross the stones. The shade has been stripped from the inlet when I see their heads bobbing on the water for a long time. Mieko comes out and she is wearing a white one-piece costume. She sits down, opening a small umbrella, covering her legs with a towel. Raoul thrashes in the calm sea. He backstrokes out a fair way, then frog-kicks to the shore where he floats with his ruddy stomach in the air. He lurches out of the water, throws himself on the pebbles.

There must be a cusp of shade growing in the rocks and they transfer there, no longer visible. I open a bottle of white wine and prepare a salad. Jean-Luc takes a mask and dives into the water to remove seaweed from the propeller. When he returns, we finish the bottle and he lazes on deck. I start rereading the Houellebecq Raoul has left on the table.

It is quiet at first, a vocalise more than a song. Mieko has returned to the shore in her white swimsuit, a sarong around her waist. Raoul sits half in the water, letting the waves slap his side. Mieko bends over and stays down for a long time. She rises, begins the vocalise again, a heartbreaking crescendo. Jean-Luc looks up, growing aware of the sound.

The breasts of the young Sainte Julie were cut off by Romans stationed at Nonza when she refused to worship their pagan gods. Corsicans believe her severed breasts were dashed against a rock wall below the village, and this produced a spring called *la fontaine aux mamelles*. Expectant mothers now come to this place as barefoot pilgrims to secure their supply of milk, it is on the trail leading up from the beach. Sainte Julie's body was draped on a fig tree and all versions of the story say a dove flew from her mouth at the moment of her death.

The Wild Beasts of the Earth Will Adore Him

My new colleagues were backstabbing and merciless and came through inching, dust-choked traffic from the hinterlands to work. In turn, they wasted no time in blasting each other over milky Liptons in mugs or warm Guinness bottles passed across the desk. Very quickly the office mystery was established as Meredith. Meredith was creamy white, with coiled blonde hair dropping down her back and the way she moved was staunch. I was informed that Meredith slept with her dogs.

The dimensions of the Accra agency were tighter than the huge Jo'burg office where I'd been stationed before, but there was just as much piss-taking with the accounts. Everyone else was sheer black except the caramel secretary. I was looked at warily (mixed-race, shaven head, *Eraserhead* T-shirt) for good reason among their yellowing business shirts, and they didn't ease up until Kwame Djoleto made a lewd crack and they could see I wasn't a jerk.

More than once, Meredith glided from the staffroom with a flowery mug and wearing a pleated apricot skirt, a shade of Sunday bazaar. Someone blurted that the husband had left her for a Nigerian hooker three years ago and she was frozen here, the sickly salary better than any amputated return to her confectioned home town. Kwame said the hooker had been squealing on top and Meredith had burst in with a gun from the kitchen, the dogs howling and the husband in grovelling tears.

This brought forth light, worn-through sniggers.

The company had rented me a house off a road of better streets and I was told that Meredith was a neighbour. She'd had to scale down when the husband's salary moved away. I didn't envisage us having stilted drinks on the porch but Meredith, one afternoon while handing in a budget esti-mate, said it was a tranquil part of town. Ingrained along her forehead and the grooves either side of her mouth were deepening lines of hardiness. I asked what breed her dogs were.

'Labradors,' she said. 'Black Labradors. They suffer in this heat.'

Never once in my life had I owned a dog, wished for a dog, even studied a dog. I find them breathy.

In the mornings a group of local soldiers jogged along the street in front of my place. This area of town backed onto the sprawling military camp with its crooked fences and colonial bungalows. The soldiers carried guns across their bodies and shouted marines' chants as they jogged to the end of the street. I watched their caps and olive shirts through the blinds. Some time afterwards, just before the driver swung around the corner to take me to work, Meredith engineered two sleek black shapes down the empty street. Their spines snaked along, their thick tails levered and whacked around, their mouths were large, pink, wet.

—

I soon realised the nucleus of my clan of colleagues was not Kwame Djoleto, who made a lot of noise and was wide and vigorous, but a thin man named Solomon who did little more than retrieve the post. Solomon sat straight-backed on his seat. He walked with a polio limp. A son of Solomon's had died recently and the funeral notice was still on the staff noticeboard, showing a bright boy with buck teeth. Though I was the boss I realised that it was Solomon who commanded the team's fluctuations and temperament. He looked congenial, long-suffering.

All hands came on deck any time there was a photo shoot as these were few and far between, dogged by many interpretations of the theme at hand. Take cooking oil. Weeks were spent on divergent storyboards, meetings were left in disgust. Brainstorming in the overheated conference room took on the dimensions of outright warfare as each colleague within the creative department (and several others without) unfolded his or her heartfelt story of Frylove. Kwame wanted a romantic scene: husband comes home, embraces wife from behind while she is cooking. There was a valid debate about the trappings of the kitchen, about whether the wife should wear Western dress; whether the husband should be fat or slim. How dark their skins should be. I noticed Meredith paying attention in a freefall way. Was she thinking about her dogs? When a handful of ideas had been cobbled together, Solomon was consulted and the fine-boned man mentioned his preferences while twisting a leaky pen. Kwame's scene, for example, didn't involve any offspring. The grasp of the husband could be perceived as sexual (guffaws). Western dress was better, though the food should be rigorously local. As Kwame attempted baldly to defend his idea I stopped scribbling and saw that Meredith's eyes like a watershed were upon me. But I was just in the way of her blinding thoughts. It was probably not the dogs she was thinking about.

Discussion reignited in a bullying way when Kwame insisted upon the wife's fair tones and narrow waist. I glimpsed Meredith roll her eyes.

The two black Labradors were also walked in the evening. That was when I sat on the porch with a neat gin. Like Meredith's, my spouse had taken off. But with good reason. I hadn't had an email since. I watched Meredith's arid walk behind the two animals with their slack leather leads. The dogs progressed slowly, heat-stricken in the musky air, heads bobbing, tongues gluey. Meredith filled out a tracksuit and wore a peaked cap.

I was still sitting there in the dark eating peanuts when Kwame and two of the others made the visit they had been promising, wearing tight open shirts. Kwame was carrying a further bottle of gin. Their faces were beaded with sweat and the youngest man wiped his temples with a handkerchief. Kwame looked up at the rusted fan blades suspended from the teak-cladded awning and said that Solomon knew a good electrician in Tudu. The fluorescent light made my skin look green, while they were a trio of dark faces with violet flints. I brought out extra glasses.

Kwame drove us up through the suburbs to a nightclub called the Red Onion. I held onto a bottle of beer as women became wavy before me. Cocks were crowing when with ringing ears we came outside into the damp. I wondered whether Meredith, in the arms of her Labradors, was awake.

Solomon was absent and the office was in disarray. It was not known whether it was something connected to the son's recent funeral, or whether fresh problems had arisen in his household. No one knew where Solomon lived. No one knew which *trotro* he caught to work. We went ahead with the Frylove photo shoot. The kitchen of the house next door served as a set. Lights on stands were placed apart and Meredith positioned fans. But there was an uncertainty, a negligence, in the air. Everyone looked lethargic. Kwame snapped at the Frylove models under the hot lights. The woman who was the 'wife' snapped back at him and folded her arms, while the 'husband' slumped in a kitchen chair and sent text after text. Any sort of orchestration dispersed. Meredith came across with her folder, standing between Kwame and the woman. I couldn't understand Twi and didn't know if Meredith in all her years of living here had grasped their tongue. It didn't seem to be the case. As she led the woman up the hall to the bathroom I heard her say, 'Now just come this way, Nana Yaa. You don't want to spoil your makeup now.'

The model 'children' rolled up bits of paper and flicked them about the room.

As boss, I knew I had to call Kwame into line and re-establish the dynamic of the day. Kwame scowled at me in anticipation, his head swinging on his considerable neck as he looked around for Solomon among the helpers one last time. The maps under his armpits clung to his skin. He went over to the cooking pot and stirred the cold stew. He checked the yellow Frylove bottle was in sharp light. He told the unruly girl and boy to behave themselves or he would take them outside to beat them. After Jo'burg's tetchy egos and flimsy models, it was hard not to laugh.

Meredith brought the 'wife' back from the bathroom. They had agreed upon a tawny girl, far too young to have produced the pre-teens at the table. Meredith positioned her over the pot, showing the lumpy 'husband' how to clasp her. Kwame nodded. Someone had handed him a mug of tea. I waved away mine and watched the white woman giving a 'honey-I'm-home' embrace to the ticklish Frylove 'wife'.

The end of the day produced two feasible shots we uploaded onto the computer: 'The Hug' and 'At the Table', the latter an alternative that showed the mother arranging a platter of jollof rice and chicken on a printed tablecloth, flanked by husband and children. Given 'The Hug' was devoid of any sort of sexual or marketing charge, I preferred the rigid table shot with its acidic yellows and greens, its gasping comedian faces. There was an irresistible lyricism at the base of its poor logic and composition.

Kwame wasn't happy with either and roamed the set like a lost dog. Two weeks later the table shot, plus titles, was on billboards about the town.

Solomon refused to surface over the next few days and voices trailed along the corridors. Where did he come from? Was it Teshie? Did he catch a bus from Nungua? A chair was kept for him at the next round of meetings, where Kwame clashed severely with a colleague called Patrice. It was about a hair-straightening product, one of the agency's ongoing campaigns. Patrice's first ideas were overturned and sliced in the belly, then given a final pounding on the head. I noticed Meredith looked distracted, someone or something had pulled the plug on her concentration. The conference room was cramped and full of bad breath.

I watched Meredith walk the dogs in the evening and almost felt like calling out to her from my porch. One of the dogs seemed to lag a little, and directly outside my scrappy hedge she crouched to the road and massaged the dog's ears while the animal licked her face. I recoiled. The other dog turned around limply.

—

A staff member who travelled a long way into town along the coast had found a funeral notice on the *trotro*. It was Solomon's. The funeral was to take place the following week. Employees gathered in the office foyer and the poorly printed sheet was passed around. Kwame pushed into my office. Shaking in his hands was the streaky photograph showing Solomon's face tilted upward, his mouth open and front teeth tugged slightly out of line. It was clear that he was the father of the bright boy with buck teeth.

Kwame cast down the sheet of paper, taking out a handkerchief to wipe his face. His trousers had an oil stain on the thigh and I saw he had tiny, clenched ears that wanted to hear very little.

Meredith entered the office and examined the page with a depleted expression. Outside a man burst into tears while a woman named Comfort led a procession into the conference room, where sobbing and moaning began. Kwame followed his colleagues and I soon heard his voice lifting above the others in a reverent, stilted backwash. Meredith and I stood staring at each other. I felt as though I were bagged inside her head and looking at myself. I saw my jaw harden and lines rippling my forehead.

Meredith flushed and we followed the others into the room.

—

What I in no way expected was to see a hired *trotro* parked outside the office a few days later and a coffin being unloaded under Kwame's sweaty direction, then slipped through the narrow front doors. The driver squatted by a roadside tree in ragged shorts as staff members filed into the building after the swaying cargo.

Inside the conference room the tables were jammed together and I heard shoes scuffing and the creaking of wood. I stood transfixed in the doorway to my office, fingers hooked in the belt of my jeans. Meredith walked grimly to the staff room, came back holding a mug of tea. I heard the box jemmied open and there was a chasm of silence, a collective exhalation mixing with the aura of Solomon's embalmed body. A chemical smell arose. My stomach heaved. I turned away to my desk and switched on the monstrous air conditioner plugged into the wall. Then Kwame was at my back looking like a man plummeting, his fists empty and his face stripped. The whites of his eyes had red hairline cracks.

Solomon's face was puffy, like he was in the process of chewing a mouthful of food. His skin looked tightened, the lines on his forehead fleeting. The flesh between upper lip and nostrils was more rounded than it had been when he sat here twisting the leaky pen. He wore reading glasses, a beige suit, a bow tie, a late-1970s ruffled shirt. A part of my brain was laughing, scavenging this experience, while another examined the cracked leather shoes that were boats on his feet, the tennis socks, and wanted to buckle over. The body already looked flattened and false, a rasping snakeskin with all moisture erased, though there was oil or shea butter combed through his hair. I stood in line around the tables as each staff member waited for a moment with the perfumed corpse. When my turn came I spoke softly, a few words. But as I walked away I felt a powerful excavation building up in my body. I wanted to shit, or vomit, writhe on the ground, pluck my own eyes from my head. I wanted rapture before it would come to me. At the door I turned back to the coffin with a pit in my chest, currents shunting in the spongy ellipse of my brain, each organ inside of me vaporous. I sat on the loo for a good ten minutes, then poured gin for everybody.

Solomon's funeral notice joined that of his bright young son on the staff noticeboard and they became a pair of comrade saints. Staff members glanced at Solomon's easy-going manner in the photograph as they passed and Kwame, hands on hips in conversation, looked up to his quiet colleague as though for confirmation or advice. Kwame's aggression moved someplace else and Patrice's ideas for the hair-straightening campaign were revived.

—

There was excellent dope to be had in this country. After a string of demolishing hangovers I had organised a good supply of undoctored weed and smoked every evening. Kwame disapproved. He refused even the slightest puff, folding his arms like an old woman and curiously watching me filling a skin. The week after Solomon's funeral Kwame sat on my back porch and stared at me lighting up, his forearms on his thighs and his large hands thrown together. He eased back into the cushions to avoid the cloud I exhaled. He had no companions this evening. His shirt burst apart in scallops and dark ovals of his belly showed through. His chest was hairless and his neck had rings of flesh. His eyes caught on the rusty fan I had failed to have fixed, its blades tilted on their axis and the knot of wires escaping the dislodged plastic cup. I knew he was kicking himself for not finding out in which Tudu slum Solomon's electrician lived, before Solomon had died.

I inhaled again, beginning to feel the easy fissuring, the wandering explosions. I dropped my head back on the thick bamboo of the chair. Kwame shifted and I told him there were more beers in the fridge. He went into the kitchen and came back outside, uncapping the bottle tops in some mysterious local way, his movement wobbling the light given off by three candles on a saucer. As usual, there was no power. The neighbourhood lay black and dense beyond us. I inhaled a third time and the memory of love in my bowels, my brain rank with it, sprang forth inexplicably. My heart rate surged and I felt my body veering. I looked down at my belly and thighs, my arms on the varnished armrests.

Kwame stared into the darkness. In Solomon's absence the office staff clustered around him and I knew he came to sit here in silence. Perhaps he had begun to understand his own deference to the slim man, and the attention of listeners whenever Solomon had whispered his words. Kwame saw me studying him and he jerked around to point out a bright beacon of electricity up the road through the trees. A generator rattled loudly. It was the house where Meredith lived, he said.

Sniggering, I asked him who the hell had started the rumour about her sleeping with the dogs, whether it was some sort of fixation or score-settling, or a sick way of wanting the broad blonde woman.

'I did,' said Kwame.

His teeth shone and we both laughed loudly, crazily, until our laughs tailed off. I did not ask him why. I felt the full throttle of the overloaded spliff and wanted to roll downward, brakeless, curl in a ball, think of Solomon meeting the buck-toothed boy in the other world, on a corner somewhere in a place as merciless and rundown as this.

—

Meredith came to me with a problem. She said that Patrice's ideas for the hair-straightening campaign had been plagiarised. She pulled out an African-American magazine she had found in the staffroom, and I could see why Patrice's lavish storyboard had initially been slaughtered by Kwame. It was damned good. A light twinkled on above Patrice's head.

I convened a meeting in the conference room. I decided to exclude Meredith and not reveal my source. I sat there, Kwame and Patrice before me nursing tea, both bristling. I saw that their newfound collaboration had thin and knotted roots.

I swung around the magazine. Kwame glowered. Patrice's eyes popped out. Kwame instantly began a tirade in the local language which I allowed him to conclude. He apologised to me. But not to Patrice who sat glumly in the chair, his first gainful moments now stamped in the dust. He confessed he had found the magazine at his sister's house; she was just back from Atlanta.

Kwame shook his pointed finger in Patrice's face and both men shouted. I wondered whether I should have told Meredith to pipe down and forget about the magazine. But the company was a conglomerate, our work traversed borders; lawyers might have been flown out. I tapped my pen on the desk and neither of the men heeded me. I had a flash of the most galvanising moments in my extinguished married life. The sense of being a faceless, fleshless absentee in the room.

'Kwame,' I said.

Kwame pushed back his chair and stood. He suggested I sack Patrice on the spot.

'Otherwise I will be leaving here this noon,' Kwame said.

This is when I longed for Solomon's counsel. I knew enough of Kwame's volatility to avoid agitating him further. I noticed the undersized ears were like creased flowers, the central folds bearing no stamen. I saw that nothing would stop him from travelling this tangent to its absurd end.

'You will choose. One of us will go.' Kwame walked over to the frosted windows with his hands on his hips. Patrice stared at the desk. I saw he'd put a lot of effort into his haircut. He was an earnest young man, an asset.

I looked at his embarrassed face and remembered when a priest had placed his fingers on my forehead at school. My prime thought had been to knee him in the groin. Until a current had passed through the intersection of our skins. Heat. Transmission.

I heard Meredith pass outside in her squeaky wedges.

'Patrice, you will leave us,' I said. 'You realise this is a very serious error in judgement. It's unacceptable, as Kwame has pointed out.'

Kwame nodded at the window without appearing satisfied or easing his stance.

I left the room. Meredith tagged after me in the hall and I turned around and looked at her face. It was downy, it had been licked by dogs. I thanked her for her astuteness and her lips pursed.

I closed my office door and made a strong cup of instant coffee from a tin of Nescafé and the kettle atop a filing cabinet. I sat there swallowing the hot, dirty drink. I turned on my computer and began an email to my estranged wife.

———

The following day a shabbily dressed woman stood in the hall and was ignored by everybody. Finally Kwame swung around and demanded to know what she wanted. I had just visited the bathroom for the third time and saw him descend upon her. Her voice was a weak whisper as Kwame bent over. She wore busted flip-flops that had been wired together and her feet were covered in dust.

Kwame turned to me with his face draped in guilt. He took the woman's fine arm, leading her to the conference room. I saw her hair had been straightened many times and she had lost patches of it. As they walked Kwame's hand opened on her back.

Before Kwame strode into my office to inform me, I knew what he would say. The woman was Solomon's sister. She needed money. I felt another cramp shifting through my gut.

'I cannot believe,' said Kwame. He sat opposite me at the desk, head rocking in his hands. 'That we have neglected his family. This cannot be.'

I asked what the common practice here was.

'Gifts of rice,' he said. 'Gifts of rice.'

I opened the top drawer of the filing cabinet and took out a wad of greasy cash in an elastic band.

'How much?'

These words seemed to devastate Kwame a great deal.

'How much is a man's life worth? And an innocent, stolen son?'

I stood there waiting. I felt very light-headed.

'Might it be better to send someone out to buy some bags of rice?' I said.

Kwame released a mighty *humph!* 'Who now shall go out to buy rice? When we are even without Patrice?'

I handed him the wad of cash. The money came from my own pocket. Kwame's shirt was tight across his back as he left the room.

Three days later a second woman was standing in the hall. Where the first woman was eroded and unobtrusive, this woman was large and gay, staring up and down at everyone who passed. She wore a bright print and her feet and cheeks were plump and scented. A glittery scarf was tied over her hair. Kwame stopped by her and the woman announced that she was Solomon's wife. I saw him march her into the conference room and command cups of tea.

I walked into my office with the armful of back files Meredith had just retrieved. I half-closed the door and sat down. The dust made me sneeze and the massive splutter travelled down the ratchets of my spine. My watery intestines had made a wreck of my body and I'd been living on flat Coke and rice crackers for days. I pushed the files aside and stared at my hands on the table. They were shaking. I wondered if you starved a human body of love or food or kinship – which loss would be the most ruinous? I continued to look at my hands, recalling the lifeless fists beside Solomon's body. I touched my fingertips to my neck and they were cold. I heard Meredith's heels squeak into the conference room. Kwame introduced Solomon's spouse. Other office staff joined the trio and I heard laughter. It sounded as though the woman was telling stories. Kwame led an eerie applause that rose through the building.

I juggled with the idea of making an appearance but felt that Kwame would have called me if my presence was required. I was not informed of the arrangement he came to with the woman, and when I next went to the bathroom Solomon's spouse was gone. The office was silent for the next few hours. Kwame and two colleagues had gone to scout for a location. Before lunch I abandoned the files and had the driver take me home, where I dropped to my bed, head pounding.

I woke in the afternoon. I showered and the water was icy on my skin. I ate some cold rice and opened a tin of local tuna. On the porch the heavy air felt chilly. I wore an old sweater of my wife's that was laced with her smell. I sat there in the midst of the neighbourhood. Children were crying out; there was an argument at the fruit stall down the road; a shoe-shine boy trudging along drummed his wooden box with his brush. I made a cup of hot black tea and sat with its fusty heat beneath my face, making me perspire. I opened my laptop to the email I had begun to my wife on the day I sacked Patrice. I wrote two more sentences before all sense, all emotion, failed me. She had used the word *irretrievable*, many times.

Meredith appeared at the far end of the street, heading out from her gate with a single dog this time, on its leather lead. I watched her pace down the road. She wore a peaked cap that shadowed her face, but today she held her head higher. Glancing left and right, she looked strangely mobile and engaged. The dog's head was low, close to the road surface, a slinking along more than a walk. The lead slackened between them. When Meredith was level with my house she looked directly into my porch and saw my eyes trained upon her. She stopped. I had the feeling she had been hoping I was there. I waved, motioning to her to open the gate. I lifted myself out of the chair and moved to the railing as she crossed the gravel. The dog followed her, nose roving over the new terrain.

'Hello, Meredith. Anything I can do?'

Meredith's erect walk became a stagger and I saw how hard she had been pushing herself before. Why the fuck had she stayed on here?

'It's Bobby McGee,' she said, hauling herself closer. 'My other dog. I think he's dead.'

After she spoke, a suffering shudder collapsed her shoulders. She removed the peaked cap and brought her hands to her eyes, her forehead shiny and flushed. The dog folded its black shape on the ground.

Meredith peered up. 'Would you mind coming to see?'

I closed my computer and went down the steps. She pulled her cap back over her coiled blonde hair. I felt her eyes comb my chest and realised I was wearing a woman's sweater. I did not wish to explain. I noticed the day-glo orange laces in her running shoes.

'This is Janis,' she said, indicating the Labrador now swinging its thick tail.

I opened the gate for Meredith and the dog, and followed them the short distance down the street. In this direction the houses increased in size before the road terminated at the crooked fences of the military camp. Meredith's place was freshly painted and ringed by leafy coleus plants, with twin traveller's palms fanning upward either side of the steps. She unlocked the metal grills over her carved double doors.

I followed her down the hall. The house smelled as I would have imagined. Soap and hair products: it was clear how much Meredith prized those long blonde coils. There were no photographs, just clean surfaces, empty chairs, a shocking emptiness. I wondered if her cheating husband and the Nigerian hooker had lasted longer than three months. It was probable that they had. I thought of young, bright Patrice who had been quashed by Kwame Djoleto, and how Kwame would soon have the final word on every project in the office. I thought of the last time I had made love with my beautiful wife, how we had lain there erased, the bed sheets blank, the room vacant, our fluids leaking from us into crevices where they would drain away and there would be no embodiment.

Meredith showed me the dead animal lying on her bed. The front paws were crossed, the hind legs a little astray. There was urine on the sheets and the belly seemed swollen. She had left the air conditioning on high so there was no smell. The dog's eyes were open. Meredith sat on the end of the bed. I stood there looking at the dense black carcass thinking of the weed sitting in a drawer of the wall unit at home, thinking that if I phoned Kwame he would know who the hell to call and what to do with this.

Three Days in Hong Kong

You fly in. He says he won't be there, there'll be a sign with your code name. *Philomena M.* He likes secrets. You know he likes living between several worlds suspended in the air. He likes flight. He risks collisions. He travels way too much.

There is the card with your secret name. *Philomena M.* The driver has pointed sideburns like Nick Cave and skin pulled tight over his cheekbones.

You drive onto the motorway into the night, past cheap housing blocks with scabbed façades, balconies crammed as though the life is oozing out of them. The city pulls you in, sucks you under, chucks you up, then streams around you. Chasms, rafts of lights, a Prada shop; the black numb sky and nowhere water.

You pull into a ritzy place. The driver carries your half-empty suitcase, lopsided by books. You see a shabby Caucasian couple, hear them speak Australian.

Your room number is 537. A slim porter manoeuvres your bag.

The room makes you start. It is layers of ruffled smoothness and finally the deep ink panel of the harbour. Buildings corded in light.

You have barely sat down on the loo when the phone rings and you waddle out, knickers around your thighs.

'You've made it then,' he says.

'Well, I was booked,' you reply.

'I can't wait to see you.'

'I'm wet as – '

'I'm full as – '

He is fiddling with something. His phone. His trousers?

'Touch yourself,' he says.

'I am, darling.' You are not.

'I can't make it tonight. Just sit tight. Rest yourself. I'll drop by early tomorrow. I'll wake you up with a little morning attention. Make sure you're naked between those sheets.'

You go to the window. The city is a wide sweep of glitter. In the story of your life you are lovestruck and yearning, lucky and crazy. But you are not. You feel like laughing when he looms over you. You don't like the *ahh* sound that escapes through his nose after sex. You don't like his bum. You run a bath, trying to imagine his apartment, his groomed wife, the people he employs to keep his life clean. You think he has three young sons.

—

In the morning you wake up to his phone call. Jet lag.

'I knocked, baby. You didn't answer. I knew you'd be tired after the trip. I nearly came in my trousers outside your door. You make me drown in you. I'm at work now. It's a beautiful day. I'd like to take you out on the harbour.'

You crawl over. You are in Hong Kong. Outside, everything is fumy with light.

'My office is not so far from your hotel. I should be able to pop in later. Don't shower. I want to savour you. I can't believe we're not in grimy London and I have you all to myself.'

You murmur. You hate air travel. You fell asleep with your book on your chest and didn't move all night. You wander over to the bathroom to pee, telephone to your ear. Your mouth is rancid. This room feels bigger than your apartment.

'Why don't you order some fresh fruit? Have them send up something. How I wish I could lather you with mango and papaya, my beauty.'

'I will, darling,' you say.

'That's a weak little kitten talking there.'

'I'll perk up.'

'You've perked me up already. I'll call you later, sweet one.'

You look at yourself in the bathroom mirror. Thirty-seven, no children, you know you are muddling along. And now you've slipped into this crevasse and you are dangling. The last time you fucked him you told yourself it was glorious. But it was June for Christ's sake, two months back. His friend's place in Highgate. You look at your face beginning to twitch with lines, your still-beautiful eyebrows in high Arabic arches. You think of the man you walked away from who loved you, and went on to marry another woman who bore a disabled daughter. How you felt so guilty over that, as if you were the one who made it happen. You had to be.

—

After breakfast you are stuffed. A package arrives at the door. You hope they haven't made a mistake and close the door swiftly. It is a Chanel shopping bag with a ribbon. There is the most delightful handbag inside and you inhale the scent.

The distrustful side of you thinks: a copy? As you hunt for the guarantee, some sort of certificate.

It's there all right.

You lounge in front of the television. You switch it off and read your book. You close that and look out at the harbour which has a hard flat light, not blue like other seas. You wonder if it is a big harbour, or an inlet. You didn't buy a guidebook; he said he would whisper it to you, write it all on your skin.

—

'You won't believe what's happened. There's been a lot of movement at the office. I've got to put in the hours today. My honey, it's just not going to happen this afternoon, our harbour cruise. Can you hold out? You didn't wash your lovely skin, I hope.'

'I'll let you do that, my darling.'

The long empty hours make you feel a form of love unfurling towards him. Is it the waiting, the stretchy irrelevance of time in this ludicrously luxurious box? You're in love with him for a minute.

'I can't talk any longer. Get yourself a bottle of champagne. I'll help you finish it off. The handbag – it's not too classic, is it? I wouldn't want to label you, my love.'

'It's adorable. You are too good to me.'

You head to the shower.

⎯

In the afternoon you doze, and then it is dark again. The day has been upended, it has swept you by. Normally you are such a productive person. This is insane. You feel drugged. Your thick hair is still damp from the shower. Frizzy. Awful. You hang up the three dresses you have brought for the three days, now minus one. You've packed slinky things, things that will slip off your skin, fabrics that will show up its warm sheen. You hope they are not too vulgar. You haven't a clue what people wear here, or where he will take you. You slide on a cobalt blue dress that throws your breasts into relief. You wish your tubby tummy didn't have to show too. You should probably take a visit to the gym downstairs.

An hour before he is meant to pick you up, your phone rings.

'This is totally unexpected. Our anniversary, I'm afraid. It's next week but my wife's sister will be here and my wife has insisted we celebrate tonight. My darling, I can't risk putting her off. But I've managed to book a table in a restaurant in one of the buildings opposite your hotel. Can you believe it? I'm so close by. I can see you, my lovely.'

You look out. Masses of lights. Layers and layers of cubicles. Some empty, some with people still working. Boats plot the harbour. Planes thread the sky.

'Where? Where are you? I can't see you.'

'My wife has her back to the window. We're in the corner. She's just gone to the ladies.'

You are standing staring into infinite rooms, infinite faces, infinite lights.

'I don't believe you are out there.'

'You don't believe me?'

'What colour is my dress? What colour are the knickers I am flashing now?'

38

'Your dress is blue and you are not wearing knickers.'

You are shocked!

'I cannot speak any more, my darling. Remove that dress.'

You stand naked over Hong Kong, your hands in tepees on the glass, your legs apart. Your hair falls down your back, over your breasts. It is hard to believe anyone is watching you. For him, you touch yourself. You are not very wet. The man you left used to arouse you in a moderate way that you felt was not enough. You would lie awake, your lips to his shoulder. You were so mad he never probed your body hard enough, that you made sure his efforts were in vain.

You want to hug his disabled daughter. You decide that when you go back you will call him and do this.

—

The next morning you rush to the door naked when you hear a knock. As you unlock the door you feel sweat between your hairless buttocks. Everything has been carefully waxed. Your sex is a peeled fruit. Your fingertips like to wander over the moist skin.

It is a woman in a mauve uniform holding flowers. You snatch them from her.

You throw them down and go to the bathroom where you look at your parts which are much more beautiful than the flowers. Then this disgusts you, the way the folds are so prominent. You love to pull a man's cock into you.

You go back to read his note.

I'm being a bore, I realise. Flowers! The most divine ones I could find, for the woman I long to embrace with love and lust.

No signature.

They are too perfect to allow them to gasp to death. You put their severed stems into a cut-glass vase on a bevelled glass table. They are orchids, the saddest of all flowers, but in the vase they spread as though in an embrace. They open to you and they are flawless.

39

'My darling! You were so gorgeous last night. I saw the way you touched yourself. So slowly. Your fingers pushing inside. Quite a spectacle you were. I kept asking myself, "What is she thinking up there?" My princess. My lover. My pristine baby. The way you opened yourself. Tell me.'

You breathe in, peering over Hong Kong. Today a grey tapestry, the lights are wounds.

'I was craving you, my love. I wanted to straddle you, feel you pounding inside me, feel your hot release.'

You know there is not much point in saying anything else.

'Have you looked outside, my darling? Have you seen the driving rain? I can't see us on the harbour. Or at the gardens. I'll be over to make love to you as soon as I've finished here. Champagne, my love. I want to drink it from every cleft on your body.'

'Oh, you will,' you assure him, shredding orchid petals. Shredding, shredding.

You commence reading your second book.

———

'Something's happened.'

He sounds upset. This had better be good, you think.

'It's worse than I thought. I never imagined. Please forgive me.'

'What's happened? How can I help?'

'It's my son, L——. My youngest. Appendicitis. Well, peritonitis, they've just announced. I'm at the hospital right now. He was taken from school in an ambulance. They operated an hour ago.'

'Oh my God!'

'I guess that rules out our afternoon tryst. I can't believe the bad luck we've been having.'

'The important thing is that he's okay. Are you worried?'

'Not at all, these doctors are the best. He's in the best hands possible. My wife's pretty shaken up.'

'Of course. What a shock.'

'But kids spring back quickly.'

'They do. Well, mostly.'

'Sorry?'

'I mean they do.'

You are thinking about your ex's disabled daughter, his rotten wage; the way she won't be springing back any time, ever.

'I love you,' you say. It moves through you, a ghastly compulsion to be tied to him at the bottom of the sea, your lungs a matted filigree.

'I love you too,' he says. You would pay to know what he truly thinks.

'I want you inside of me.'

You hear his breath catch, you feel pathetic. You are testing, pushing. He is whispering to you from a walled-in space where his groaning long-ings are compressed. You hear the noise of machines and a voice on a loudspeaker. You feel power.

'Come to me afterwards. I need to feel you. We can still make this happen.'

'I will. I'll just get my wife settled. Unfortunately, it might take a while. But I'm with you, *ahh*, I'm with you.'

⟶

You wake up, still drowsy, head throbbing. There is an empty bottle of champagne near your pillow and a bright-faced woman looking out from the television screen, talking on mute. A perfect face. Hong Kong harbour is chafed by light.

'My darling.'

'It's my last day. I haven't seen you yet. And I'm leaving this evening.'

You are crying, there is too much riderless emotion within you. Perhaps it's the trip, the displacement. Too much inertia, the jet lag. Too much time studying your face in the mirror, bending and hoisting and scrutinising the descent of your body. You've never had the time for such corrosive nudity.

'I've come all this way to see you.'

You are falling, you have fallen into this room, this lavish fabrication.

And now you haul yourself before the astounding panorama which is thinly luminous. Your tears are wet with theatre.

'You've been so patient, so unbelievably patient. L—, my son, had a turn last night. We were down there again. His blood pressure dropped. It all went off-kilter for a moment. It was an emergency but he's okay. The doctors here are the best around, the very best. You understand, don't you?'

You know what is implied there. That, childless, you live in an obscene gulf. You can never know these things.

'I guess you'd understand if you had kids,' he says.

You end the call.

That night you tell the receptionist she can go fuck herself and you are not catching any flight to London. You order champagne, you stand by the dramatic window with its view of light-pocked buildings behind buildings and the harbour heaving in its black bucket.

Naked, quite drunk, you plaster yourself on the window. Rolling your body over and over on the glass.

In the morning the hangover passes quickly and you feel normal, more like yourself than you've felt in a very long time. The jet lag has gone and you've eased into this time zone. You dress elegantly and step outside into the city's warm cauldron. You wear a huge horny smile on your face. You are *Philomena M* and this is your fourth day in Hong Kong.

Genitalia

Her periods are messy. They have just moved in together and each month, at the height of her flow when the plump moon beams on their mattress, she groans with her cramps and they awaken in the morning adhered by red wounds. She heads off to the bathroom with butterfly stains on her knickers, then returns with a warm cloth to diligently wash his pink penis which has a metallic aroma.

He asks her if there is some way it can stop. Not her menstruation – of course not! – but the excessive blood loss – surely she must be anaemic – and then there is the battleground of their mattress. Would it not be possible to use wider pads. Or stockier tampons?

She stands up and there is a dribble down the inside of her leg.

She tells him that once, in a hotel room in Budapest, encouraged by a man she loved as a student, she painted a line of hieroglyphics (she is an Egyptologist) on the yellow wall.

He asks her does she not feel guilty about that? The woman who had to clean her *blood*? His parents are people with menial jobs.

She tells him that for sure the hotel has been bulldozed down by now and the piece of mortar she painted would be lying in a pile of rubble along the river. Where it gleams at night.

'Be serious,' he says.

She tells him that when women are pregnant they do not menstruate for nine months, and often when the mother breastfeeds, also, her periods do not return. She has a New Age older sister who breastfed for three years and did not shed blood in nearly four.

He feels very ignorant. His parents were anatomically contained and he did not know this.

43

Now his girlfriend is pregnant. The full moon dances across their bed and the mattress has been turned, and he proudly watches the drum of her belly when she sleeps and the flicker of an elbow or ankle of his own son revolving within. There is no blood, no washing of his pink genitals or splattering of hers, no sense that they are compelled by the Earth to be.

The Book of Bruises

Renzo brought his sister Monique to the station. He had half-wanted her to miss the train and hovered there as her quilted jacket and trainers climbed the steps. Monique paused in the corridor, tucking her hair behind an ear as someone pushed past her. It was a Romany girl with a dragging brown skirt. She blurred across Monique's body as the train pulled upon its agonising physics and began to move.

Renzo stood for a moment beside the empty tracks.

Outside the evening sky was still cerise in one corner. He stepped into a bar and drank the glass of red wine Monique had refused an hour ago, she'd preferred another coffee before the voyage. He sat there, fingering his glass. The wine was not good. Last night they had finished a bottle of Merlot and he had brought their father's mountain grappa onto the table, filling a pair of shot glasses. He had watched his sister's eyelids grow heavy, the way she licked her teeth and asked for water; he followed her lilting walk to the bathroom. Monique had fallen asleep on his sofa. Renzo paid the barman and went outside to smoke, sat on a cane chair as people pushed past. Some went back up to the Gare du Nord with their trolley bags, others to the metro around the corner. He noticed a second Romany girl as she wove along. Pregnant, he saw the expelled belly button at the centre of her freighted body.

He felt like eating noodles but he went past his usual *traiteur* and wandered into another bar. He ordered a Calvados. He was familiar with the woman sitting alone in the corner, but he ignored her. Several times he was aware of her eyes cast towards him, then they would return to her glass. Renzo wouldn't see Monique again until after Christmas perhaps, when they all rallied around the minute porcelain woman their mother had become. Monique's husband Serge would make his annual appearance, with his ponytail and wide shoulders and a hand often resting on the back of Monique's neck, under her hair, an engraved silver ring on one of his fingers. Monique would wear short skirts and black tights, boots with a stacked heel and metal chains around the ankles. They would take their mother to her favourite restaurant in the 4th arrondissement, where Monique would shepherd talk and locate harbours of recollection, until the old woman asked them all to leave her in peace or she'd call the manageress.

Once *Maman*'s descent was in place, Renzo and Monique's father had left Paris and gone back to his hilly town in north-eastern Italy. Age had skated over him. The last time Renzo had seen him, his father had been wearing a fine blue sweater the same colour as his eyes. Gesturing to a listener in the dusky courtyard of his brother's farmhouse, the vivid azure of his irises had been emboldened by the dye of the wool, caught in the last light. In an older man it had seemed especially flaunting. Renzo had turned away and walked down to the cold lake. Where his father had been a boy there was a brutal, scarred riverbed Renzo and Monique had roved during school holidays, hunting for gun cartridges or buttons from the young men blown apart by mortars at the end of the Great War. Their father had told them of this last crop of underage boys, brought to the front when all the other soldiers were maimed or gassed or wandering shell-shocked through the villages in rags. They were the *Ragazzi del '99*, born in 1899, clutched by their mothers and sweethearts, given misfiring weapons and cardboard boots and the blood-splashed uniforms of the dead. They were shot down in the dirt, just footsteps from the trenches. While Renzo had loved these stories Monique would look idly about, her damp black fringe pressed to her forehead.

The reason Monique had come this time was that she and Serge had had a fight. She did not show Renzo, but he knew there were wounds on her somewhere. She wouldn't tell him anything further, said it was not so bad this time. Serge had the kids holed up at his mother's place in Lille. Even so, Renzo knew from the start that after three days Monique would want to go back to him. There would be no calls, no contact, just a magnetic pull that would reach into her and start hauling her northward. Monique would become robotic, she would book her return ticket. At the outset

Renzo had warmed to Serge, thinking the big ponytailed man had tamed his sister, who'd had abortions and slept with a raft of men. Until Monique turned up with a newborn in a shawl and a purple welt on her face. Renzo had watched the bruise turn violet, then green, then yellow. She wouldn't get it checked. He saw her pat it sometimes, hold her palm against it.

The woman he had ignored now came to the counter and leaned in next to him.

'Hello, Renzo.'

He nodded.

'I'll order us both another round. You don't have to talk to me. I can see you don't want company.'

But she sat at the bar with him when their drinks arrived. Hers a cognac, his another Calvados. Outside it had started to rain and the shower swept down the street. The woman held an unlit cigarette. They went out together under the awning to smoke, feeling the bluster between them.

'I saw you had your sister down again.'

'Yes.'

'She looked well.'

Monique's train would be crossing the flat dark north now. She would not be reading. She would already be communing with him. And Serge would be waiting for her in the unlit house, the children long gone to bed. Renzo's mind couldn't produce any other thoughts. Would Serge pull away his sister's clothing? Trace her bruises or push his fingers into them? Renzo had seen Monique's body when they were children bathing naked in the river near Vittorio Veneto, their father watching in rolled-up trousers from the bank, alpine water coursing in green furrows between the shoals. Monique had splashed icy water over him, made him shriek, her nipples pressed into her chest and her tiny pleat opening as she leaped away. Elfin, with her helmet of black hair. As a young man Renzo had waited to shed those long boyhood years. When Monique started to go out drinking and clubbing he had studied in his narrow room, hearing her bang furniture or moaning when she came home with a boyfriend. But Renzo had been desperate for a celestial love to invade him. At twenty he had moved to Rome, spent ten years there savouring the scrolled façades and the swallow-sketched nightfall. He'd been melded to the carnal, obliging city. And he had loved profoundly too. Every tributary of his mind had gushed with love.

He looked to the woman at his side and saw her grey, serene eyes were upon him.

'I had trouble with my ex-husband,' she said. 'I've seen the bruises on your sister's face the other times. You always go back to them. You always do.'

Renzo stared at her.

'It's an awful thing to see happening,' she said.

He wanted to kick away from her and charge down the street in the rain. Not looking back, swearing at her. But he finished his cigarette and ground it into the pavement. They had a final drink at the bar and when they returned outside a night wind had cleansed the sky and they saw stars. He hoped it was a good omen for Monique's homecoming. But any thoughts he had of his brother-in-law made him feel sick.

The woman said she would walk a stretch with him. Her name was Caroline and she had been a dancer. She walked with light abbreviated steps, her spine stretching upward. It made him walk more erectly.

'I loved my husband as I love water, wine, the night,' she said to him. 'But he was the man who finished me off. I was nothing after that man.'

Renzo listened to her. He had grown used to her talk.

'I hope your sister can get away from him,' she said. 'Do they have children? I remember I saw a boy once.'

'A boy and a girl.'

'I see. That's difficult.'

They were both smoking again. She was wearing cascading, muted clothes. She dressed like this always. He saw her skin was pearly and fine.

'What did he do to you? Your husband?' he asked.

'My husband? You mean the violence? Oh, I cannot tell you that. Each of us is different. We do not have the same wounds. But I can smell it on a woman. I can see it in a man. I can see it on your sister. She is expecting it. Perhaps you had it in your house.'

'Not at all,' he replied.

As they rounded a corner into a dim side street three young men overtook them. They jostled Caroline from behind and she gripped Renzo's arm. They joined as a phalanx in front of them and demanded cigarettes. Caroline gave them three from her packet. They insisted Renzo add some money to that. He shook his head and waved them off, said he'd have none of that in his own quartier. The one closest to him pulled back his fist and drove it hard into Renzo's cheekbone.

Renzo's body jerked against the wall. As his coccyx hit the ground he thought of his father's *Ragazzi del '99*, those young boys climbing over the trench walls into the sunlight, chests stung by metal, the caress of hot blood before they even knew their bodies had begun to die. Renzo had seen his aggressor's fingers clench and his hand forming its soft club, but why hadn't he tried to block the swinging arm? Was this how it happened with Monique? Did she stand there as Serge balled his fist and it crossed the air?

Renzo smelled blood trickling down his cheek. Caroline dropped to his side as the thugs ran off.

'Put that away,' he said as she pulled out her phone.

'Don't be foolish. You've likely broken your cheekbone. It's not looking good.'

'No doctors,' he said, feeling nauseous. 'Just let me sit here a minute.'

He banked to the other side and vomited on the pavement. The vomit smelled of Calvados and the prawns he and Monique had eaten at lunch. Caroline handed him a tissue and crouched by him, her garments skirting the ground. He moved his palm over the surface, smelled the fustiness at the bottom of the building and saw the city above as a reeling firmament.

A couple walked past, arm in arm. They stepped wide around them, the man turning back to stare.

'Come on,' said Caroline, helping him to his feet. 'You're not a pretty sight on the ground. Let's get you at least to my place. It's just across the road.'

Renzo stumbled and he felt the heft of her arms as she pulled him upright. His feet plonked one after the other.

'The bastards,' Caroline said. 'The bastards. This is when being a woman is so useless. And there were three of them.'

They crossed the road and she punched numbers into a keypad by the door, pushed it open as her arm reached out for the light. Renzo looked up into the stairwell. It was the same in his building. Flared creaking steps and a sinuous banister, bony doors and a stack of muffled lives.

As soon as they entered her apartment she led him down the long hallway to the bathroom and handed him clean men's clothing. He had never seen her with a man and he wondered where these had come from. His eyes strayed over her jars of cream, an open box of tampons, her eyeliner placed near the mirror. He bent down to wash his face but the nausea rose again, so he leaned against the tiles and tugged off his shirt.

Renzo wandered back to the main room which had an elongated shape and heavy velvet curtains. It was stuffy. There were three papier-mâché sculptures at one end. They were dancing humans or swooping birds, and each figure had half-melted skin like plaster casts he had seen in Pompeii. They circled in immense agony. He smelled cats.

'This is not my place,' she said from the kitchen. 'Just housesitting for a friend who's gone abroad. It's a tad depressing, isn't it?'

'I was just thinking that,' said Renzo.

She brought out two mugs of tisane on a tray. 'Here, you'll like this. Let me take a look at your face. Oh Lord.'

She came over to where he was sitting, peering all around his left eye. As she dabbed, little puffs of her breath collected on his face and the pain thundered to the surface.

'Perhaps it's not broken after all. Just an almighty bruising.'

When she had cleaned away the blood and rubbed oily arnica into the bone she sat down hunched over her tea, ignoring the cat poised there waiting to tread onto her thighs. Renzo had a feeling she disliked cats. She had pulled her sleeves back and her arms glowed in the lamplight; they

50

were performer's arms. He now knew that they would speak until dawn in this light. Renzo thought back to his father shrugging and gesturing in the dusky courtyard, his azure irises and the fine cerulean sweater, how these reverberating hues had been radiant. He remembered the snap of leather down the hall, and the first weals he had seen across Monique's thighs. He remembered bruises darkening in a grip around his mother's neck. Renzo also remembered the woman he had dearly loved in Rome so many years ago. How that time it had coursed through him too, and he had struck down this woman's beauty and she had stared up at him from the marble floor.

He looked at Caroline, whose hands were closed around her cup. He had never thought that his voice would be heard.

Pelt

Rolfe triggers it. In the way that is the way of all men. In his case a type of athletic bragging ruined by the self-defeat he hangs his hat on. I feel a plock and, with his surprised, involuntary retreat, my waters come splashing out, gay and heralding, whereby he bounds back to inspect the folds of his manhood.

My *obroni* baby will come this day. I roll onto my back and raise my knees in sweet excitement, the baby nestling inward even though her head is plugged within my pelvis. Soon after, Rolfe is agitating with a towel, peering cautiously at my mysterious opening. *No action there, darling*. He looks perplexed. Despite his 39 years Rolfe is unfamiliar with the mulch of his own body. A fever sends him into studied ecstasy. The tumbleworm in his butt, whose head and long wrinkled body I inch into the light, is repellent and edifying.

At the apex of his growth curve I suspect I must place myself. This is the man who continues to daub his hands on my back and breasts. He told me that in Ethiopia, his last posting, the Ethiopians called girls like me 'slaves' because of our broad noses and skin a shadow cannot cross.

This is Rolfe's first child. His wife Karina was barren. I have led Rolfe to believe that this is my first although I had two others before. They are at the village with my aunty and I send them money. The midwife will no doubt perceive all of this.

—

Rolfe has been a maniac these past weeks. His wife Karina wrote him an email that she is coming here for a conference on small investors and banking. I have seen the flags up at the Conference Centre. It is going to be big. Rolfe and Karina have been working in different countries for 18 months. There was a sort of split, Rolfe said, and they each decided to go their own way with work.

Karina is arriving this morning from Namibia via Johannesburg. Though Rolfe hasn't said it in so many words, I know this woman does not know of me, nor that I am full of Rolfe's baby. There is a certain satisfaction in that.

It is not an early flight so we stay in bed for some time as he has taken the morning off work. The girls have arrived, rattling in the kitchen and complaining about their lives, as we make love in the slower, inflicting way he does in the morning. The last twinges as he rakes my buttocks are disturbing, so I pull away and his apologies are profuse.

Out of the shower he wears an uneasy grin and retrieves old cologne from the dresser. He traces a little elbow or heel that crosses the elastic of my belly then kisses me with guilt and pressure.

'It will be okay,' he says. And for some reason, '*I will never harm you.*'

Two hours later Karina arrives from Namibia. Blonde, tanned, petite. Small eyes placed at the extremes of her face. A fine bridge from the forehead to the nose where a slight bump interrupts the descent into cartilage. Thin lips and a wide downy jaw. Little breasts. Flat arse.

Rolfe brings her into the living room where I am sitting under a fan in an embroidered boubou and headscarf, naked underneath. Then there is a commotion in the yard with the driver and Rolfe is called outside. We two women are left alone.

Karina fights the first jolt. I am used to being treated as Rolfe's house-girl by visitors if Rolfe is not there to explain. I try to rise, but am impeded by my big belly and the lowness of the couch. Karina stands shocked on the other side of a carved wooden chest. I climb upward. The woman takes a step back, treading on tall Rolfe's bare foot, her eyes fixed upon my bursting stomach.

She falls to Rolfe releasing mad ugly sobs.

———

Rolfe takes his wife to the guest room where the girls have made up the bed and left the best towels. There is an ensuite bathroom attached although the water pressure is not good. There are shelves with some unread books in their language. I think she should find some comfort.

When Rolfe went back to Germany last year I was just pregnant. He couldn't take me. I do not yet have a passport and visas are very difficult to obtain. He told me all about the trip. His town far in the north where his mother is postmistress and the owner of a hotel. How he skated on the frozen lake with his nephews and went on skis. Though I asked him to send me photographs he sent none. He bought me a prickly set of underwear and a box of wooden blocks for our child.

Rolfe and his wife remain behind the guest room door for a long time. She is crying mostly. Long broken wrenching that comes from a subsided place within her. I hear Rolfe's tones, a murmur in their language, though these do not convince. This is such a Western thing, the dialogue and the praxis. I would have torn out his hair by now.

One of the girls – Comfort – asks me with a giggle what is to be prepared for lunch. Their assumption is that the real Madam has turned up, and I am just another hussy-made-good carrying a milky baby. No doubt this will be the speculation of the day.

When I met Rolfe he had just started out on the Obensah Housing Estate, where crooked villas creep over hillock after hillock of red soil cleared outside the city. I was working in the office. He had a girl with him in a big jeep. A student type with straightened hair and good clothes. Later it turned out I was right. She was a student but she kept on with her hometown boyfriend on the side. In the beginning Rolfe begged me not to do that, made me promise I wouldn't fuck behind his back. Before he even fucked me he made me do an AIDS test. Oh, he couldn't keep his hands off me and let me jack him off, but he wouldn't put his thing in until my results came back clear.

Sometime after midday Rolfe emerges from the guest room and draws the door closed. The woman is no longer crying. They have been inside for one hour and 53 minutes. I am still sitting on the chocolate velour couch the same tone as I am, the couch where Rolfe – when the girls have gone – likes to make me lie naked. But I have been sitting out here watching the clock he ordered online from Germany, feeling our baby flicker in sleep.

Rolfe stands looking at me from the other side of the room. He appears very white. His eyes are glassy small discs. Other girls say the same thing about their *obroni* men: when their old wives turn up they become little boys.

He glides past me, drops down and wraps his head with his large hands. '*Was hab ich getan?*' he says. '*Was hab ich getan?*'

You don't need to speak German to understand that.

—

Karina comes to the lunch table in a green flowery dress that sucks in at the waist. It falls a touch below the knees, showing her swelling, resolved calves. She wears tiny rounded black shoes with no heel. Washed, her blonde hair now shows its icy cut.

She and Rolfe can find no way to address each other's faces, though she smiles briefly at Comfort lolling in the kitchen doorway. Her eyes look like she has suffered bee stings, or punches from a wild boyfriend, although I know Rolfe would never do that.

I touch Rolfe's bare foot under the table. He jerks it away.

It is uncalled for because I have made his favourite – *banku* and okra stew – hoping to calm his mood. His head snaps back in Comfort's direction.

'Cutlery!'

Comfort scurries off, skirt flaring in the hall. Titter from the pots. This is a meal which, in my company, he will eat with his hands, on occasions eating from my fingers. Comfort reappears with her boulder-white eyes over spoons and forks arranged like surgical instruments on a metal tray. Keen to see what will come next, she leans on the doorframe once more, her toes twitching on the tiles.

'Go off from here, you silly girl,' I say to her in local language.

Her grin crackles.

Rolfe and his wife eat in silence. She pulls away a wedge of *banku* with the spoon, assessing its consistency and dipping it into the sauce. She knows I am watching her. My baby moves a limb, high up against my rib cage. She brings the *banku* to her mouth, glancing at me before she parcels it in warily. Her eyes water. She is forced to look to Rolfe, struggling. Comfort brings a jug of water and sloshes it into our glasses. Scant words are spoken in German. She perseveres with her meal while Rolfe's plate empties. I am playing with my food now, nudging a shallow indentation into the *banku* which pools with sauce, breaking apart the last shard of fish, knowing the heartburn will come later.

Rolfe pushes his chair back, going himself out to the kitchen for a beer. He gives a bottle to Karina and her eyes take this in with some relief. Rolfe throws his down while Karina drinks with jerky rapid slaking.

It is time to leave them alone.

I turn on the fan and lie down upon our bed. The food makes me sweat. I pull off my headscarf and my hair spills out. I wanted to have extensions done before the baby. Rolfe wants me to crop it short and tight around my skull – *sakura* – but he does not realise that schoolgirls wear their hair in that way. I am hardly a schoolgirl. I am uncomfortable. The food has started its burning passage up and down my oesophagus. Right now, I feel like sex.

But out in the living room they have started again. The woman, in a different register now, is talking more solidly with few breaks. Rolfe must have his head down, nursing his beer, the way he is mumbling.

'*Nein, nein,*' he says like a weak animal. '*Nein –* '

I put on the little Rex Omar CD near my head and remember dancing to *Abiba-eh* in a tight red dress.

—

I wake up at sundown. Mosquitoes. The baby tapping my inner spine. Rolfe gone. His wife too.

Out in the kitchen Comfort is asleep against the wall. She knows better than to wake me when she wants to be dismissed. Cecilia has already taken off. I look into Comfort's open pink mouth and realise I will sack the pair of them as soon as I have the kid.

'Where are they?' I say.

Comfort's eyes open, lucid and cocky.

'In the car, Madam. They have left in the car.'

The only time I have ever gone behind Rolfe's back is with Joseph who is a Ga. Years ago, Joseph fell into a learning programme for street kids and met the coordinator, much older than him, from Canada. He has been to Canada twice and they are married. When he is in town he still sells stereos and cameras he has been passed. He knows the gangs that break into *obroni* houses. I think of Joseph and Miriam in their little house on the beach, the way he pats her on the head as if she has taught him to do it right. Joseph and I together, we are something. After Joseph, I cannot even walk.

But I don't want Joseph now. I sit in front of the television and watch *Sunset Beach*.

—

They come back in the stifling dark although Rolfe does not come to me. Because of the baby I shift in and out of sleep all night. They remain murmuring in the living room, opening more beers. At times, the woman releases a small, sad laugh.

Somehow, though there are no specifics, I sense the movement of their bodies together. There is a change in volume, electricity. I sense their searching for reasons has fallen away and today's steeliness has finally eased.

With a shock, I hear them progress to the guest room.

I half-rise, cramping my upper belly and pushing the baby downward. She jigs, then begins to hiccough. I wait for each hiccough to tap-tap-tap inside of me. Down low where the head is already lodged above my pussy. Every tap is a drop of rainwater on my tongue setting off a shiver and recoil. I cannot hear them. They say that European women scream like cats and like to sit on a man. Well, this one does not.

Rolfe, though he doesn't stay too long (there is pleading), accomplishes

57

his feat. He comes into the darkness around me, washes lazily in our ensuite bathroom and throws his whole exhausted length on the bed sheets where in moments he is asleep. He does not touch me or the wide berth housing his child. The woman by contrast is still awake, I hear. She is restless, charmed and defrauded by her man. Can't she see? Of course she can. She is weeping in her room to the lip-lip-lip of the fan.

Later I am pissing in the hall toilet where I can flush, with my thong at my knees.

Karina is standing there watching me, the dim light glowing on her nightdress. I pull up my thong which she observes as it travels to the pouch below my massive belly. I always sleep naked. My full breasts swivel towards her. These are the breasts her husband sucks.

But she doesn't back off this time. Rather, she holds out her hands towards the baby's warm halo.

'Can I?' she says, her eyes hurrying to my stomach.

She plants her hands there quickly. With her short square nails they look like colourless sea creatures that fishermen trawl up, webbed on my skin. But the baby is asleep and there is no movement.

She removes her hands and I know what it is that she can feel. It is the whir of my blood, the blood I have given to Rolfe's baby. She turns down the hall and I hear her close the door.

Back in my room Rolfe snuffles in his sleep, branching out for me. I fit to him. He swells and we sleep at length in this way.

—

In the morning Rolfe discovers that a thief has made off with the rear lights, spare tyre and both headlamps of his four-door Mitsubishi Pajero. The driver, asleep in the boys' quarters, also protests that his bath towel (grey if I remember, bone thin) and his *charley wate* are missing. Evidently, we were all lost to sleep. Rolfe sacks the driver on the spot and calls forth the garden boy, a towering northerner with a machete. The boy begins to whimper. Rolfe's Western discourse about trust and honesty falls upon keen ears however. The boy is listening for the word *police*.

Karina is watching from the terrace in her bathrobe, adding apoplectic asides in German to the guilty parties. Rolfe storms between the two men, this way and that, knowing the unscrewed pieces were passed over the wall to eager hands on bare feet, and carried to a taxi at the end of the road. They will already be in various stalls in the spare parts market. I turn away. Rolfe looks so handsome in his drawstring trousers with his thing bouncing around. I'm sure Karina has noticed that too.

Karina comes to breakfast in a yellow dress which follows her form but slinks away from it. It is synthetic and moves oddly, adding to the oddness of her proportions. She has a brown ribbon tying her hair back and drinks juice, then harsh black coffee from a small drip filter she has brought with her. Rolfe is too angry to eat. He takes a short shower and goes outside to smoke. The woman's curiosity of late last night has withdrawn into a single tear that collects in her eye and wanders down beside the hillock of her nose. I hear her swallow in her throat. It is difficult to see the way that Rolfe would fuck her, which games they would play in the rooms of the house. She stands up and collects a briefcase and a laptop. The taxi Rolfe has ordered is honking at the gate. He urges her out the frosted glass door.

The day sets out to be long and cantankerous. Rolfe telephones me from the office and tells me to call Joseph to find out what I can about the parts. I tell him I won't accuse Joseph of theft. Rolfe replies that Joseph will most certainly know where the parts went. His voice is growing exasperated thorns. While I know this is not the case, I lie. 'He's travelled,' I tell him. 'Last week.'

Rolfe's thorns break into my skin. He says that is bullshit, that yesterday he saw Joseph on the beach. 'Oh?' I say, sweat welling. 'So you softened her up at the beach?'

Rolfe's line goes dead.

I call Joseph and he is around here in ten minutes, sitting on the other chocolate double couch. I send Comfort to do the shopping. Cecilia has not even turned up.

Naturally, Joseph wants to know if that was the old German wife Rolfe left behind. 'Well,' he says laughing. 'I didn't think she was his sister.' He calls her 'no-bum' and 'tuna legs' and 'fish-head-soup face' and seems to derive great satisfaction from this. I give him a beer and he presses behind me, so hard in the morning, but I move off, burning softly. Not today. Of course he knows who took the parts, but he won't get them back without a show of cash for his trouble. I try – my knees fall open – but Joseph will not be tinkered with in this respect. Soon after he gets up to leave, the beer bottle sitting in a lake miles away from its straw coaster. I hear his bike clanking along the road.

Comfort comes back, prepares *wackye* and serves it up for the three of us for lunch. I wait for a taxi to trundle up in the sand outside the gate but neither of them arrives. Comfort minces in at regular intervals to remind me that Master Rolfe and Madam Karina have not come home. By three o'clock, too incensed to yell, I throw the bottle of Malta Guinness I am drinking in her direction, which shatters somewhere behind her on the wall.

I drag my body off, tearing away my clothes, standing full and canti-levered in the shower. The water pressure is good. Water skitters off the chute of my upper belly, now emptier of my baby's limbs given these too have dropped into my pelvic cradle. My lower belly thrusts out to hold the heavy teardrop of liquid and flesh. My inside-out belly button, the lobe of skin that Rolfe likes to lick, trembles pale and divulged under the water.

It is too hot to lie on our bed. I wrap up my hair and choose a dress. Outside on the road I tap the roof of a taxi. A pair of heels is kicked out of the passenger window. The driver takes me downtown to the hotel that Rolfe and I frequent, where I have learnt to swim under his instruc-tion. It is an inner-city place where the *obroni* do not often come. There are too many mosquitoes and the food gives you the runs. The pool has blue molten lights and we swim under the black blowsy palms at night.

I pay the driver and walk through the lobby to the garden outside. Certain air crews stop over here – the Ethiopians and the Egyptians – and I dislike the stares of these men over my body. Rolfe never wants me to come here alone for that very reason, also because I think he is worried I might drop like a stone to the bottom of the pool. With our baby.

It takes some courage but I remove my dress and walk over to the open shower, while two local Lebanese teenagers eye my ample form. It makes me feel sticky. There is nothing so exposing as having your body's naked act and its consequence on show for all to see. Then, under the far palms, I see them. Rolfe and Karina. On two loungers pushed together on the grass. Inches apart with beer bottles collected on a cane table.

Rolfe scratches his back, then transfers his open hand to her flank, while hers cups one side of his face and he nuzzles it.

I step down out of the shower recess onto the cement surrounding the curved pool. Though the Lebanese boys have made rude comments, the two Germans have not seen me, so avid is their talk. I look across to my handbag with its possibility of retreat. If I walk away, maybe this moment will never have occurred. But then I glance over and Karina catches my eye.

It is not hard to decide what to do next. I pace towards the wide tiled steps dissolving into the shallow end of the pool. I walk up for the grandest entrance imaginable, breathing in sharp each time the balls of my feet make contact with the grainy hot surface. I think of Joseph and Miriam in the beach house. How he pats her on the head. How he fucks me so well and then rides his bike off. How these people always try to make fools of us.

Rolfe rises. Karina pulls away. His face blurs. The waiter pauses to watch and attracts his colleague to the scene. The water journeys up my thighs, through my panties, up the bulwark of my belly. I begin the breaststroke, frog-kicking my legs as I have been taught, dipping my face into the water as my forearms clear a path.

Rolfe is standing. His balls and cock are squashed to one side from the way he was lying down. Though they soon fall into place. He opens his mouth to call my name, realises he has quite an audience, and instead rubs the back of his hand across his mouth. He reaches for his beer on the low table, Karina taking this chance to whisper her startled opinion. I am gliding now, past where their toes were almost intertwined before, and Rolfe can but follow me with the circling, desperate steps of a tall man on a hot strip of cement.

At the far end, in the embrace of a bending palm, he seethes at me, crouching.

'This – this – you realise – this is foolish – you take yourself home. Take yourself home now!'

His eyes are locked on my face and yet do not centre upon my own eyes until the words have been spoken. Then they fill with sorrow and shock like a wound filling with blood. They darken.

'Just go home. I beg you. She will leave. She is nearly gone. I beg you,' he says as he bends closer.

But no extended hand or kiss of confirmation. No *I-love-you*. He rises, adjusts the squished balls again and returns to the other couch with its pair of eyes.

Before leaving I order a tonic water, which I used to drink with gin before the baby. I ask Osman to put in some gin. Perhaps this is why it happens so afterwards.

———

I return to the house promptly, put on my indoor dress and turn on *Sunset Beach*. Comfort is heating palm oil for fried plantain. It smells as though, of her own initiative, she has prepared bean stew. Already I feel the heartburn and the long lonely night.

Rolfe and Karina clatter through the gate. This time the taxi has been soundless and I have not heard them bartering for their fare on the street. There is some talk in German on the steps as they carry up their bags. Over the television show, I can hear Karina bossing him.

I walk out into the kitchen to look for a Malta Guinness and there they are, Karina handing Rolfe a cold beer from the fridge. Comfort has just thrown the first disc of gingered plantain into the sizzling oil, the way Rolfe likes it.

I move over to the pan, grab the heavy handle and manoeuvre it into the centre of the room, the contents swaying and spitting. The oil splatters a little onto the linoleum. Rolfe puts a protective arm across his wife, whose eyes leap towards him. Comfort lunges into the laundry. The pan is heavy and so far I am holding it with one arm only, although we can all see that this is beginning to wilt. Oil slurps over, again, onto the floor. The plantain has in this short time become a crisp.

Rolfe's face staggers. I watch its transformation. His barren shock goes someplace else, gradually. It is pulled apart, the terror dissolving into little shards of reckoning, little mushroom clouds of capitulation. One by one his features transform: his eyebrows lengthen, smoothing the labour of his forehead, his nose loses its hitch, the muscles supporting his mouth begin to fail.

They are trapped, too, at this end of the kitchen. The woman opens her mouth to speak but Rolfe's eyes flare at her. He turns to me. It is apparent that my single arm outstretched beyond the arc of my belly could at any moment collapse. And yet Rolfe's features have attained the expression I desired.

He begins to smile. Recognition and hunger are plunged in deep strokes on his face. I have never seen a man hungrier.

Gently, he moves. With his help, the pan of oil is returned to the cooker.

That night Karina packs her bags without tears. Rolfe escorts her formally to the front gate. She moves into a hotel for the duration of the conference, the one closest to the airport.

As Simple As Water

Vasilis K and Marj B are embracing at an Athens train station (it is Ambelokipi) when Vasilis feels Marj's legs fold under her and sees her eyes roll back, and the woman he has made love to in a hotel room far above and with whom he argued (he knows he was being unjust) falls in a dead faint at his feet as the airport train rolls in on screaming rails.

A woman in a suit rushes out of the opening doors and loosens Marj's scarf and tight jeans (he sees her white belly) and checks her airways, laying her in a recovery position on the stone slabs of the train station floor.

A minute ago Marj's tongue had been enwrapping his own, and her eyes with their hazel curlicues had spoken of wanting while his had (Marj said) been wearing their dark shields, which was what she called his retracting each time before her uncomfortable fading away on public transport, taxis and planes.

Vasilis thinks now Marj will miss her plane and what will he do with her. Vasilis's day is lined up, as hers was too in another country a short flight away, and now she is lying on the station floor with a woman crouched at her side. The seams of the woman's pants stretch over her hips.

Vasilis who has been making love to Marj most of the night (except when she wept sitting on a corner of the bed and he waited) wonders about the pelvic cavern of all women which is filled with jostling organs and squelching tubes and lengthy orifices like vivid botanical sections drawn into slithering life. He wonders whether this woman too has mauve toenails within her brown boots.

'Who is she?' The wide woman turns back and asks. Marj's small suitcase stands by the station wall.

'I don't know. I saw her fall down.' Vasilis who had not known these words would come from his mouth stares at Marj's pearly face on the ground as another train releases startled passengers who funnel away until he and the crouching woman and Marj's body are all but alone.

The doctor comes out and he has black hair with dandruff captured at its roots. Vasilis feels a charge of sadness to think of the doctor raising Marj's wrist and laying it by her side, lifting her eyelids and shocking each pupil with a flashlight. Vasilis still has Marj's saliva in his mouth and some (she is a vigorous kisser) has dried on his cheek and neck.

'We're doing preliminary tests,' the doctor says. 'She may have simply hit her head, or it could be some pre-existing condition. Or even the early stages of pregnancy. We may have to keep your wife here overnight.'

'I see.' Vasilis's heart is in stiff points under his skin, barred in his rib cage.

The young doctor with dirty hair stands there, looking at the language on Vasilis's face. Then he turns back to his patient, slouching up the hall with its seam of lights.

Vasilis walks outside up a concrete path and he calls his wife who would just be opening the shop on the island, and his son who has an anthropology exam in the afternoon. There had been a way to loving Marj as there is a way to loving all women, but in Marj's case it was a silken rope, a water snake with a ribboning tail, and at dawn they had been clasped at the hotel window (Marj's cheeks were dry) staring out over the flushed city and now Marj is in a bed under lights and Vasilis is walking, walking.

The Woman Whose Husband Died in a Climbing Accident

Helga Pfenning lost her husband, Jan, in an accident on Aconcagua. His companions told her Jan had been fretful and disoriented when they bedded down that night, and in the morning his sleeping bag was an empty tousled shell. As it snowed heavily before dawn, there were no tracks.

The men were sorrowful and each man telephoned Helga from the country where he had returned to his wife and children, or partner, or solitary life.

Jan's body remained on the mountain.

Helga later wrote a book gleaning as much information as possible from Jan's climbing companions via email. She noted that they were reticent, and this tugged at her heart. Perhaps there had been conflict? But a Frenchman called Claude, in charge of the expedition, said this had not been the case.

In her book Helga portrayed Claude as a guarded man who undermined the men's psyches. But in truth she knew that Claude was shy and admirable, where her husband had been hot-headed.

In fact, the evening the news reached her that Jan had wandered from the tent and been slaughtered by the mountain, Helga had not been surprised.

—

Helga's book became a bestseller in Europe and she gave readings in bookshops all over the continent. In the beginning it was harrowing speaking of Jan's last texts and photos (some had been explicit and she had put these in a secret file), especially when people in the audience asked her did she intend to retrieve her husband's body.

In Copenhagen a journalist asked her about the other climbers, whether she felt rancour towards them and if they had remained in touch. Helga thought of Claude running his abseiling business in the south of France, with his Spanish wife and two daughters. Claude and the other men no longer called her. When approached about Helga's book, Claude had refused to speak to the press.

Helga's publisher wanted a sequel to her book so it was suggested she develop a manuscript about retrieving her husband's body from South America. Jan's body had now been frozen on Aconcagua for five years. Helga hired an assistant, Pieter, to help with her research for the new book. Pieter thought that they would have to enlist at least one of the men from the fatal expedition, to help them retrace Jan's steps that night. In her hotel room in Zurich, Helga wrote emails to all of the other climbers, asking if any of them would join a possible expedition. Helga had begun to train, hoping she would be able to reach one of the base camps.

None of the other climbers replied.

That summer Claude was killed by lightning in the Pyrenees, and Helga, though it involved an expensive battle with her publisher in court, abandoned her project.

Magaly Park

There is a murder in the new apartment block on the Point, in the garage downstairs, it's all cordoned off. It isn't anyone who lives there as they're not up for sale yet. A jogger on her way to the bay saw a side door ajar and ran over when she heard a scream. She saw a guy pull a knife out of another man's gut. The guy knocked her down and ran off. I watched her interviewed by a journo after the police, as a paramedic tended to the scrape on her arm. 'It was the last thing I was expecting! The very last thing!' Her voice is hyper and she sounds excited, like she's met someone famous in the loo. She has a badge on her tank top from Tai's school, Sydney Girls High.

The action is all over now and I'm sitting on a bench in the park. A RiverCat goes past towards the city, rousing the water and mucking about with the boats. The cops and men in puffy white suits have gone away and the ambulance crawls back to the main road with the siren on a slack dead man's spin, the red light clocking around.

I call Tai to tell her something's happened on the Point. Her mother's been on the balcony all along, shifting up and down the length, going back in to top up her coffee. Coming out again in her jute slippers and baggy pants. Tai is doing statistics problems today and won't answer. I guess Nora's seen me, she doesn't miss much. Down by the water there is a bloke with a fishing rod. He doesn't like the dog that's come up behind him to sniff his bait.

'Cassie! Cassie! Don't do that!' A woman in a peaked cap drops onto the sand from the stone wall, runs to the nosing Labrador. The fisherman is barefoot in rolled-up trousers.

'I'm sorry! I'm sorry! Hope she didn't eat any of your bait,' she calls as she clips on the leash. The man looks at her. The woman is wearing a pink pair of plastic croc sandals and an open white shirt. Beneath this her wobbly breasts are contained in a too-small top. She pulls her shirt together. She and the Labrador walk along the sand towards the ridge.

Further along I see the woman who was interviewed about the murder. She has finished her run and is exercising now. She lunges, one leg bent at the front and the other stretching out behind, her butt pushing towards the grass as though a palm is putting pressure there. Her arms are pointed above her. It's a yoga position I've seen Tai do, but she isn't as good as this. Tai is tiny, but not nearly as bendy as this woman. I can see the woman's heart is not at rest and her face is taut. How alone she looks in the still park.

She pulls out of the pose and walks to a bench, sits down and covers her face. She stays hunched there, crying. Why haven't the police taken her home? She is probably a tough woman who said she was fine, just a little shaky. That the jog would help.

I walk over. When she feels someone approaching she braces herself and looks up.

'I saw you interviewed up there,' I say. 'Thought you looked pretty shaken.'

'Oh, I am, I guess. It was pretty crazy.'

'It must have been. Was he a young guy?'

'I didn't really get a look. I mean, I did, but I couldn't tell. I was supposed to go to the station with them. They're coming to my place tonight. I'm not looking forward to that.'

She is older than Tai and me, too old for high school. There are wrinkles around her eyes and across her forehead. Somebody's big sister. Her hair is pulled back with a faded headband.

'He was rolling around on the concrete, you know. There was blood everywhere. You know I did first aid once. I did a course. But I couldn't go near him. I just turned away and started calling. I pretended he was a dead dog or something. You know, one you've smashed on the road. Now I think his soul must be floating around above us and he never said goodbye to anybody. I'm thinking, I didn't help him leave this life. I must sound pretty fucked up.'

'I think anybody would be,' I say. Another RiverCat pushes by, sending

69

out its long, deep-bellied concaves. The fisherman backs away on the sand, watches the waves splash. A man has released twins from a double buggy onto the fine grass. A football travels between two boys.

'I told the police I didn't see anything. But they're still coming to the flat tonight. I ought to tidy the joint!' She stands up and her legs are restless. Her tears have left dried salt along the sides of her cheeks.

'My name is Giselle.' She puts out her hand and shakes mine.

'I'm Grant.'

'Wouldn't it be nice to live down here near the park?' She looks at the arc of new, overpriced apartments that have risen on the bedrock. There seem to be more of them each month, crowding around every inlet cluttered with boats. The brief, sandy beaches are no good for swimming but cleaner now than ever. The guy near the water has caught a fish. Giselle looks up to the Point where the apartment building stands, shining with new chrome and glass balconies. There is plastic sheeting on many of the windows.

—

Giselle lives in a block of flats under a huge Moreton Bay fig tree. They protect them now. You need a permit to cut one down. The pods fall to the ground, crooked husks that look as though they could still be of some use. There is a row of carved grooves inside if you open one up. Giselle's front path has been swept clear and there is a bank of coloured disposal bins.

'I shouldn't really be inviting you to my place. I've had a murderer knock me down today!'

I am wondering whether Nora saw me approach Giselle in the park, or watched me walk away with her along the footpath, by the swimming pool that only residents can use. Tai was adopted from China when she was two months old and Nora has always chained her to her desk. Nora wants manic Higher School Certificate results. Tai wants to change her name and find her real parents.

I check my phone and Giselle glances at me. 'Cuppa or a beer? I guess you're old enough for a beer.'

She places a can before me. She opens a smoky-blue cupboard door that has been painted over many times. She pulls down a beer glass. Giselle's upper arms are bulging with muscles and her waist is narrow. I am certain that guys have tried to circle it with their hands and she has laughed them off, then become annoyed.

'They asked me if I got a good look at him. But I had to say I didn't. He just pushed me out of his way. I was looking at the other fellow, trying to understand what was going on. It wasn't clear at first.'

Giselle sits opposite me. She pulls off her headband and her hair is greasy and thin.

'I think I'll have a beer too.'

As she moves I watch the stubble in her armpits. There is a slit above her nostril from a piercing and her earlobes have rows of silver studs.

'I wonder what he's doing now, the killer I mean. He could be sitting somewhere having a beer, just like us. I bet he's headed interstate. Up north. Well, you would, wouldn't you?'

I see two guys pitted against each other in the garage on the Point, the walls still smelling of wet paint. A knife pulled out. Pants shitted.

'Do you think they knew each other?'

'I'm pretty sure they did. Maybe I'm imagining it, but the vibe was there. It was something that finished badly. Maybe he didn't even want to do it, you know? But they knew each other all right. I'll probably tell that to the police. I mean, they'll want to know why and I'll say it's just a feeling.'

'Maybe you should be more careful from now on.'

'I'm always pretty careful.'

'Well, I think I might head off.'

'Yeah, I've gotta shower and see these guys.'

'I guess you won't be jogging in the park for a while.'

'I could do.'

She takes me to the front door and I see a room in shadow I hadn't noticed before. There is a yoga mat rolled out beneath the window, which opens onto the arms of the massive tree outside. I see a warm bronze

Buddha sitting on a shelf and a pale orchid in a pot. One day I would like to watch Giselle do yoga again. The way every inch of her body was tuned, a triumph of equilibrium. Tai isn't there yet. She shakes and perspires and it is a pain to watch her. My other feelings take hold and I have to rake these back. Tai has decided to remain a virgin until it's the right moment.

On a table by the door is a picture of Giselle and a much younger girl. Giselle's arm is around her shoulders. The photo is from a few years ago but its meaning is clear. The girl has died. Placed near her box of keys, it looks like a reminder.

Giselle looks smaller behind the half-closed door with its Yale locks, she is glad to be relieved of me. She can't be that careful if she ran into an empty building and saw a man stabbing another man.

—

I decide to walk back towards Tai's place, though I imagine Nora will have penned her at the dinner table by now. Her phone will be off. The news might be watched afterwards. Or Tai's hands might flutter over the piano keys while Nora knits. If the sliding doors are open, I will hear her. She has to stop by nine o'clock otherwise the old man downstairs will call the police. Nora drops chunks of soil or cherry tomatoes onto his balcony, which juts out far beyond their tiny strip. The old man reports Nora for hanging out her washing, which is not allowed.

If the old man listened to Tai's music he would be healed. He has a tumour.

Tai and I were at the same high school but I really noticed her at my last swimming competition before I quit school. She was in the junior girls' relay team, she did breaststroke. I was captain of my squad, a couple of years above her. I swam butterfly and had the best time in the state. Tai wasn't a bad swimmer but the team lost. She wasn't selected for the district team and I guessed she wouldn't swim any more with her exams ahead. I went on to the nationals from there. I came in fifth on a bad day, the very worst.

I don't train any more.

I kept thinking of Tai's small face in and out of the water, its fierceness compared to the other girls. She had the propulsion and slinkiness of a rodent and when she climbed out her skin shone. I watched her shiver with the other girls, all hiding their brazen new chests. I saw how resolute she stood among them, how the losing cut into her.

After I quit I followed Tai home from school one day. I sat on one of the benches in the park, directly below her place. She knew who I was. She came out onto the balcony to look at me, then went back inside. I watched the bay. I remember a man came down and unlocked the metal gate to the marina, with its rolls of barbed wire like a punk bracelet. He walked along the jetty to his boat, turned on the engine, opened up the panels enclosing its frisky noise. A woman stood on the grass as though on a stage, reading from a book to a bunch of sailing boats.

Then Tai came outside, walked past me but didn't stop. On her way back she sat on the bench beside me. She took my hand and placed it on her thigh. That was a year ago now.

From Giselle's flat I walk out along the peninsula in the dusk, taking the road the ambulance went up this afternoon. The first stretch of apartments has been sold. They are two-storey duplexes, curved in a terrace overlooking the bay. Some of the gardens have climbing plants in bark-strewn beds or terracotta vases either side of the front door. A man beeps his car alarm and pushes open his gate. These places cost the most. Tai's block and the ones with the better view on the Point are smaller two-and three-bedroom apartments, probably some studio flats as well. The man has paused at his front door, staring at me as I pass his car. He's probably heard from his wife or girlfriend or boyfriend inside that a guy was knifed a few hundred metres away and he should watch out.

I reach the site of the murder. There is a portable fence around the whole garage area, tape over the doors. I stand where Giselle was standing when the policeman interviewed her. The concrete driveway has a black seam down the middle and I'm pretty sure this is where she was standing. There are two garage doors behind me, with two side-doors flanking these. The one to the left was the one Giselle entered when she heard the screams.

I turn back down the footpath to the bay. As it grows dark I begin to hear the halyards clanking against masts, waves slapping hulls. I slept here once, on a beach towel inside the cave on the rock shelf. Lights have come on in the terraces backing onto the park and in the block where Tai lives. The heaving water seems to rise into the sky, merging with its glittery molasses. I lie down in the grass and my brain feels like an entire galaxy. Tai has told me she can feel the same thing.

I wonder if the old man with the tumour will sleep tonight. The motion of the water, it would help him just to hear this.

I look up to Tai's apartment and there is a grey fuzz. Nora's watching SBS no doubt, some movie from Serbia or Ireland. I could walk around the back of the building where Tai's bedroom lies, just to be beneath her slowly undressing body. I know how much time she spends in front of the mirror. I know she's shaved herself down there. She says it's itchy but she won't let me touch her. She says all the girls do it. My ex-girlfriend from the swimming team had a tufted pod that showed under her costume. I imagine Tai's folds and my mouth fills with saliva. But wanting Tai has made me cleaner. The abstinence roars through me and there are days when it turns into a boundless force. I could climb rock faces, or swim to the other side of the river. It allows me to lie here ridden with stars, my tongue curling in my mouth. I am not even hard for her.

Tai said she had an older man proposition her when she was 15, on holiday with her cousins at the beach. She is the only Chinese member of the family. She wore big hats and didn't tan. He was a businessman from Hong Kong. He came up to her when she was reading Henry James in a café. He asked her if she'd like to come to his room. Tai filmed the guy on her smartphone and her mother called the cops. Now, Tai says, she would never have done that. She would have asked him for money and never told Nora. She would have just fucked him and had it over with, she says. Got rid of her virginity just like that. More than once. She says this with regret – she wonders if perhaps he had come for her, maybe he was family. She'd just been too young and dumb, too conditioned by Nora to see every man as a different shade of danger, just because Nora had had two of them and they had taken off. Tai says that perhaps she might have flown away with the businessman to Hong Kong, where he would have found her a job with a merchant bank. She is gifted with numbers. I have listened to this story expand. Sometimes she imagines she is sitting behind him on the aeroplane, watching him eat through the gap between the seats. Sometimes she meets his immaculate wife in their apartment. When she talks, I wonder if it is because of where she comes from that she needs to travel so far and so accurately. I know that in her life Tai has hardly left this suburb. Some days she says Nora should have left her in China where they'd have slit her throat.

Tai isn't pretty. She has a mole on one side of her nose like the final island of a long archipelago. The skin is denser there, flecked with dark hairs. It seems as though it was given to her at the last moment. She can't get it removed yet, the dermatologist has said. Tai is worried that with Nora's views arching over her, the mole will have to stay.

I sit up, the waves are short and agitated. The tide is about to turn. When I trained I used to know water. I could feel its cohesion, the way it is a cousin of the air. Water has a grip, it just pretends to be porous. Some days even the water in the pool felt like a clinging syrup and you wouldn't be allowed to stream along. Other days it was a buoyant liquid that thrust you down your lane.

I try to voyage like Tai does. I try to modulate the past and make it swing to my command. But for me this is impossible. I see Tai in the shack where she was born, the mother who hated the squall of her voice, who left her for days in her own shit. This is the only story I see on her smooth skin.

—

The following afternoon I walk along the footpath in front of Giselle's apartment block. I see where the branches of the Moreton Bay fig tree brush her windows with dark leaves. You could almost climb inside and tumble onto her yoga mat. It is brighter today than yesterday. The sky is sharp and the bricks of her block are burnt yellow. Giselle comes outside in a zippered hoodie and jeans, her hair fluffy. She holds a carton of paper rubbish.

'Hello there,' I say.

'Oh. Hello.'

She opens up the bin and tips out a carton of toilet rolls and pasta boxes, then a stream of newspapers and leaflets.

'How'd it go last night?' I say.

She frowns. Today she has put a silver ring through the nose piercing which changes the composition of her face. Everything now radiates from this puncture.

'You mean the police? It was pretty pointless. They showed me photos. One of them did a sketch on the computer. They wouldn't tell me anything about the dead guy.'

She throws the empty carton into the bin and turns away. There is no continuity from last night.

'Have you been down there today?' I ask.

'Where? To the park? Not yet. I'm headed down there now. I got in late.'

'Might catch you there.'

I imagine the pair of big constables filling up the stairwell with their shoulders and boots. Polite rapping on the door and two Anglo names announced.

She walks away and enters the building. I back off and cross the street, worried she might stand there watching me from the yoga room, thinking I'm a nutcase. Along the main road the eucalyptus trees lift and whir with the wind carving up the water. They are ragged trees with the bark torn away, or with cinnamon curls stuck to marbled trunks. They are inmates who know this land's burning colonial past: the smoke drifting after battles, a bullet tearing through black skin. It is written in them. Blue-green leaves lie on the footpath and I wonder if the murders are written into us too.

If the map of blood Giselle saw in the garage will have its edges scrubbed hard and some caustic acid thrown onto the cement by a foreign cleaner who knows we are a murderous people. That we have killed here, over and over, dark-skinned bodies thrown into the salt water.

I don't like the piercing on Giselle's face. I guess she inserted it before the police came, pushing the silver through the hole and stepping back to see herself in the mirror. Probably it makes her feel stronger. They might have told her to take it off at work.

I pass liver-bricked Federation houses with trellises and brass bells on brackets clinking in the wind. These homesteads have names like Stepney, Mile End, Rudley's Chase. Sometimes an Italian woman in an apron comes outside to cut roses. Sometimes a worn Lebanese man is rolling a cigarette on a step. I cut through to the new estate carpeting the Point with its signs saying SOLD! SELLING FAST! Tai says we are a bunch of cowboys here, that we will never amount to much. On days that it suits her she goes on about Chinese history and culture, other days she stares cross-eyed at Vietnamese ladies on the bus. Giselle jogs past me. Her pace is swift and the muscles of her thighs are at work. She ignores me and descends to the park.

I follow her down there. My bench is occupied so I walk along the stone wall above the sand strip, then cross over to a vacant one in the shadows. I am close to the terraced houses backing onto the park. The place behind me has its own swimming pool wrapped in a glass fence. A little girl wearing floaties jumps into the water. She climbs out, runs around, jumps in again. Giselle begins her yoga with some loose stretches, then drops down, flattening her hands on the grass, printing them there. She rises slowly, lifts her heel into her crotch, one leg bent up, arms raised over her head, palms pressed together. She holds each pose long enough for someone to sketch her on a page. From here, she looks supple and poised, but yesterday when I was closer I could see the effort the poses required of her, each one a departure point into a gulf that was bodiless. Yesterday, until she broke down and cried, Giselle travelled to that place. I wish Tai could do this. I would love to see Tai's body extended as a bird's, swooping down to the earth. But I know that Tai is not ready to consign herself to anything or anybody.

When she is finished, Giselle comes over to me. Her features are razor-sharp, the nose ring moves with her breaths.

'Look. You're freaking me out. What the fuck do you want from me?'

'Nothing. I'm just watching.'

'Well stop it, would you? I know people like you. People who check up on you and hang around and try to be nice. I was dumb enough to bring you up yesterday but I was in shock, you know? And now you're freaking me. If I see you again I'm calling the cops. I'll say you're harassing me.'

'I'm not harassing you. I always come to this park. My girlfriend lives here.'

'I don't care where your girlfriend lives. I said you're freaking me out.'

Her arms drop to her sides and I notice a pulse on her stomach skin which is exposed below her tank top.

'I'm sorry,' I say.

'Yeah, the fuck you are. I can't believe you even know where I live! You try anything and I swear I know who you are. They'll find you.'

She twists off, the graceful bird gone from her. I stare out to the water, pushing away my shock. Mostly, these boats are never unmoored. Their wood is sodden, bird crap splatters their decks; they spend their lives yanking on chains.

Giselle half-jogs a few metres then turns back. She stands in front of me, her face fallen.

'Look. I'm sorry. I know you're not a freak. I have seen you here before too. With that Chinese chick. I know you're all right. I'm sorry I lost it on you.'

'That's okay. You've been through a lot.'

'I don't think I should have come here today.'

'Maybe not.'

'Are we fine then?' she says. 'Are you sure we are?'

'We're fine, Giselle.'

She jogs away through the trees.

On Saturday mornings Tai is allowed to see me. It's the gap where she used to play netball, so Nora can't really protest. Tai can't study endlessly. Besides, her exams are not for seven months. At first Nora stands watching on the balcony. She is an ex-smoker and her hands twitch in the sun. Below her the old man moves about on his terrace with an aluminium watering can. He stoops at each flowerpot and earthenware vase. From here it seems that there is a neighbourly rapport between them. Tai and I normally do not touch, but today she leans on my shoulder. I think of the businessman from Hong Kong, working up the courage to approach her reading a Henry James novel in Coffs Harbour. I see his silver-framed glasses, a horizontal slit etched in each oval, the café reflected in the glass. One day I know Tai will kiss me and our mouths will explode.

Tai has decided she wants me to be the first one. She says she used to think it should be a stranger, in case it hurt or she hated it. But she's touched herself down there, put things inside. She tells me she thinks she can feel what's going to happen. Tai says Nora has a vibrator hidden in her drawer, and at times there are snatches of her cries in the night. Listening to Nora has made Tai despise bald, noisy emotion. That is why I wouldn't be surprised if, when the next businessman asks her, she lets him take her away.

It's a crazy thing, entering a girl's body, just to contemplate that you are inside the confines of her skin. I think that I would be overwhelmed if I entered Tai's body. I'm worried I might go blind, like a man who has stared at the sun, or that I could freeze inside of her and we would be stuck together forever – I've read online that it happened. I know it would not compare to the other girls I've been with, their squealing and clenching. I would be engulfed. Just now I have begun to think that if it were possible I would prefer Tai to enter *me* and feel her pushing *my* organs. I would sooner have her within me rather than invade her. I could not handle hearing her disguised grief.

Nora goes inside. She watches the Italian news at ten o'clock, the last night bulletin from the other side of the world. She can't see us from the couch. I have waited all week to smell Tai next to me and now her hair is beneath my lips. I part it with my nose and sense the thick strands flaring from her scalp. Tai draws away. She looks at my face, her gaze moving over every feature. She takes my hands which are furnaces within hers. She releases them and they return to my lap. She slips her fingers under her thighs, tilting, so her hair falls in a black quiver. Her body inches away from mine so that we are no longer touching. My head is reeling, but this is how it is. There are days when she laughs a lot and tells me about her English professor whose freckled hand lingers on her forearm. There are others when we sit like two old people who have no mirrors in the house because each is the reflection of the other. These are very moving days.

Down on the strip of sand, a father walks into the water in a pair of baggy shorts. A small boy bounces around, clapping and skipping. They have a radio-controlled boat. The father sets the boat in the water. It is a racing boat, not really meant for the jerky shallows. The waves push the boat to the shore and the father splashes back to retrieve it. They walk out further. The father holds up the boat and the propeller starts to buzz. He places it on the surface and it does one furious circle.

I know Tai hasn't got much time left before Nora calls her up and tells her they have to go food shopping. I look at her knees, shaven too, and the opaque lengths of her thighs. Tai's phone lights up and she doesn't answer.

There is a cry. The speedboat has gone straight into one of the anchored sailing boats and lies still, already far away. The father wades in a little, then pulls back. He is a non-swimmer. The backwash tugs the boat around the other side of the hull and soon the tiny craft is being drawn out through the moored vessels, its red plastic less and less distinct. The pair stand on the shoreline as the boat reaches the body of the river.

Tai turns to me. 'Why don't you swim out there and get it for them?

You can do it.'

I look at her, to see where this request might be coming from.

'It was a stupid place to put it in.'

'If you swim out there, I will do it with you. Today. Now. We can go to the cave in the rocks.'

My heart jolts. It is a seedy cave, horrible with fires and brutal sex.

'Don't say that.'

'You don't want to?'

'No, I don't. Not there I don't.'

She moves as though she is getting ready to go. She swings her dusty feet. 'You won't do it?'

'No.'

The boy is crying. The father's shoulders have rounded. I think of the green water gripping my legs. The water is cold here and the riverbed is clean enough, but years ago it was full of trash and jelly blubbers and putrid slicks. Not even the sharks came upstream. It's probably about 100 metres out there, two lengths of the pool, something I used to thrive on. I've done ocean races where the waves slap you about, currents snaring your limbs and sea creatures tracing your thighs.

'Kiss me now,' I say to her.

Tai's jaw moves. Her toes splay in the dirt and she looks out. There is a RiverCat crossing the bay now, the racing boat is drifting towards its path. The boy squats in the sand with his arms wrapping his head.

The father tries to see through the masts.

'It's too far now anyway,' Tai replies. 'Look at that fool.'

When she leaves she says sorry, it just came into her head. I watch her walking back to her place. Nora is on the balcony.

———

I don't go to the park for a few days. I have my own stuff to do. There are times when I forget Tai. Not for long, but she is far from my thoughts. She calls me once, but I see the call afterwards. I do not call her back. I will wait until next Saturday to see her in a better mood. When I am in a big shopping centre I see Giselle sitting in a café, wearing a blouse and a plum-coloured skirt. Her hair is pinned back and sits in a curl above her neck.

'What are you doing around here?' she says.

'Just picking up some trainers. My old ones have had it.'

'I'm on break for another ten minutes. Like a coffee or a juice?'

'Sure.' I edge through the tables and sit down opposite her. She looks well-rested; the nose piercing has been removed.

'I work in the building society over there. Been a slow one. Haven't seen you around lately. Look, you don't need to stay away.'

'I'm not staying away.'

'So you'll be back then?'

'Yeah, I will.' I order an orange juice and a bright cupful is poured out from a machine.

'Health freak, are we? Did you read about the guy that was stabbed?'

'No.'

'They were cousins. The dead guy owed him money. The killer came all the way in from the country and then he caught the train all the way back. He was waiting for the cops in his kitchen. Came away without a fuss. They even looked the same in the newspaper. Crazy, hey?'

'Yeah.'

'I guess that'll be a hard block to sell. Or maybe not. People can be weird.'

The orange juice is chilled and acidic with metallic-tasting strands. I used to get a navel orange in my lunchbox when I was a kid. I thought they had something to do with the sea, the navy. There is a swirl of pulp and liquid at the bottom of the glass.

'Your girlfriend doing her HSC?'

I nod. 'She doesn't get out much. Her mother is strict.'

'She looks really brainy. Not because she's Chinese, I mean. I bet she studies hard.'

'Yes, she does.' I feel like telling Giselle that Tai is perfect. I imagine putting the words out there, seeing Giselle's face take them in.

'Well, I'd better head on otherwise my boss'll have a fit. See you at the park one of these days, then? Maybe you can pop upstairs and we can have some pizza.'

'That would be great.'

She slips through the tables and pays, walks a way down the main thoroughfare and then through glass doors into the place where she works. In the darkened yoga room, under the boughs of the Moreton Bay fig tree outside, I can see our bodies pushing together. Giselle would be firm and soundless, never looking into my face. She'd be glad when it was over. I watch the woman opposite eat a big piece of fluffy cake with caramel icing. She forks it into her mouth slowly, staring at passers-by.

I end up at the park on my usual bench. The sun is still high and the water is drained out. The fisherman is sturdy in the sand, newspaper cupping his bait like a desert flower. I look at his line sloping into the water. The boats all point east, none of them bucking against the tide, no sound except for the *cark* of birds. The fisherman looks back at me, nods. I turn to Tai's apartment, knowing she will be wandering down from the bus stop now. I'd pick her up from there but her mother won't allow it.

I see Nora on the balcony in a pair of red ballooning trousers. She sees I am on the bench. Tai says she is exasperated by my constant presence. She has told Tai I am a dropout who is surely on drugs. I think of Tai's offer the other day, being played by her. I might have held her in the filthy cave last Saturday. It could have happened. I reel back to what I should have said, but the only way I can regain some sort of control is by imagining my limbs slicing through water. I imagine swimming hard, against a current, a gruelling distance.

I get up and walk along the sandstone wall to the rock face, climb up to the same level as the cave. I round the Point and stand in front of its mouth, now an open tomb layered with pebble-smattered rock. I crawl in but it is too much. There is a whorl of wrath and the hole smells of shit.

I move outside, standing with the burdened peninsula at my shoulders. If it were possible to dive here I would spring into the shallows and swim as far as my limbs would go, no matter the ferries and vessels, I would just swim and swim until something carved me into shreds.

I see Tai approaching me on the rocks in her school uniform. Her white socks are rolled down. She is coming to apologise for last week. I sit on the ancient stone, turning away from her. We will walk together to our grove, here above the water's milky tissue.

The Russian Girl

When Louise came downstairs the next morning the Russian girl was tying up rubbish bags with swift double knots. To anyone else Louise would have said there was no need, but she let the young woman shuffle outside with the two smeared bags. Louise even pointed to the bins by the gates of the small villa so that she might feel obliged, and checked out the girl's pert bum screened by a pair of rose capri pants. She couldn't recall exactly what the girl had been wearing the night before but it had been busty and sheeny, and she knew the males had groaned after her, holding their loaded crotches. Louise also had a gut feeling that the Russian girl had ended up in her brother-in-law's tent. How else to explain this act of contrition?

Louise glanced at the kitchen counter, now freed of her husband Daniele's stoned cooking efforts. A coffee percolator sat on a blue ring of flames. Louise put on the kettle for some green tea. The Russian girl's name was Yulia. She was new to Verona and a friend of someone's girlfriend, invited to help redress the gender imbalance. Louise always provided far too many men at her annual summer party, single men who thunked to AC/DC when the couples had melded into the dark corners of the garden.

Yulia came through the back door holding Louise's son Angelo on her hip. Louise opened the tea tin, feeling hangover-lousy.

'Did you wash your hands after touching that rubbish?' she said, not really wanting Angelo's outstretched arms.

'Of course. We play now. Where are Angelo's toys?'

'They're out the back on the terrace. In a big trunk. Those are his outside toys.'

Yulia smiled a gooey smile at Angelo and swept outside. Graceful, Louise thought, after all that gyration last night. Louise heard the toy box open, and Angelo pitching trucks onto the tiles. She exhaled. She knew that the right thing to do now would be to call Francesca, her brother-in-law Diego's wife, and see how she'd passed the night. Francesca had a stitch in her cervix and the baby was due next month.

But Louise walked back to the cooler front rooms of the house with her cup of tea. On her divan was a sleeping man wrapped up in one of her *kente* cloths. It was Ross, Daniele's best mate, who'd flown out from London for the bash. He'd also been vying for the Russian girl through the first phase of the night, until it was clear her brother-in-law had somehow scooped the evening's prize. Louise was almost certain she'd seen Ross throwing himself about to an AC/DC track on his own after the DJ did a runner, which was when she noticed Yulia and Diego hand-in-hand crossing the wet grass. Around dawn she'd finally tucked under Daniele's shoulder as Ross rolled yet another joint, a dozen empty prosecco bottles across the tables between them.

She unlocked the door to her study and sat awhile. She heard the gates creak open and a car drive out up the hill. As the day drew on guests would either drag themselves back to town or dig in for the day-after party. Someone would revive the fire, some younger person would put the music on full blast, jazz or mild hip-hop. The dogs would lie sated under the trees, bellies full from the barbecue last night. There was still a plastic bag of meat in the spare fridge.

She could just see one end of the bright blue tent her son had helped her erect yesterday afternoon. She'd set it up for Diego who'd had a stressful year and didn't much like to be bothered, who had driven in alone from Milan, sweaty and strong-smelling, and headed straight for the downstairs shower. This was before she had rushed inside to finish the flans. Now the tent zipper was open, wafting, a woman's summer skirt. No sign of Diego. Warm sunlight was starting to douse the grass and two men she didn't recognise were shifting a cane chair under the trees, both with bare tattooed chests.

The door pushed open and Ross popped around the corner.

'Louise? All on your lonesome?'

'I thought you were dead to the world,' Louise said.

'I think I was for a while there. I can't sleep any longer on that godaw-ful sofa.'

He turned to the window as Angelo crossed the garden kicking a ball, a robust Yulia behind him. She was all muscle and flying raven hair.

'Hey,' he said. 'She even comes up good in the daylight.'

'They all do, don't they? That kind.'

'That's a bit harsh. You said you needed some fillies to join up the dots. She's a great-looking filly.'

They watched her tumble to the ground and let the child's ball pass towards the fence. Yulia rolled over and Angelo straddled her belly, bouncing while the young woman laughed. 'You were tailing her for a good while last night,' Louise said. 'Looks like Diego beat you to it.'

'It wasn't really like that,' he replied.

'What were you talking about all that time?' Louise had seen them on one of the outside divans, Ross wearing an unusually disarmed face.

'We were talking about education, really.'

'Oh, come on.'

'It's true. She said she's brought her son to Italy because the schools are rotten where she is, and she got out just before the war. She said her husband used to beat her. He cracked her cheekbone twice.'

'Right, pull the other one,' said Louise. 'Next you'll tell me her family perished in Chernobyl and she walked all the way here in those nasty stilettos she had on last night.'

'She did lose her grandparents there. And both her parents died young. She grew up in an orphanage outside Moscow. She told me her daughter died of leukaemia last year. She was four.'

Louise gasped, her eyes knitting together, propelled towards her son. They both watched as there was a flutter or beckoning from Diego's tent and Yulia fell to her hands and knees and crawled inside.

—

Louise settled Angelo in front of a cartoon in the only childproof zone of the house, and went upstairs to the bedroom. Her husband Daniele was still outstretched on top of the sheets. He opened his eyes as she walked in.

'*Vieni qui, bellezza.*'

'Not now, Daniele.'

She sat down on the rumpled bed, thinking of the pale-faced daughter in the hospital ward and Yulia's bone cracked by a man's fist, her cheek swollen and the bruising seeped around an eye. It couldn't be true. She told herself that Ross had been swayed by the dope and the loud music, the girl's cupped breasts. Daniele nuzzled her back, cradling himself to her. She pulled away from his hot body and went to the bathroom, where she sat on the laundry basket. From the window she saw the bright blue tent in the middle of the garden. A couple lay entwined in the hammock and the two bare-chested guys drank beers in the shade; a woman from her office sat cross-legged on the grass wearing a burgundy straw hat.

Daniele came in, sat on the rim of the bath.

'He fucked her, didn't he?' she said.

Daniele was the older brother and now his face remained steady. He kneeled down on the bath mat, a little cautious on his dodgy left knee, opening her with his chin, stroking her thighs with bristly cheeks, pulling across her panties and reaching her cunt with his cool tongue. She clasped his head, felt the oil in his scalp. Louise had been to Moscow for a conference once and hated it. The men with grey swabs under their eyes, the statuesque silken women who would one day decompress into their pillowy mothers with pincushion faces and arms. She had marvelled at the flower stalls on a freezing Saturday morning until a colleague told her they were 'forgiveness flowers'. Forgive what?

Forgive me for beating the shit out of you.

—

Louise stepped out of the shower and her son handed her the downstairs telephone. The music was on loud outside and she shut the bathroom window. Louise sat on the laundry basket again. It was Francesca, Diego's wife. Francesca had spent the last five months confined to her bed. Most nights, apart from when he had his tennis matches, Diego had been stationed in the next room reading the newspaper.

'Do you have any idea when Diego's heading out? I've had a pretty bad night.'

Francesca sounded teary, ever so bleak.

'Sometimes I can't feel the baby moving any more, you know? And then I lie there waiting. I even tap my tummy to get him to move. Is that stupid?'

Louise remembered pushing tent pegs into the soft ground, wanting Diego to be comfortable, feeling guilty that her cousin and her kids out from Bristol had taken up half the house. She had thought he might feel out of the fray there, able to bed down if he got tired of the dancing under the portico around the back. She had never imagined the warm enclave might provide a shroud for two fused bodies.

'It's fine,' Louise told her. 'It used to happen to me all the time.'

'Is Diego anywhere nearby? I suppose they must all be sleeping still.'

'Well, yes. I've hardly seen anyone yet. They're beginning to surface downstairs and someone's just put the music on. I haven't seen him so far.'

'Another long one, hey? Gosh, I bet you worked so hard. I'm so sorry I'm stuck here and can't give you a hand.'

'Don't worry, Fran. You just sit tight. Next year we can get legless.'

'Next year I'll be bloody breastfeeding.'

Francesca was on the verge of crying but all Louise could see were Yulia's flimsy capri pants being thrown aside, and Diego ascending her flesh. They were sensual stocky brothers, both with round, jutting bottoms and heavy lips. Before her love for Daniele had triggered, it was Diego that she had wanted. She and Diego had once kissed.

'Are you okay there?' Louise said.

'Yes, I am,' Francesca replied. 'I'll be okay. I just don't like being on my own too much. I'll be fine. Tell him I called.'

Louise stared down at the blue tent in the middle of the garden. The couple in the hammock were snogging, arms wrapped around each other. The trio in the shade were leaning over eating sections of watermelon.

Daniele pushed open the bathroom door and turned on the shower.

'That was Francesca,' she said.

He opened the linen cupboard and took a towel from the top. Water splattered against the glass door until he reached in to lower the pressure.

'What must it be like,' she said, 'throwing yourself at anything that moves?'

Her husband took two tired steps towards her. She loved him infinitely for what he was about to say, but knew she would do her utmost to batter it down.

'Louise,' he said. 'You are not responsible.'

Now Louise recalled the look on Diego's face as he danced with Yulia. Astonished and bold, a face activated by rebellion. And Yulia so vulgarly agile in his arms in that shiny dress falling from her shoulder, bending her body around his.

'I am responsible for my lies.'

Louise took a short sundress from the wardrobe and rubbed suncream into her face. She stayed barefoot and went downstairs. Fresh coffee sat brewing on the stove and she greeted her cousin's teenage daughters, all part of the tireless dancing clan last night, who were teasing her enraptured son. Biscuits were stacked on a plate and croissants were being tipped from an oven tray into a basket. It was a good thing the Russian girl had bagged so much rubbish before as the bins were quickly filling again, and these young girls had no intention of tidying.

Ross, shirtless, was sitting outside in the sun wearing a pair of women's sunglasses. He was drinking from a jug of pinot grigio someone had refreshed with ice. She poured herself a full plastic cup and edged into the shade. The tent was a dozen metres off in the middle of the bleached lawn, whose fringes were now dotted with chatting people lounging in the shadows. A smoke plume rose from the barbecue. The tent flap had been zippered, its blue flanks were still.

'Do you think she tells the story about the dead child and the smashed cheekbone to every sucker she meets?' Louise said. 'It must be rather stifling in there by now.'

'Louise,' Ross replied. 'They left an hour ago. She had to pick up her kid and Diego gave her a ride into town.'

⸺

Louise looked at the painting above Francesca's head. It was by Daniele's grandfather, a provincial painter who'd managed to sell a lot of work. His was a strain of localised surrealism, unfriendly to the eye and – Louise had always thought – to women. In this work, long knuckled fingers clutched at elusive shapes. The dynamic seemed uncomfortably sexual, bearing a wet pulse, and revealed a cloying internal diorama. She suspected maternity to be the muffled subject: the parting of childbirth, the moistness of the organs; the renewed filling of that gulf by penetration. It was as close to an heirloom as the family possessed and she had never wanted it in her house.

Today, the painter's great-grandson lay in Francesca's lap, her massive dark brown nipple pressed to his face. Francesca was sweating, her neck and breast glistened as she touched his damp curls. The strain of these months, the final bursting through of the child, had left her a ruin. Louise filled her glass with another nip of foamy Guinness.

She heard the men in the kitchen. Daniele was tipping pasta into the colander and a hot chute of water coursed into the marble sink. Diego was setting out plates and cutlery. They were laughing together as brothers and speaking in dialect.

That day, that blistering morning after the party, Louise had shaken down the address from someone. She'd made a stubborn, torn Daniele drive her into town, had sent him upstairs into the ugly apartment block near Porta Nuova station. Twenty minutes it had taken. Then Daniele had brought his younger brother out onto the footpath like a criminal. Diego had stood there collecting himself, his blunt hands dropped before his jeans. As they pulled into the street Louise saw the Russian girl come outside and stand on the narrow balcony. She leaned over to see who was in the car, watched them drive away.

Life

There were dark, earthen children in the school. The war had ended, and the people had been swept from one end of the country to the other, and now the sombre faces of these new refugee children enclosed riotous teeth. At the nursery school they had crept in, and then there were many.

He leaned on the school fence, making a study of their movements in the playground, wondering whether they were hardier or possessing different skills.

He was ushered away from the school fence by a woman with a whistle.

But he asked her, 'Those dark kids who have come here, are they any different?'

He was a curious man who watched many documentaries, especially about distant places. Perhaps if he had lived in a peaceful country, he might have earned the money to travel. As a man he would have liked to speak to a dark-skinned man, from a village like his own with clambering goats. About his life and his wives (he knew that some tribes allowed several), about the seasons and the soil. Then he would shake this man's hand and know him better.

Earlier in his life the man had raised his two sons after his wife died when her brakes failed on a mountain road. His sons had been active joyful boys. But the war had taken them, and they had not come back.

Foundation Song

He describes the persimmon tree as an equilibrium of weight and colour; a tree Gauguin would have liked. They stand at the bottom of her wrangled garden. The wet branches are clotted with scathing orange balls you could plunge a finger into and it would come out sullied with orange jelly, like you were poking inside breasts.

In her language the fruit is called *caco*. There is no path between the two words.

They go to a concert which is *King Arthur* by Purcell. When the King dies in the snow she can feel the capitulation of the army of her cells and the oozing inertness of her body.

After the concert he collects their coats. His phone rings and he stands on the ruffled carpet of the auditorium with his phone cupped to his ear. In the car he tells her that his son has a disease and he will fly back to his country tomorrow. The disease is in its early stages and curable. He says he will stay there as long as it takes the boy to fight this malady.

How she misses him already. It's like a tourniquet applied to thrusts of blood.

Nathalie

The plane was held up in Lomé. Mona didn't bother leaving the house. She checked that Miguel was sleeping. He was. The slow fan wheeled above him, his hand clenched a fistful of mosquito netting which she loosened and let drop. She went out to smoke on the terrace, the city air a giant belch of open sewers and fried food, a gassy decomposition. Mona had seen travellers gag at the channels of waste snaking through the city. Where old women straddled and pissed, where a fallen coin might as well have plopped into magma. But for her it was the most acute of honesties, the travails of the city were naked.

Nathalie called again and Mona's stomach eased. The plane had landed, she sounded intact. Mona was relieved she would not have to spend the night visualising local technicians fingering the plane's entrails on the tarmac. She could sleep. From the liveliness in Nathalie's voice she must have met some fellow traveller on the flight and shared the wait. Mona's envy unwound. The only people who talked to Mona on planes were women as chiselled as herself. They were a robust tribe, nationless and colourless, they made lean talk.

Mona parked in the new carpark and shushed away the watchmen closing around her. She pointed at a bright-faced one and the others slouched away. She strode up to the dense triptych of the airport entrance and saw her daughter standing to one side talking to a tall man; a returnee, she ventured.

'*Maman!*' Nathalie broke free, nestled her face in Mona's neck, the shameless child who used to sit on her belly and tweak her nipples. '*Tout va bien? Et Miguel?* Why didn't he come? You left him sleeping at the house?' She placed her cheek against Mona's, her skin still so soft, a loving gesture.

'This is Seth, *Maman*. His family is from here. He's working in Paris too. He's been commissioned for a project in the north.' Nathalie made space for Seth's long arm to wend out and their hands shook. Mona's thoughts: edgy, cool, burning for success. They would sleep together before Nathalie flew out.

Seth had a ride coming in from Teshie, an aunt who was a nurse. He was fair-skinned, with fine freckled features and trendy thick-rimmed glasses. Mona was staring. Chaos surrounded them now. Another plane had released its passengers and they pushed as a many-headed mass through the glass doors as porters stormed towards them.

She wanted to take Nathalie home, to have her on the terrace sipping a mug of green tea. She tugged Nathalie's arm.

'Miguel is alone,' she said.

'Of course! Seth, I'll call you tomorrow, *d'accord*? We'll most probably go to the beach, okay *Maman*?'

Mona took Nathalie's camera bag and pushed past the hustlers and vendors, down the steps and under the neem trees back to the carpark. She didn't want Nathalie to see the tears that had sprung into her eyes. Her jealous tears. She had wanted Nathalie to herself.

In the car Nathalie chattered. 'I was so certain we would be catching a bus from Lomé! You have no idea how full the plane was until Abuja! I'd forgotten. It's been too long, hasn't it Mona? Just how have you been in your little house on the roof? Are they paying you properly in that silly school? Does your lover still visit when Miguel has gone to sleep?'

She pinched Mona's side and Mona could feel the skin stretch. Months ago now, her lover had returned to his town when his young girlfriend had died delivering twins. He had asked Mona for money and disappeared, leaving Mona feeling robbed.

'How long can you stay with us this time? You're not going to go north with that guy?' Mona said.

'Oh, *Maman*! He's a photographer too. It will be good to work with someone else. He has funding, you see. He is working on a book.'

'What of Xavier?'

'It's over, Mona. I told you that. Don't make me go there again.' Nathalie spilled a knot of tobacco into a skin and rolled up fast. 'Here Mona, take a drag on this.'

Mona inhaled and it rushed into her blood.

'How is that little monkey, Miguel? Is he still your sweetbread?'

The truth was that Miguel was a challenge. He had the same flints in his eyes as his rogue father. He was disobedient. He loved to trick her, lie to her. Mona began to cry in the dark.

'Oh, *mon choux*!' Nathalie touched her hair, smoothed her neck. 'Don't cry, *Maman*. It will be okay. I've missed you so much. Now we will be together.'

They brought her bags up the damp concrete stairwell to Mona's haven at the top. Four rooms, a detached shower and washroom, the apartment was an afterthought on top of the block, with views from the sea line to the fuzz of cheap cement houses spotting the scrub, all the way to the blurred violet ridges behind the city. But it provided the sky at all hours, in all her moods. Mona prepared tea while Nathalie tickled Miguel in bed. Later they sat out there in silence, Mona having forgotten all she had wished to say to her.

—

Miguel charged into her room and wriggled under the thin sheet. Mona had put Nathalie in her studio, where there was a spare mattress propped behind her easels. Last year Nathalie had brought her boyfriend Xavier with her and they'd been intertwined, interchangeable, every comment and glance. Mona, whose loves had been unequal and endured, adored their complicity. But something had erased what had thrived between them. Nathalie had moved on and Xavier was a thing of the past.

Miguel pinched her soft stomach. 'This is my home, *Maman*! My old house! Wake up so we can go to the beach!'

She felt his wet breathing on her neck. The two of them, Nathalie and Miguel, were the only ones who still identified the parts of her body that had produced them. Her hardy breasts, her old womb, her shabby middle.

'Get off me, Miguel. You are too hot.'

She was surprised to see Nathalie already up in the kitchen in a T-shirt and shorts, her city skin so pale.

'*Bonjour, Maman*! I've just called Seth. You don't mind if he joins us at Kokrobitey? I know you will like him. Look! Here is your present. I brought you some tools and paints.'

Nathalie opened the box of Japanese tools and Mona saw knives for slicing through linoleum, scalpels for her buttery paintings. The gleaming tubes in a row.

'And I saw your work in the studio – *juste un petit peu* – you must show me afterwards. I am so happy to see you are working!'

In an hour there were deep in the sluggish traffic through Kaneshie, the market thronging, churchgoers pacing along the overhead bridge, mothers close to the kerb with dangling children sashed to their backs. If Mona painted more longingly here it was because at home she was constricted, she could hardly explore her compulsion. Here she had found colonial villas painted toothpaste blue, and flaking stucco archways and statues dappled with tiles. There were lopsided hotels over the Atlantic from the post-Independence years, with dry shattered swimming pools and perilous diving towers.

Mona worked hungrily. In the beginning, nobody but Nathalie knew. After school Miguel went downstairs to kick a football with the children from the block and she went into the hot narrow room with its ceiling fan and glass louvers rusted into place. She sketched, she also worked from photographs. The young boxers in the square downtown, their faces twisted masks. Children soaped along the fetid canal while in the background, football players scrambled in the dust.

'Miguel, have you been looking after *Maman* for me?' Nathalie had asked her brother about the school teacher he detested, and before that about the dog downstairs that had disappeared. Of their two fathers, Miguel's had been more passionate, but crueller. He had grafted Mona onto his life when his partner left him. Slowly, he had enthralled her, leached her, he had almost stolen the child.

'Where is Xavier?' Miguel had asked.

'Xavier has gone back to his old girlfriend,' Nathalie finally revealed to them both. 'That wimp. He's gone back to London.'

The road behind the beach huts was sandy and knotted with bumps. Mona's low Peugeot revved and laboured along the latticed palm fence on one side, that marked out the private plots of the foreigners. Diplomats had started to upgrade the area with concrete weekenders fanning out from the coast, some had walls crenulated with broken glass, and uniformed watchmen carrying batons. Mona had been lucky. She'd been handed down an unpretentious wooden hut by the cultural envoy at the embassy. He hadn't liked his successor, and offered it to her. Sitting at the end of the sweep of beach, for the moment it was the last construction before the rocky point.

She pulled into a gap in the fence but there was a car parked in her spot, a white Suzuki with churchgoers' stickers on the back window. The aunty from Teshie. Seth had borrowed a car. Mona looked around for him and there he was, stepping off the porch to greet them.

'Who's that?' said Miguel. 'There's someone at our house!'

'It's okay, Miguel. It's my friend Seth. He was on the plane with me from Paris.'

Nathalie hopped out quickly and they walked towards each other, exchanging kisses on the cheek. Miguel stared.

'Come on, Miguel,' Mona said. 'Help me with the bags.'

A shirtless villager rushed up behind the car. It was Jacob, their watchman, wearing a pair of Mona's old shorts with a woman's plaited leather belt. He opened the boot and brought Mona's cool box and baskets up the steps, fishing for the keys in his pocket.

'Hello again, Mona,' said Seth.

'Seth, this is my little brother, Miguel,' Nathalie said, holding her brother's shoulders. 'Miguel, meet Seth.'

Miguel sized up the tall man with an impressive Leica on a strap around his neck. For years now Nathalie had no longer lived with them and her visits were short, exquisite eddies. The last time she and Xavier left, Miguel had shouted at Mona, he had screamed and sobbed at her on the terrace, until he had folded into a chair and slept. Miguel turned away from the pair. He ran down onto the sand to play.

Briefly, Nathalie helped Mona unpack. But Jacob took over, flinging out the printed tablecloth and pegging it in the wind, putting out glasses and a jug of cool water immediately. After years in the employ of her high-ranking predecessors, Mona had failed to rewire his zest. At times she sat back and was grateful for it. Twice, though she shrank to think of it now, she had paid Jacob to stay away. She had sent Miguel to a friend's house and had brought her lover here. The young man had waded into the thick night waves, beckoning her. She had thought of their bodies washed up in a putrid cove in the city.

Mona opened three bottles of beer. The surf frittered along the beach and the wind tugged her hair. Nathalie threw out her towel and sat down in her bikini. Seth watched her and gingerly lowered himself. As he crouched on the sand in his jeans and grey T-shirt, his heavy boots still laced, Mona became curious to see his body. She rotated him in her head, naked, seeing the long heavy thing and his tight high buttocks. She saw that Nathalie's body was laid out for him. Mona hadn't had that sort of youth. Love had come in taut trickles and then gone furling back. Men had come to her in defeat and moved onward. Even her lover, the way he had allowed her to photograph his body, the way he'd stilled before her, she had seen his imminent departure written in his eyes.

Nathalie sat up and waved to her and Mona brought their beers onto the sand.

'*Tiens Maman*. Sit here with us. The sun is so rich!' she said.

But Mona shook her head then returned to the porch and drank alone. She watched Nathalie laugh. She saw her small hard breasts and flat stom-ach, her flexing thighs. Further away she looked at Miguel playing in the sand. Jacob walked down with his bucket and spade and helped the child dig. Other village kids raced up to the fair European to try to snatch his toys. They were dressed in rags with amulets around their necks to ward off the deadly spirits prowling the village. Though Mona wouldn't have minded, Jacob chased away their red furry heads.

After a while Nathalie trod back to the hut, sand stinging her feet. She tied on her sarong. She put sunblock on her arms and turned to Mona to smooth it into her back. Seth watched mother and daughter on the porch. He looked expectant. Mona felt a slither in her gut.

'We're going to walk to the point, *Maman*. Seth wants me to show him what's on the other side, and maybe take some shots. You'll watch his car, won't you? He says he has his camera stuff inside.'

Mona watched them walk away. When they were far enough, almost hidden behind a ledge, Mona saw their bodies hook together and share a probing kiss. Mona's eyesight was excellent.

—

Over an hour passed. Miguel and Jacob came back to the shade. Miguel was hungry. In the meantime, Mona had bought four baby barracuda from a pregnant girl with an aluminium basin on her head. To lower the tin the girl bent perfectly at the waist, her spine thrust straight out as the cumbersome belly dropped downward. Mona had seen this action over and over, and each time thought of how she would convey the extending vertebrae and the swaying breasts, the membrane harnessing the curled child. It would be hard to reproduce these kinetics. She too was hungry and had finished her second beer.

Jacob had lit a fire and now the coals were ready for grilling the fish. There they lay on the wood pallet with their slit bellies and numb eyes, just degrees away from life. Miguel had helped Jacob. He pushed the serrated knife into their slimy pouches, pulling out the squidgy stuff, watching the organs collapse in the sand.

Mona had begun to worry. The beer had a sour chemical taste. Everything was too warm and the wind had blown a veneer of grit over the table. She walked down to the water's edge, past the indentation Nathalie had left in the sand. She was wrong to fret. She paddled her feet, wishing she were the type of person to cast herself into the sea with abandon, to roll on the bottom and watch the waves from underneath. She wondered if this Seth were to be trusted, or if they were simply making love on the bed of a rock pool, the sea trailing over them, mouths cupped together.

Miguel shouted. She saw Jacob take off running. She looked to the point and saw Seth half-carrying, half-supporting her daughter down the rock shelf. Nathalie was limping, struggling with a knee, crying. There was blood on her thighs.

Mona gasped and began to run. As her throat dried to dust she had a quick déjà vu, indecipherable, merely an evil flare. Focussing as she ran, she saw that Seth looked as though a horrible poison had travelled through him, and his camera was gone. Mona saw Nathalie throw up on the sand.

Nathalie fell into her arms, pushing away from Seth. Jacob stood transfixed, Miguel grasping his waist. Mona wanted to shield her son's eyes, wanted to censor another image burnt into his memory, *the day my sister was attacked on the rocks*. Mona couldn't look at her fully. The soiled body, the sarong sticking to the blood, the wet shapes on her thighs. Mona wanted to scream at Seth. Broken sounds fell from her mouth.

She held Nathalie close. 'What happened to you? Who did this?' She smelt the acid in Nathalie's sweat, saw there was a small cut on the side of her neck. 'Oh, my baby!' she cried. 'Can you hear me?'

She began pulling Nathalie along. Nathalie sobbed with each step. Miguel held fast onto Jacob, who said something about the police. Seth strode along with them, hard-faced and silent.

When they reached the hut Seth dissolved. He climbed into his car and covered his face with his hands. Then he manoeuvred past Mona's car and drove off.

Mona ignored this and sat Nathalie on the rattan chair on the porch. She covered her scratched shoulders with a towel. Nathalie shook as the tears dried on her face. Jacob smothered the fire and began to pack their things.

'Miguel, help Jacob put the things in the car,' Mona said. 'I'm taking you to the hospital.'

'No.'

'Just tell me what happened.'

'Doesn't that seem rather obvious?' Nathalie said, turning on her. It wasn't the first time.

'Did he hurt you? Why didn't Seth do anything, for God's sake?'

'Oh, shut up, Mona. Just shut up.'

—

Mona had had her first exhibition at the French Cultural Centre a month ago. Nathalie, filming a documentary in Berlin, had been unable to come. Mona had sold three etchings which a friend of hers had framed. Two paintings were bought for inclusion at the Nungua Gallery, where a good deal of international tourists passed. Mona had received her first payments ever for her artwork. After so many dismal years, this was a triumph.

But the image she adored most had to leave her. It had been inspired by her lover, just before he had disappeared. One night Mona had taken out her camera. She began to photograph his body against the cool bathroom tiles, which was where they had just made love as Miguel slept. The canvas she painted afterwards showed a man on hands and knees pretending to prowl, his spine hanging low between his rump and high shoulders, the genitals concealed. Not prey, not a hunter, but a harrowed mythic creature. When her lover left her soon after she finished, she knew the painting belonged to neither of them.

Mona drove past the gallery on their way to the clinic. Nathalie had agreed to see Mona's gynaecologist, an older Ivorian woman who ran a clinic on the outskirts of town. The doctor cleaned Nathalie's wounds, took a swab and blood sample, while Mona listened to her daughter release weak cries. Mona felt dizzy. When they were young she had wanted to absorb their pain, to steal their fevers into her own skin. But this, the idea of wanting it, was ghastly.

'Have you gone to the police?' the doctor asked.

'No, my daughter didn't wish to.'

'Why on earth not? You don't think this is a crime? Were there any witnesses?'

There was Seth.

Nathalie called out from behind the screen. 'I'm not going to the police.'

'I recommend you think about this happening to someone else. Some other woman like yourself. It makes for a very unpleasant experience.'

They drove home through the traffic, Nathalie staring ahead. Mona had left Miguel at a friend's for a few days, without saying why. It was beginning to feel as though she had brought this on, the walk with Seth to the point, the sickly kiss. Is that what Nathalie was thinking?

'I'll take you home then. Maybe you should get some rest.'

But she knew Nathalie would not. She knew the man's smell would be there, the prick of the knife, the shocking organ steady.

'I'll make you a good cup of tea.'

They paced up the damp stairwell. Mona stumbled on the steps, grazed an elbow on the concrete wall, regained her balance. Up on the rooftop the evening wind channelled through the rooms. Nathalie walked directly out to the terrace and for a moment Mona worried she would cast her body over the rail. But she lowered herself onto a chair. She moved with pain, clutching her abdomen.

'Would you like a cover?'

Nathalie didn't answer. Mona brought out an old silky piece of *kente* cloth with rippling blues and golds. She tucked it around her. In the kitchen Mona prepared green tea and pulled down two cups from the shelf. These actions made her feel useful again, as though a healing could begin. She thought of her art, she thought of Nathalie's love of her craft. They were strong women, they would overcome this awful day. Mona brought out tea.

But outside Nathalie looked so much older. The lines Mona had never noticed on her face had become grave and harsh. Her eyelids were fallen, discoloured furrows beneath them, and the cheeks were those of a gaunt woman whose good health had been stolen. Mona was silent. Everything had been taken from them. This was the day that would never pass.

Love and Death and Cell Division

It is eight months since Shaun has come out of a North London hospital. He parks the silver car and steps down first. His hair has grown back curly instead of straight, the waves are reaching out, conspiring and rich, blacker than logic. Shaun has fought off the same malady that leached my brother's bones. He used hardiness supplied by his Slavic mother, the one who ran off. Shaun also fell in love with one of the nurses who is now eight months pregnant, whose elbow within a denim jacket he gently lifts out of the car; her hair is arranged in neat braids. She is brown and sleek with a basketball plumped above her jeans.

They walk steadily together and Carlotta barks. Their kiss is a small note of harmony. Shaun points to something at the back of the house.

Carlotta rushes at Shaun with instant recollection and I recall the months Shaun stayed here, helping with odd jobs and the garden. How, listening to the young man moving about the rooms of the house, I would place a hand upon my heart and feel an uneven rocking. Minor things used to disappear from my cabinets and one day I found Shaun collapsed in the garden. Blue-lipped, his skin drained. A spreadeagled Bacchus in shorts. The paramedics rushed wordlessly through the house with a stretcher banging doorways.

Shaun runs his hand along Carlotta's bristly back until she flips over, presenting her teats and recent scar. The girlfriend smiles, tucking her hair behind one ear. Shaun prevents Carlotta from lunging over to sniff the new odours of her person. The dog sits, eyes moored on Shaun's face.

Introduced, the girlfriend extends a hot hand that has been planted in a pocket. Shaun leans across for a pertinent hug.

'You've shrunk, Vivian!' He seems taller, fair skin aglow, on the verge of a strategic, masculine beauty.

'And you look so very well,' I say to him. 'Do come inside.'

Shaun throws their jackets onto the coat pegs and follows me down the hall, to the living room where a fire pulses.

'You see what a wonderful place Vivian has? It's like this all the way through. Stunning, Viv. Looks as stunning as ever. Who's doing your gardening?'

'I have two older chaps. They come over from the estate.'

Shaun stands still on the carpet for a moment, rubs the back of his hand across his eyes.

'I'm sorry, bit overwhelmed for a minute.' The girl folds her arm around his waist. 'Thanks, love. Thanks, babe.' Shaun's hand steadies on the ball shape above her jeans.

The day the ambulance took my nephew down the lane, I stood on the flattened patch of grass made by the paramedics kneeling around Shaun's strewn body. I tried to understand what had taken place. My own heart had felt a surge of palpitations that slowed into incinerating relief – for I had failed to warm to my brother's son, and I knew I was once more in full possession of my house.

I felt a luminous sense of liberation as the ambulance changed gears on the hill.

—

Shaun assists Efua with a flourish as she lowers herself onto the chair. 'This is the woman who saved my life. It's all in her hands.'

Efua's fingers knot together beneath her cargo.

'This lovely lady used to read me stories after the end of her shift. It was mesmerising. She comes from Ghana. She took me to her country. She's made me see everything, the lot of it. Illness, disaster, joy, simplicity. I owe everything to her.'

I make a round with the teapot. When he was in hospital I visited Shaun rarely. He was in my brother's former ward, lizard-like.

'We'll be getting married traditionally in Ghana after the birth. And then the official thing in London after that. My mother – you remember Dina? – she's making the dress.'

'Dina? She's resurfaced?' Unfortunately this comment escapes.

Carlotta trots over to Shaun, provides her broad head for a rub, before she reclines at his feet. Carlotta's jaws slacken and her tongue lolls on the carpet. The fire-spun air in here is soft. Cinders reach up into the chimney shaft. The girl removes a cardigan.

'You all right there, Effie?' he asks.

She nods.

Shaun looks around the room, at the floral wallpaper and pretty oil paintings, the urns on the sideboard and porcelain platters on the walls. He massages the dog's belly and I am alert.

'It's so good to be back here, Vivian,' Shaun says. 'I know it wasn't always easy between us. I know bad words have been spoken. Perhaps – perhaps there's a chance it was the illness talking. We know it had already seeped in.'

In an argument, Shaun once let fly what he thought of me: *You are a frigid, uptight bitch who hasn't been humped in an age.* The words were muttered as he slammed the glass door across and stormed down to the garden shed. I don't think they were meant to be heard. Shaun had come in late and vomited in the downstairs bathroom. Carlotta had finished off the mess on the bath mat and stank to high heaven.

'I've seen the bottom, Vivian. It was hell,' Shaun continues. 'I can't even explain. I had to learn to trust in my body. Trust in a bunch of cells. I can see goodness now.'

Efua leans across and touches his knee. She has a fresh point. 'We had the baby screened, didn't we, Shaun? They did a genetic test. They said everything's normal. Nothing to worry about.'

She halts, perhaps remembering something blurry Shaun has told her. My malformed daughter, born when I was 44, her distressing face mistakenly shown to me. A nurse should know better.

'How is your mother?' I ignore the girl and question Shaun.

'Dina? She's all right. She went home for a while. Then came back to London to start a business. I have a kid sister, you know.'

I see my poor brother's emaciated body turning in his grave.

Efua asks to use the bathroom. She looks quite frantic. Carlotta waddles over to sniff her boots and she shuts like a flower.

'I'll take her,' Shaun says. 'I doubt I've forgotten the way there.'

———

He saunters back into the room. Efua follows, pulling the cardigan around her shape.

'Those windows don't look very secure out the back,' Shaun says. 'Have you had any more burglaries in the area?'

'I have Carlotta. And an alarm. I sleep well at night.'

I cast my eyes out over the garden. The roses are thriving, catching dabs of sun. Several of the trees show off their shaggy moss coats while the lawn gleams. I am pleased with my new gardeners.

'Dina asked after you,' Shaun says. 'She wanted to know if you were still hiding out in the woods.'

'I'd hardly call this hiding.'

'Don't miss the big bad world?'

'I've seen enough of it.'

My visions of his mother come forth. Shoulders. Breasts. A way of steering her body into a room. How my brother hungered after her and the upholstery used to soak up her scent. And then this son, brewed from the pair of them in Dina's womb.

'What does she look like now?'

'Dina?' he says. 'She looks older, I guess. She still packs a punch.'

Shaun runs his hand through the black currents of his hair as though even he can't believe it has burst back. Before his cells went wild he was so reedy, a slice of my brother's physique. We are a tall, fine-boned people. It is easy to recall the boyish frieze of his body. But somehow, the illness has heightened different, vital genes. His features have widened and his eyes have a stinging elemental quality, now directed at me.

'Viv, the truth is, Efua and I would like to ask you something. I don't have a job yet. And Efua is about to give birth to, well, we weren't going to tell anybody, but your great-niece. You wouldn't care to rent us out a room for a couple of months? The back wing – I know you never go there. We'd keep to ourselves, of course.'

I look at the woman with my nephew's offspring folded within her abdomen, her body a vessel Shaun has filled over and over with wriggling matter.

Those foul words Shaun once muttered about me were correct.

The afternoon they took away his blue-skinned form in the ambulance, I at first stood in a stupor on the grass, wrestling with this drama. When the garden sharpened into focus I saw that my flower beds were being assailed by a strange flat worm. Seconds later, my hands were holding a cloudy rubber condom. I looked about and there were further congregations everywhere. Hanging from the rose bushes, draped across the azalea and hollyhock, crushed beneath the peonies and zinnias; even hurled over the papyrus stand on the artificial island in the canal.

Near the garden shed, I found a stash of coloured wrappers kicked into the dirt.

I remember standing on the grass, my outrage crisp, recalling cars along the lane and the summer-long moans in the dark. I thought back to fleshy shapes on the lawn and Shaun gulping glass after glass of water by the kitchen sink at first light. That day, while the paramedics revived my nephew's body, I plucked out Shaun's used condoms from my plants using a washing peg. One by one I watched them descend into the bin.

As we sit in silence Carlotta comes across and rolls over at my feet. She's grown a little stout after her operation. She gives me the closest expression to a smirk that could be expected of an animal.

The Mafia Boss Who Shot His Gay Son on a Beach

It was a good day for a killing. The summer had been good. There had been rain, and his arthritis had not bothered him for several months. His wife had gone to her sister in the hills. Ornella, his long-time lover, had passed earlier in the afternoon. She had paraded her naked splendour through the house, serving him coffee while he sat in bed. She then moved her nakedness over him.

He had wanted to tell Ornella as she nursed his head, the thoughts had been so close to her hands. There had been secrets passed between them before. But Ornella had looked down upon his ruined face and told him he was her beauty. He had gazed at her, snakes in his brain, a pit of them.

He had watched the dust scrolls chasing her car.

At sundown he drove into the centre. The bars jostled around the piazza and serene evening light bathed the basilica façade. He parked his car around the corner and walked to his son's apartment. Upstairs, the balcony shutters were opened wide. His son was at the computer, stroking a cat.

He sat down. What they had told him, he had verified first. But there had been no need. The boy himself had announced his habits. Told him that he liked the Scandinavians who came in the summer or the Africans outside the station. But now they had informed him that his son had begun to deal in the clubs, with his thin addict boyfriend who patrolled the high schools. His son looked at him carefully.

When he asked his son to accompany him to the beach he knew that the boy would inhale. He poured them two glasses of amaro. The young man dressed. They drove north along the coast to an area neither had ever seen, a dull stretch of sand with the water still and green in places. On the rise was a half-built house with girders scratching the air, three date palms spaced unevenly. The young man asked if he might swim. He removed his shirt and trousers, walked into the sea.

The boy later knelt and was shot.

For some time, looking at the way his son's fingers curled into the sand, and strands of seaweed twisted around an unfamiliar ring, the man wondered if he should turn the gun on himself. He put the odorous muzzle into his mouth and took it out again. The sea rushed back and forth. He kicked sand over the body and walked back up to where he had left the car.

As he drove he recalled how Ornella's pupils had contracted and he had watched the brown tissue of her irises, which concealed a niche of revulsion. It had aroused him to see the flames surging over this.

A Young Man Reflects

The country where he was born had scorched hills and quixotic animals and wise elders with spectacularly gnarled toes. But it also had knife crimes where there was no mercy and people barbecued dogs, and those elders were diabetic drunkards full of *juju* balderdash.

The Coptic Bride

Last month my brother unexpectedly came back to Sydney with a fiancée from Ethiopia. Adam had woven a career as a development consultant across the world, bought a house by the harbour and an apartment in New York, and had crossed the Sahara on a motorbike. He left us 18 years ago and there was a week of turbulence whenever he came back.

I met them at the airport. The girl was not the fumy supermodel like David Bowie's wife. She was compact, chesty and not very dark. I spotted Adam parcelling their documents away and steering the heavy bags on a trolley. She followed behind.

'Adam!'

'Jim!'

We came together and I felt his resolve had softened and he was no longer working out. We separated and he introduced Laila who, though she had a jewel of a smile, had bad skin and unremarkable features. My first thought: strange, given Adam has had a run of flawless women.

We drove out from the airport and Adam briefed me on the trip. They'd been back to headquarters, where he had to chase up some tenants subletting the apartment. They'd also had a rest and done some shopping, he said, *finally out of that place*. He glanced behind at Laila watching out the window. I looked up in the rear-view mirror and she smiled back, her hair in loose springs against my tan upholstery.

We crossed the Anzac Bridge into the suburbs. Adam explained the Madonna's bra concept and I saw her cottoning on. In Ethiopia they'd had Bono campaigning for stick figure kids and here we had a bridge wired up like Madonna's D-cups.

They were staying at Mum and Hadley's place in Drummoyne for a day or so as their place was rented out, before we all headed up to the lake. Mum's second exhibition had just opened in Woollahra so she and Hadley weren't at home. I found a parking space and Adam and I pulled out their two suitcases onto the footpath. He breathed in deep, looking down to the sailing club where he had smoked so many joints, where he used to take Leanne Gordon into the bush, where he'd even torn the rudder off a Flying Eleven on a broad reach. The bay was glassy, it had that untroubled hue. But in an hour the wind would be tossing it.

'You heading back to work then?' I had taken the morning off, but sensed that Adam needed some breathing space before Mum hurtled home.

'Yes, ought to rush. Catch you tonight?'

Adam opened Laila's door and his eyes fell upon her dozing. She had more hair on her cheek than a woman should have, on skin that was a tired sallow olive. Her eyebrows were ragged above her firmly closed eyes like Frida Kahlo asleep.

—

My mother adored Laila. Halfway through the afternoon she called to share her joy. I suspected it was hardly Laila she adored, but the prospect of a brown daughter-in-law and mixed-race grandchildren requiring the occasional visit to New York. Mother, on the overcrowded and whirring canvas of her life, sought such flares. She had married a plumber, given birth to Adam; lived with a sculptor and then had me. Now there was Hadley, a serious interior designer who pushed her photography and had taken her to New Mexico.

'Have you spoken with Laila?' I asked her. I had Reuben with me, in the St. Leonards office.

'We've just had coffee,' she said. 'I thought I'd better get back and prepare them some lunch. Adam's on the divan asleep.'

Working in the Eastern Suburbs and a stay in London last year had brought about an upgrading of Mum's vocabulary. It was sad to see 'couch' turfed out.

'She's so adorable. I'm so happy for them. Are you coming over for dinner? When will you be following us up to the lake?'

I replaced the phone and moved away from Reuben's eyes. In the aftermath, you wonder how you ever loved, as if it were some abject emotion that had to be slaked. Light from outside spooled over him as he released my apartment keys onto the desk. I watched his shoulders retract, the sweat peppery on my lip, my neck muscles beginning to unclench. In a year from now the pull will have left the pair of us.

The next day the traffic was hell out of Sydney. I organised food for the cats and read Reuben's final audacious message, picturing his broad fingers smudging the digits. I switched off the phone. The northern suburbs were pinioned out down to the last house on stilts between the trees. I opened my window at a pile-up just beyond the Hawkesbury. The scent of eucalyptus came through, perfume of the stolen land. The traffic filed through two sandstone walls quilted with dynamite triggers. In the car next to me I saw a pair of young urbanites in profile, metal piercings tucked into their fair skin. I thought of Reuben's blue-laced tattoo dissolved into his brown chest. How arcane it had been at the outset; how quickly it had begun to date.

Mum had rushed away from Sydney with shopping bags of delicatessen food, not to be diminished by a son who employed cooks and servants. Traditionally, she overreached for Adam, and this time the foreign fiancée compounded her will to impress. The fridges were stashed with local wine and Tasmanian cheese and tubs of pâté. Hadley hoisted up cartons of beers from the boatshed down on the water. That was where Mum had put the visitors, in the wood-planked room over the jetty sliding into the blue lake. I was in the spare bedroom in the main house. I unpacked my things into the pinewood set of drawers, pulling on old porous clothes steeped in salt. In the bathroom out the back I had a quick wank and released the drama of the last few days.

Mum was in the kitchen pressing the base of a cheesecake.

'Hadley's rigging up,' she said.

Sure enough, I saw the mast of Hadley's prized 20-footer down by the jetty. The mainsail went shimmying up.

'You're not going out, Ellen?'

Mum's eyes lifted at the untimely use of her Christian name. Now that

Adam was here with us, it belonged to another intimacy.

'No, darling. See if the others are interested. Mind their beers are cold.'

But it seemed Hadley was heading out alone, as we all knew he preferred. I saw Adam push him off the jetty and turn around, walking with tender feet over the grain of the wood. I saw the looseness in his thighs and the curve to his belly. Even his arse looked rounded and shook like a woman's. He disappeared from my line of vision. I wandered down the lawn and made my way to the steps.

They were on lazy chairs in the sun, close to the water. Laila had gained some colour and appeal, lying in a white bikini with her hair unreeled around her. She lifted onto her elbows and her breasts rolled down comfortably, she opened to him. Adam sat up on the other chair, leaning over to spread his palm on her belly and they kissed hard, the first expression I had seen of my brother's conquest. Hadley, now beyond the shelter of the point, hit the mild nor'easter and tacked too early, sending the sails luffing. As always, he took an age to cleat the sheets.

—

After Mum's rich seafood and heavy-handed salads we sauntered down to the waterfront. Hadley set about lighting a fire kneeling with his stringy tanned legs folded and a packet of BBQ lights. Laila watched him stoke the flames as the dry gum leaves and twigs crackled. Hadley stood back as smoke lifted towards Mum on her way down the steps with a tray of drinks.

'We have eucalyptus trees all around Addis,' Laila was saying to Hadley in a light, thoughtful voice. He and I listened to her, neither of us able to tend the conversation.

Adam stepped in. 'They were introduced by the Dutch around sixty years ago to combat soil erosion.'

'Well, no,' said Laila. 'You're wrong, Adam. They were brought in from this country by our Emperor Menelik when he made Addis Ababa our capital in 1895. They were lacking in wood and he believed the species would be favourable in our climate. In fact, as you have seen, they have flourished.'

In terms of dinner party theatre, Adam had years of training. In Nairobi I'd seen how polished he had become, his resilience. Yet here was his agronomist girlfriend with a PhD who worked in some outpost reminding him of history's wonky path, catching him out here in front of us. Adam sank down, grew into sulky Adam whom we all knew well, and began to bite his thumbnail, a 40-year-old habit. Hadley stood up so fast you could see his eyes quiver. He staggered over to uncap another beer. Mum who was oblivious plonked the tray on the table and rubbed her eyes from the smoke.

'I heard the Gordons arrive earlier,' she said. 'Adam, you remember Matt and Rosemary? You used to sail with Daniel.'

Poor Ellen hovered her omission of Leanne, Adam's long-time girlfriend, Daniel's little sister. When I saw Leanne last, she had three kids and was still whippet thin. She had just divorced. Laila, who knew about her Emperor Menelik but could not know about Leanne, walked over and prepared twin whiskies on ice. She handed one to Adam.

'No, thanks,' he said uncaringly.

Laila paused in front of him.

'I'll take it,' I said.

I heard them at it in the night. I'd left Hadley and Mum some time alone in the house and was taking a solitary walk along the waterfront. I went to the end of every jetty that wasn't fenced off and stood listening to the stays clanking on the masts and the hulls rocking and the slapping water. I felt Reuben's absence along my skin and the times we had come here together from the city unfurled in my head. But Reuben and I had not given our intentions good government, and he hated the finicky rules of sailing and the slimy bed of the lake. Now the sounds muffled together in the dark, providing generous consolation. I gave Hadley and Ellen enough time to make love and drift to sleep, the curtains skating over their interlocked bodies, then headed back around the boatshed. Two doors down from us the lights were on at the Gordon's house and I heard the kids were still up watching a noisy car chase on T.V. According to Rosemary, a long-standing tennis companion of my mother's, Leanne's ex had gone interstate and she was seeing a Māori guy.

In the boatshed I heard Adam and Laila arguing. My brother issued a sentence and the girlfriend spliced it blade thin, until it wobbled and fell flat. From Adam's tone I could sense she had just about pushed him too far. When Adam's fuse frayed to the end you needed an almighty head start: as a kid I had climbed roofs and stayed bolted in the spare bathroom for hours to avoid his fists. I tried to picture them. Adam hunched on the couch trying to shut her out, gritting his teeth for control as her high-pitched voice climbed in circles. The girlfriend in the unfamiliar boatshed with Mum's early black and white prints of the lake in cedar frames.

I heard the wicker chair shoved back and the table grate over the floorboards. Someone was taking a lunge. I heard a body fall unevenly and a quick scuffle on the wood. Against everything that I had considered proven within myself, I grew hard.

—

I woke up to the sounds of Mum and Laila taking off on a shopping expedition into town. My room in the brick house had a hint of air passing through in the mornings but by midday it reverberated with heat. Consequently it was not possible to sleep until late at night when the damp of the lake wended through. I rolled over and retrieved a book. Occasionally I let my mind wander to Reuben in slumber, his paws suspended in endearing inactivity on the sheets. But I closed this away. I thought of his silver jeep reversing in the parking lot, how minute and pretentious the car now seemed, how its arrival had once unsteadied my gut.

Adam was in the kitchen wearing a loose shirt with a Coptic cross embroidered over his chest. As he opened the newspaper one of the long sleeves dipped into his mug of coffee.

'Bugger!'

He squeezed out the coffee and settled at the table.

'Comes with dressing exotic,' I said.

'Oh, hiya,' Adam replied, his pale eyes crystal clear this morning. I

117

wondered about the fiancée and the skidding furniture last night.

'Hadley?'

'He's out in the old boot. Praying he remembers where he sank the crab nets.'

'And you guys? What are you up to today?'

Adam mumbled into the newspaper. Born Sydneysider, he still suffered the real estate. 'I was thinking of taking Laila over the other side, over to the beach. Like to come?'

The tautness around his eyes saying, *Whatever you do, don't come.*

'No thanks, I think I'll stay here.'

I poured some coffee and shook out some supplements.

'You still on that stuff,' he said without lifting his head. Ten years back, before he started the good life and broadened, Adam's body had been sublime.

'Can't let down the team.'

Adam looked over. On a packed suburban school bus decades ago, Adam had been wearing nearly the same expression when he shot the calf between the eyes. *And which team is Jim on?* he had cried, cracking up, joined by the whole bus. Every face had swung around to the blanched kid in shorts.

But now I was unfazed. I returned the usual hardy smirk. The year Adam crossed the Sahara a group of Scandinavians had been kidnapped by some Tuaregs and a man the same age as my brother escaped into the desert to his death. I used to play with the idea that it had been Adam lost in the dunes, crying like a baby, nursing his last thoughts. Whenever Adam came back this image was never far off in my head. That way, my gratefulness that it hadn't been him, Adam never realised he had to earn it. I opened the television section of the newspaper. I saw *The Guns of Navarone* was on in the blind spot from two till four. I pictured Mum and Hadley downing pinot grigio on the water, and Adam and Laila tiffing on the beach.

'When did you guys decide to get married?' I asked.

Adam closed the newspaper and took me in.

'It was a reaction, I guess. Two of our friends were wiped out in a car

118

smash this year. Outside Addis when the trucks break down – which they invariably do – the drivers leave them there with a trail of branches as a warning along the road. Tobias and Irene didn't see them. They ploughed right into the back of a broken-down truck. We'd been at this lodge out of town for the night and they'd left early. Laila and I found them the next morning. After that – I know there's no correlation – we thought it was time to get hitched.'

His voice faded and I couldn't help thinking of poor Tobias and Irene who'd been hoovered up into Adam's history. He breathed in roughly. 'There are no greys over there. Everything is black or white. Crazy things happen. A hundred crazy things would have happened while we've been sitting here.'

'You must like it somehow,' I said. 'The Indiana Jones factor.'

'Not when it comes to seeing your friends' insides mauled by wild dogs.'

'Oh Jesus, sorry. I didn't mean that.'

'Who the hell ever knows what you mean?'

He stood and moved to the sliding door looking out over the lake. A group of skiffs in a race tore downwind on the nor'easter towards an orange buoy in the water. Habit grown deep, we both watched the twin leaders setting off on a new tack, sails set beautifully. A fine-looking race. Tomorrow I might take out the two-man canoe.

'They thought Laila's brother was gay, you know. That's why she was really interested in meeting you. Her Mum is Italian and her father has a transport company. Apparently her brother Bisrat went to Milan to study and lost the plot. He's back at home now, working with her father. He married a gorgeous girl, you know. Utterly gorgeous. They're having a kid.'

I thought: poor sleepy-eyed boy wearing beauty's noose.

'Great story. Maybe we should all just marry stunning women and procreate.'

'It's all very well for you to sit on your perch out here. We are talking about a culture with a three-thousand-year-old history. Not a truckload of white bums in leather.'

'Are you saying that in three thousand years they've never had a man who loved another man?'

Adam backed off. His head was framed by an old 1970's photo that Mum had blown up. It was Adam and I with floppy haircuts and BMX bikes.

'You know nothing of what's out there. You know nothing of humanity,' he said. 'You're a sick bugger.'

—

After the film, the sandy-skinned return of the couple from the beach, and Mum and Hadley's emptying of a couple of pinot grigio bottles on the veranda, most of the party were senseless. Adam, wearing a different Coptic shirt, saw Laila to the end of the lawn and she headed down the steps with a torch. He turned back to me. It was apology time, his eyes looked contrite. He grabbed my shoulder and squeezed. In my mind, I released him from the torment of the baking dunes and he wandered back to the oasis.

Mum and Hadley were expiring in front of the television. It was a documentary about deforestation in Africa, now part of their extended neighbourhood. I went outside down to the water, treading onto the jetty. Sounds travelled all the way across the black-skinned lake. I heard the bikie gangs on the other side with their kero lanterns and beers. Someone called out, *Bob! Where the fuck is Karen?* The lights in the boatshed were out. I started moving along the waterfront until I heard Adam's voice and stopped still. It was coming from the patch of grass below the Gordon's house, down by the water. He and Leanne Gordon were talking in the dark.

' – and when he refused to stop, I left him. Not before he lost his job and raided our savings. He used to lay into Kyle.'

'You told the cops all of that?'

I slipped behind the Gordon's shed and leant against the rock. I could just see Leanne open a couple of beers and hand one to my brother's back. The bottles chinked. They both sat down on the grass.

'Ellen told Rosemary you're tying the knot,' said Leanne. 'Now, that's a new development. I never thought you'd get around to it.'

'Rosemary told Mum you're with a Māori guy. And he's heaps younger than you.'

'Only eight years. That make you jealous?'

'You'd better keep him out of Jim's radius. He likes a bit of colour.'

'Oh yeah? You can talk. What about your Ethiopian?'

Adam didn't answer her. I waited.

'Hey,' he said in a lower voice. 'Why don't you turn over and let me see that arse of yours in the moonlight?'

A trawler gurgled across the lake with its triad of lights. White at the top, red on the port side, the starboard green. When the wash passed I couldn't hear them as clearly as before. Her voice was further back, suppressed, and I couldn't make out what she was saying. It seemed that Adam's shape was over her, but whatever he said was blurred too.

Often, you can recognise the very last wave of a high tide as if it were tagged pink. After which the drive of the motion works on a different torque. I twisted upward and saw a cigarette lighter flare under the Moreton Bay fig tree way up on the Gordon's wooden deck and my back prickled. For a while the cigarette burned against the massive tree five metres above. I hoped it was Rosemary outside smoking, or Leanne's oldest kid with a joint. Then I heard them moaning. I slid deeper between the old man's shed and the sandstone cliff until my body was jammed against the rock and I could just see them. My brother's white haunches were gaining rhythm over her and her fingers clutched the grass. Then I heard feet jangling down the metal steps old Matt Gordon had sunken into the stone and a huge hand the same as Reuben's threw the cigarette into the ferns at my feet. He hauled Adam off as the screaming woman rolled over pulling down her clothes. The tall Māori kneed Adam in the groin and began to sock his jaw.

—

Laila came to watch me pull the canoe out of the boatshed. She smelled of coffee and bruised sleep. She asked if she could come out with me. I asked if she could swim. This canoe, handcrafted wood that I sanded down myself, was an unsteady thing you had to keep moving, that a deep trawler wake could easily capsize.

'I think I'd prefer a life jacket,' she said.

The sun was ruthless and narrow-eyed through muslin which meant that tomorrow or the day after it would rain. Today was a day to nail.

'Then help me put her out.'

She wore her white bikini alone under the life jacket, she wasn't interested in covering herself from me. Her hair settled on her shoulders though she ran her fingers through it, revealing an odd gold earring hanging from the top curve of her ear. She turned around smiling.

We paddled off to the east as the light pooled on either side of us in heavy globules. There was no wind, just gassy mirrors of sheer cloud. Far off a couple of trawlers were crossing back with their nets hauled high. Though I gave her an oar, she merely dipped it from side to side and let me do the rowing. Eventually she stopped, settling the oar across her thighs. I pulled hard into the roil and felt the schema of my shoulders, like a kit put together well. I might have stood a chance against the Kiwi last night, but I stayed sandwiched between the boatshed and the cliff, breathing lichen while Adam's head twisted on his neck.

There being no resistance we arrived at the cove along the promontory on the other side and I asked Laila if she wanted to get out. We cruised into the shallows and I hoisted up without letting the hull scratch, though the rocking made her tense. I helped her off before beaching, then tied the bow to a rock I threw in from the shore. There was much scraggly bush cover, burnt grass, old stamped-out fires and crushed beer cans. At Christmas and Easter water-skiing families camped here, burning up and down the smooth water on wakeboards behind boats called Maverick or 4-Play. But this morning there was no one, just embers and the vague smell of shit. We had to cross back before the nor'easter churned up the surface. In the distance, on another arm of the lake, the Dora Creek coal stacks released cords of smoke towards the faded mountains.

Laila crouched by the edge of the water on a strip of sand. Her thighs were dimpled, she hugged her knees. A fringe of pubic hair escaped coverage deep between her legs and made me feel fonder of her. I lay out, elbows dug into the sand.

'You've never made it to Addis,' she said, leaning into the final 's'.

'No. Though I visited Adam in Nairobi. That was a long while back,' I told her. 'He was trying to sort out the office there and I turned up in the mayhem.'

'I've never been to Nairobi. Although my father had business there and in Somalia prior to the war.'

'So how did you guys meet?' I asked.

'It was through my sister, really. I don't suppose Adam told you. Iri. Irene.'

'No.' But the name snagged.

'Adam had been so close to our family. They were to be married.'

'What happened?'

Laila looked downward. 'Tobias is a German. She is expecting his child. Iri is the woman your brother wanted.'

I paused for a moment, thinking of what Adam had said yesterday. 'You mean they are still in Addis?'

Laila slowed, she made sure she caught my eyes now. 'Iri did care for Adam,' she said. 'And I have always admired your brother. We are not bad people.'

She allowed me to watch her face. Tobias and Irene. Tobias and Iri. The couple Adam had slaughtered in the car wreck in his head. His beloved bearing another man's child, mauled by wild dogs. And now Adam himself, the escapee flailing in the desert with his vile secret, his tongue bursting in his mouth. Laila turned to the other side of the lake where you could just make out the boatshed where Adam lay asleep on a leaking ice pack, his jaw wired, stitches in his chin.

'I am very glad to have met you,' she said, as the wind rose in oily scented puffs.

In Venice

Donna Carmichael felt the full weight of her name when she and Noah were in Italy. Every time she handed over their passports to a hotel receptionist, the sleek man or abundant woman would show teeth and say '*Donna!* You are a *Woo-man*, Signora Carmichael!' Several hotels into their trip an American explained that *donna* meant woman, meaning that Donna's Melbournian parents had christened her with a name that merely flagged her gender.

An amused Noah started calling her *Woo-man* when they were lying undressed on hotel beds. Noah was a man who almost always invited sex into the room, in ways that were exploratory and tender. But when he called her *Woo-man*, he encouraged Donna to perform lavish and servile acts.

One glum morning in Venice they climbed back to their room after breakfast, having decided to spend the day in bed. Donna felt tingles of anticipation along the bridge between her legs. They reached the door to their room and Noah inserted the brass key dangling from a burnished ball of wood. They stood looking through the doorway at the rumpled bed sheets they had left an hour ago, the day now reframed.

Noah closed the door. Donna undid her jeans. They stood fondling each other, clothes flying off, until they dropped to the floor and crawled to the centre of the gritty room. Noah breathed the word *Woo-man* in Donna's eager ear. Something in the muted marine air or beyond the peaked gothic windows made the game edgier and soon Noah – this was a first – found himself fiercely slapping Donna's rump.

When it was over, Donna rolled on the carpet, her bottom still burning as she returned to the raft of her body. Noah lifted away and went to the bathroom, where he stared at a creeping smile on his face. A boat sloshed past below and Donna looked at Noah's Casanova translation, fallen to the floor.

Donna walked out of the Peggy Guggenheim Museum holding Noah's hand. They were not particularly satisfied; it was an arid, motionless place. What had really stayed with them was something they had seen yesterday in a costume museum. It was a pair of platformed chopines for tiny feet. The woodwork was a chipped sage-green, painted with flowers, and the clogs were impossibly teetering, designed for the high tides that slew through the lagoon town. They were so tall a courtesan would require two maidens to help her walk.

Over drinks Noah and Donna talked about Noah's fierce slapping that morning, and whether they wanted to continue in this vein (or should even), and where it might lead them next. Excited and frank, they looked at the arousing city surrounding them, immersed in the sultry lagoon. Both agreed their urges belonged to a wider carnal history they were keen to plumb.

Asunder

He parks the rental car at the train station, which is a post-fascist box with marble planes, diminished by concrete extensions on either side. After the unchecked sensuality of the baroque city he kisses Rachel on the cheek, and she gracefully walks off. He thinks of the sculpted effigies on top of buildings (mostly naked males) and how these posed bodies seemed to be pondering, absorbed by all but the urban fray below. It was sublime what they could do with stone here. It seemed that for centuries men had stared into unhewn blocks and seen glorious bodies to be retrieved.

Rachel, whose Italian is admirable (she studied opera singing but never performed), needs to change their tickets. These are things she likes to do on her own, so he remains in the carpark, a recently tarred scallop along the main road, knowing that it may take some time. He knows that Rachel will probably engage the flirtatious ticket officer with his greasy hair, or she might stray into a café for a secret espresso, or get into a conversation with a young mother holding a heavy child.

From where he is parked he observes the tattered wing of the station, seeing how the post-fascist intent lapses into a series of grubby cement alcoves along the final wall. Between this and a railway shed there is a path leading to the platforms, which must have inveigled its way through. A woman in black tights and a bomber jacket walks there now. It seems as though she has no skirt, or the briefest of shorts perhaps at the top of her thighs, or perhaps not.

The woman reverses into one of the alcoves, pulls down her tights as she squats low, and begins to piss. He watches the ripples of her vulva as the spray gushes onto the ground. Her inner thighs are yellow and her parts are violet. Her eyes shoot past him carelessly as she finishes, pulls up her tights and walks away.

He looks around and there is no one but him in the carpark. A bus has just passed so the shelter is empty. He switches on the central locking of the car. Right now he cannot remember the face of the young woman, just the rich floral colour between her legs, how he had sat there watching the dab of hair, the gushing water.

Somehow the warm piss has reached him and his hands feel wet. And he's sure that when Rachel comes back she will smell something. Culpability, or a new strand of information she will beg him to surrender, while she leans over inhaling his face.

He will tell her, feeling horrific candour.

But he will never tell Rachel that now this other, vivid aperture will be what he sees always, it will make him faint and bring him to a shocked brink, he will see it every day of his life.

Young British Man Drowns in Alpine Lake

Tom's father frowns at Corinne again. This is the moment I expect to scroll down and see into her face, a clear and unwritten page.

But Corinne's eyes close and her lips grow thin. Another spasm passes Tom's father's features and I see there is a primal animal in there. He wants to raise his builder's hands to Corinne's neck.

Tom's father wants to know why, in the middle of January, his freshly graduated cardiologist son dropped his jeans and went skinny-dipping in a mountain lake.

He nears Corinne's face one more time. He is gleaning it for ashen traces. Of which there are, for one who knows her. He cannot see how the colour of her lips has dropped a shade towards the blue end of red, a drop in blood pressure as much as a realignment of pluck, and that her huge white forehead, the template for her sticky righteousness, lies galvanised beneath its compelling shirr. They say the hydraulics of the face are spellbinding. Corinne's face is giving him so much information I am appalled.

Corinne's face now pulls apart. The unwritten page is provided. Corinne crumples and begins to cry.

I take her into my arms again, kissing her temples where I imagine the blood in its wiring runs close to the surface. She feels so cold. Tom's father backs off, swearing at us.

Tom died in the ambulance, somewhere between Lago Santa Croce and the hospital in Belluno. That's what I was told. Amazingly, he was still alive when they pulled him out of the water, the resilience Tom displayed in abseiling and wintry sailing put to its final test. We followed the ambulance which took off at a crazy speed, but lost track of it quickly. We took the wrong carriageway on the autostrada and ended up in Vittorio Veneto, then wound back to Belluno on a state road, sliding on day-old snow. We simply got lost, had to ask directions to the hospital, the slowly resounding obscenity of what had happened dove-tailing with the very banality that was taking place.

—

Tom's girlfriend Mary sees dots on the mountain flank. We work out they are skiers heading downward in tight S-curves – the ultimate motion – along a lush blue pleat in the snow. The mountain is colossal. Some sort of palpable convection pulverises your thoughts and sucks you upward, makes you feel ethereal, or on the very skin of being alive. I enjoy being so reduced. We look carefully and see there are still more dots making their ascent to one side. They are climbing almost vertically towards a sling of whiteness between one outcrop and the first shoulders of the peak. The biggest slide in the park. They will never make it to the top. Tom says they can't. In twenty minutes and two more espressos to the unnecessary beat of Jamiroquai, they have.

The girls drink coffee, losing interest in the skiers, maintaining their guise of getting along. It's not working, the Mary-and-Corinne thing. It's far from the first time our unmatched girlfriends don't hook up. Tom seems tired and I know he'd rather conserve his best energy for the snow, not Mary's delights on a pine-framed bed. Thankfully Corinne's seasoned stubbornness is more pliant. I watch her eyes drift over the peaks then back to her nails, to the grain of the wood, to a declaration of love some teenager has carved there. For a second, I think of eating raw fish. It must be the purity of the elements: the zinging air, the grey seamed wood; Corinne's flesh.

Tom watches the skiers trace their compass-set arcs. In my head I try to project myself up there too, away from the bar and the bright sports clothing, the bombastic nature of every Italian conversation now accessorised by the full-volume Supertramp some retro has fished out. The silent combustion of the mountain caught in its geological yaw. The taut air pulsing in my throat in burning breaths. Breaking the pearly crust with an easy plush-plush-plush.

But Tom and I are crap on the snow, and though Tom thinks he is champion material, he is no more than decent. Right now no dream feels more elusive.

Tom's eyes have gone over to where our snowboards are overturned next to the girls' skis. 'Let's do a run,' he says.

We strap our front bindings over our broad boots, pulling the serrated tongue towards its comfortable *click*. Tom waves a gloved hand to the girls as he paddles off to the top of the slope, collapsing to the ground again as he fits in his rear foot. I don't see if the girls respond. My eyes are still on the last skier of the group, his final slices leaving a graffiti squiggle before he disappears below the tree line. Tomorrow morning the massive mountain will have erased all traces of his path.

I reach the spot where Tom had been fastening up and catch sight of him already at the base of the first part of the slope, arms splayed and knees braced as he finishes his last curve. Irritated that I have to chase him, I bumble on downward. I am no athlete and Tom has spent almost a decade reminding me my efforts are entirely valiant, exclusive of both talent and skill. I reach him, out of breath, as he shuttles off for a series of swift curves close to the edge of the slope, out of the radius of a couple of beginner skiers. His pelvis engineers the back and forward tilting of the board as he picks up speed, his extended arms keeping his upper body balanced and on course. He looks back towards me, he wants to check I am watching. I wave. Then I see what Tom has not yet seen. A snowmobile jetting up his side of the slope, about to accelerate over a bump that obscures Tom's vision. Two locals with hawk eyes and broom moustaches sit braced together, now connected to the crescendo of a motor's buzz.

But Tom turns away in time and up-thrust fingers are exchanged by both parties. Tom heads back to the middle of the slope. Burnt fuel dissolves on the air.

I reach him at the lift. He's been studying me on the last part and is keen to give me tips rather than harp on about the near-miss. Much of Tom's brilliance lies in his flawless memory and technical exactness, though it means he's had a string of Marys wheedling in the night. We do several more slopes. By the third, Tom's tips begin to pay off and on the easiest incline I feel both the board and my feet strapped to it are becoming marginally more obedient. The board cuts from side to side and my spine stays in place, as I ease my pelvis and thighs onto the arc of the curve. Inside my boots, my toes are clenched so hard I can't tell whether they are hot or cold. Sweat soaks my bum crack and lower back.

Then I stop. My goggles are fogged. I unzip pockets hoping I brought some of Corinne's tissues. The slope is empty but I'm so happy with my progress I don't care if Tom is a mile further down. A fogginess has lowered onto the world. The fresh snow we saw forecast for this afternoon. The first flakes trickle down uncertainly, a dreamy shower against the wet green of the trees. But it is too warm for the snow to stick yet. I put out my tongue and I can feel the same needles I did as a child.

I find Tom at the bar halfway down the slope rearranging his jacket and gloves on a heater built like a tiled ceramic box. He has ordered a beer and is trying his Italian on the bored waitress with curly long hair and green eye-shadow. I recall that the slopes empty quickly when it snows. The carpark below will be choked with revving vehicles and city people on their knees trying to put on snow chains. I wonder if the girls have moved inside close to the fireplace. Surely Corinne must have delineated a field fit for conversation.

Tom and I drink three or four beers each and take turns going out the back to piss. The waitress has a name now – Ambra – meaning amber, as in the resin that is sometimes flecked with prehistoric gnats. I've come close enough now to see her challenging nose piercing and quite big teeth, and how Tom has taken a shine to her. I see he wants her, in the way he often wants a woman when he has a perfectly useful one at hand. Over the years there have been women he hungers for and takes home to bed, only to – I sense – leave them hurting in the dark. For a woman Tom's body is probably too powerful.

Apparently Ambra's brother was one of the skiers who freestyle-skied down the mountain this morning. Ambra asks if we saw them earlier, putting an endearing effort into her precise English. Tom is stoked by both factors, and Ambra's desirability climbs. I don't even ask Tom if we should hunt down our girlfriends. My phone has no reception in this depression at the bottom of the run and the snow is gathering along the window panes. I walk over to take a look outside. The snowflakes are larger, falling steadily now. A few more skiers come onto the terrace, stomping caked boots and shaking off white shoulder pads. They enter. They are suntanned with broad bony faces and might be from nearby Slovenia. Ambra prepares them a tray of mulled wine and slides back to Tom. He asks questions about her brother, who is close to Tom's age it seems, and an instructor with one of the ski schools. She says he goes up when conditions are good, which wasn't really the case today, describing these in meteorological terms which are music to Tom's ears.

—

I found Corinne weeping on the boot of my car after a hard night in the city. Mine is a dull area and finding a beautiful sobbing French woman was akin to finding a real fairy at the bottom of the garden. I couldn't get it out of her, what had happened, whether she'd been gang-raped by punks or her cat had been flattened by a car. Despite being in incredibly bad shape and having an early start the next day, I urged her into the house, made some strong tea and set her up on the couch. As I took my last look at her wilted eyes and pale forehead settling under the emergency duvet, she beckoned me.

I made ruthless love to her, the fact that I knew I'd never see her again meant I sought no democracy and nothing divine. The stuff I'd smoked make me draw into her and imagine I was expanding and could stay inside her for hours. But she wanted it. She hovered on the brim for a long time. A strange thing, she cooperated, and occasionally smiled at me, though I looked away from her. She was fit, fitter than I was, and you could tell she loved her own body and inhabited every organ, every cleft within it.

Afterwards I left her, cleaned myself, and she turned to the wall.

Tom never believed in the Corinne-and-Markus thing. He made jokes about the fat Brit and the smashing Parisian. *She's sleeping around, you can be sure of it*, he would say. *Don't think you could ever be enough. I've seen it in her.*

Early on, Corinne told me she was abused as a child. We were sitting on Ikea stools in Tom's kitchen in the dregs of the night. I thought it was a poor line – who hadn't had an uncle's fingers skate across their balls? She said her mother had had a string of oversexed boyfriends who all laid their hands over her. It turned me on, the dirtiness. I liked it when she didn't wash and, at a party, she pretended she had no interest in me.

I told Tom she was the woman I would take to the grave.

Ten months later she disappeared back to Paris, claiming her mother was ill. She telephoned me in strange whispers or in a hoarse halting voice. It took longer than I wished to let her go. I'd wake feeling her feet rubbing mine, or my soft cock nursed by the crook of her arse while she half-snored. Never had I relished the articulation of my working days with such bliss, book-ended as they were by her *séjours* at the house.

Tom took me under his wing after she left, buffering me from myself. We turned 26 the same week and drove up to Edinburgh. Blind drunk most of the time, we made an effort to go to some Fringe shows and round up some female attention. Tom reeled in a dancing understudy called Jody and was set. I knocked about with a student called Erin until her weird body smell overcame me and I kicked her out one night after midnight, man down and full of shame, went to the bathroom and puked.

In the winter Corinne came back. I found her standing at my front door with a suitcase and her mop-faced terrier in her arms.

———

Tom swaggers over with another frothy beer. It appears Ambra's concentration has lapsed and the beer is half head, half amber nectar. A metaphor for Tom's current condition. He leaves me at the encrusted window and goes back to the girl with green-hooded eyes and a washer from a tool box threaded through her nose. I imagine them at it – it isn't hard – Tom thrusting into her as he would thrust over the mountain, past the skiers he wishes he could impress. I sit down. The other skiers are speaking in Slovenian, I am almost certain, probably about their return to their hotel. They look doubtfully outside. Their eyes fall upon the varnished tabletop and they call Ambra for fresh drinks, grappa this time. Ambra comes out from behind the counter in low jeans with firm flesh showing below her T-shirt. She has a small waist and an ample bosom hiked up firmly, she must have to shop well to keep those beauties in place.

As she returns to the counter she strikes a pose next to Tom, who knows her body is on show for him. He manages to stroke her side, she touches his forearm. I let my head fall back and it hits a hard pine curlicue.

I see shapes outside. They become tall men shaking off jackets. They thud into the room bringing a wave of wetness and a dense clean smell. Everyone turns to them. Already I know they are the skiers we saw on the mountain this morning. How many were there? Five? Six? Or seven? I drink my foamy beer and watch Tom trying to read them, already placing himself in competition. Ambra shouts out to them in what sounds like a dialect and Tom is thrown off-balance. He tightens up, straightening his shoulders.

The group of men orders a variety of drinks. Hot milk, beer, a hot tea, some grappa. I can understand that much. They are members of an elongated race. Even Ambra looks misshapen next to them and I can feel Tom's insecurity pushing, unfurling. I have known him long enough to know how callously he feels these confrontations. Ambra points to him and the tall men suddenly notice him holding up the bar. He puts out a sheepish palm. They extend hands, their group loosens. Ambra chatters with all of them, her eyes open wider and her gestures are those of a busy sister, a busy future wife. Tom notices this. Gone are the seductive touching and slowness. She has him meet her brother, a lean carbon copy without the eye-shadow and vulgar piercing, a giant man with her round face, the same face Tom has been thinking of pushing between his legs for the past hour and a half. Ambra's brother is shy, he teaches foreigners to ski all day, speaking English embarrasses him. His sister doesn't seem to notice and sends Tom another drink gaily.

Tom brings himself over to me and sits down. He begins peering out the window at the heavy woollen clots. I can't see anything now – the fold of the slope, the triangle of trees, the braid of pylons and lift seats. I have a comfortable entrapped feeling, as though I don't care if the snow presses us into the earth like a capsule with pine curlicues and fake geraniums and stuffed falcons on the wall.

Tom stands up and removes his gloves from the heater. The Slovenians glance at him. I know Tom feels they have witnessed everything. The girl with the big knockers has gone back to her brethren. The silly English are drinking beer alone. If the warmth and alcohol hadn't already burnished our features, Tom would be blushing. Tom walks over and settles our bill. There is a catch between Ambra's green-hooded eyes.

'You go outside? Now?' The ring of mountain brethren turns across to frown. 'Stay and drink, no?'

Tom just grins at her, salutes the Slovenians and the tall skiers, cocks his head and expects me to spring into place.

'In this? Are you mad? I'm not going out in that,' I say to him. 'Let's have a grappa and wait for it to pass.'

'I'm not staying here any longer,' Tom replies. 'We're nearly at the end of the slope. You can stay here and have a grappa if you like. Make your own way down later and I'll see you at the hotel.'

Tom's eyes abandon mine. This is why women take such a long time to leave him. Tom *does* take off and his girlfriends *do* follow him into whatever fray, craving his unsparing logic. I figure poor Mary is down to her last rations of humiliation and resolve.

I swear under my breath, picking up my gloves as a jostle of mirth travels around the group of tall skiers. They have seen idiotic foreigners before, crossing their mountains. I would have liked to have made a minor appeal on Tom's behalf. *Believe me, he's a great guy, he's a competitive bastard is all.*

He's come from nothing, you see. Has his father's bloody chip on his shoulder.

Only it would have sounded naff. Still, standing just behind him as he opens the stained pine door and an eddy of snowflakes pushes in, I feel I am on Tom's side against the world. I also feel an inkling of being physically thwarted and this startles me.

Our snowboards are buried under inches of snow and we are drunk. I try to ignore this fact as I ram my boot into the binding and miss, and the edge slices up and over the top of my gloveless knuckles. I look at the exposed epidermis filling with blood and let a couple of drops fall into the snow. Tom is up, both feet strapped in and he is flippering about like a penguin. I pull my foot on course, jimmy in the binding tongue, and fix the rear one too. I put my goggles on but they are full of snow and useless. We should be wearing helmets but one of our bags was lost on the flight and Tom refused to fork out for trendy Italian equipment.

'Which way?' I call out. More than anything, I want to slow Tom down before he takes off like a bat out of hell, whether or not his audience can see him.

'Over here!' I hear Tom shout, but already he is covered in blobs. The quiet, the heaviness, feel asphyxiating. I can't remember if this is a blue or a red slope, whether we have done it before even. But we have, I remember we've done it every day we've been here. With the girls before and after us, Corinne an agile experienced skier and Mary with her determined snowploughs, well-chosen accompanists for our middling curves. How different it had all been yesterday! Now I can hardly see the ridge of trees and Tom's body looks like a yeti on a dying screen.

'Tom! Tomas! For fuck's sake! Wait!'

I wonder if Tom is as drunk and blinded as I am, or if he is charged by the apparition of the real mountain men, challenging them in a rush of endorphins riding the beer. But he'll get down there, it's a given. I am bumping through wedges and pillows of snowdrift, the goggles on my forehead providing a brief shield from the driven flakes. I think I am going downward, but the board slows and the ground is flat. I make out a tree, then a bank of them, each one fattened with white carousel arms. I read a bestseller about climbers dying like flies on Everest. The ferocious white-out and the trail of ice-blackened bodies, each one propped against the snow in a mauled stupor.

Then I make myself think logically. I remember watching Corinne's tight pants whizzing over this last section of the slope yesterday, entranced by her perfection, proud of it. Corinne, who has a Frenchwoman's adherence to rules if only to upend them, will be angry we have taken off in such idiotic conditions. She has an unpredictable tolerance for Tom's enterprises.

I hear a quick whistling sound behind the whiteness. It is not Tom. Two of the skiers materialise, one of them is Ambra's expert brother. Tom is not going to like this. The word 'rescue' will kill him. But perhaps he is already at the bottom, taking a leak, pissed off that he has let Ambra slip away.

'*Stai bene? Vuoi seguirci giù?*'

Whatever they said, I nod hard. I assume it wasn't, *hey, we've come for your girlfriend*. They stand there in lax positions, leaning on their ski stocks for support, the snow falling on their faces.

———

Tom's father is staying at little hotel close to the slopes. He wanted it that way, not near the lake or the hospital, God forbid. He wanted a couple of days before he flew out with Tom's body. Mary organised everything. Mary has evolved from the girlfriend Tom was preparing to cast off to a tear-streaked organiser. I guess she still has a store of resolve, haunting her probably. Tom's father smokes in the hotel carpark in the sunlight, watching families pack their gear and have their squabbles before leaving for the slopes. He takes everybody in, eating them with his northern English eyes. Everyone knows about the tragedy. Mary sweeps up to him. She cries into his big chest and dwindles within his massive arms. Tom was so wiry, a spare man whose physical strengths were technical and acquired. I'm sure the old man beat him.

I wonder if – for Mary – they have a whiff of the same scent.

Corinne and I begin to pack. Corinne won't face Tom's father again. She lies in bed. This morning she went for a walk in the woods and I was certain I would come across her body curled under a snowy tree, the same way Tom's had been folded on the ground and gently covered, already so lifeless.

From our balcony I can see the end of the slope Tom led me onto the other afternoon when it was snowing. Ambra's slope, I now call it. Today the sky is brilliant and the snow is still hooked on the trees. Tom would have been up in the fresh powder, paddling off-piste, telling me what a tosser I am and how Mary liked it up her backside. I turn back to Corinne. She is asleep.

—

The night Tom died we set out to a concert by the lake at the opening to the valley. It was an outing Tom cooked up with Ambra, and there were only the three of us in the car. Somehow Tom had managed to tiff with Mary and she stayed at the hotel. On the way down we were lucky the local snowploughs had been so deft, and Ambra's directions proved decipherable and correct. It looked like the right place. A wooden hut with a bar, and a small stage platform next to it. Big speakers. Guys setting up chrome microphone stands. People in beanies chugging beers.

Tom parked the car in the cleared area. Other jeeps and pickups started streaming down the hill and an older guy in a fluorescent traffic jacket waved his arms, directing the vehicles. Tom said he was going over to the bar to watch the band set up. Corinne and I walked down to where the lake stretched out black like a maw in the side of the earth. Fresh snow covered the surrounding mountains in sheer iridescent moonlight. A high-altitude discotheque. The moon was a disco ball with a galactic spray that pattered over the surface. All around, the land descended steeply into the body of water, trees braked along the edge. There were no boats or jetties in sight, no relic of any other season than this. We stood there awhile. I knew Corinne was ready to go home. She was sick of Tom's behaviour and the way Tom and I kept gliding down the slopes on our adult learning curves.

Corinne had mastered skiing when she was a kid. But she said nothing and looked out over the water. There was a pause in the murmuring and clinking of bottles behind us and a sound that was complete nothingness expanded, a volume that would pound through our ears later when we were calling out, trying to spot Tom's body. We heard a bass riff shooting into the air and spinning apart.

Back at the bar I spotted one of the Slovenians from our afternoon in Ambra's snow-buried bar. He looked into my face and waved, to my surprise. I waved at him, taking it as a sure sign that Ambra would turn up and Tom would get his home run. The band started up with an old Clash song, sung in strangled English words learnt in a mountain class-room. I couldn't help thinking that it was admirable, the head-banging becoming grammatical research, or vice versa.

I looked at Corinne and she rolled her eyes.

Tom came up to us after another wander through the crowd. It seemed that Ambra hadn't appeared yet, but who knew what hamlet she hailed from, how many round-faced brothers she had to cook for, and the potency of her car. Tom nodded with the music, holding his beer bottle by the neck. He'd put a black cashmere scarf over his boarding jacket, urban-meets-mountain, to be lost on the girl with the clunky washer in her nose. I touched the small of Corinne's back. She turned around to me and I saw the face she was wearing when I got back to the hotel room that day. In soapy bath water up to her neck, face reddened, hair wet, watching me peel away the shrouds of my clothes.

She whispered something to me that I didn't hear well; the music had morphed into some Bowie song but I couldn't recall which one. Corinne loved Bowie, I didn't. Perhaps she wanted to dance. She dragged Tom away towards the stage. I watched the odd pair they made, printed one over the other, zigzagging through the crowd.

I remember the music changed to the worst rendition I had ever heard of *Purple Haze*. I realised this was just short of insanity, standing on a strip of sodden earth between the creaking templates of mountain and lake, listening to ruptured Hendrix. I was so cold my body smelt pungent, as though the sweat was stoppered in my pores. And there was another smell I couldn't identify, lifting on the air. Like overturned earth, or the entrails of water. I looked above the nodding heads to the carapace of blackness. It was the inverse of our comforting burial by snow. It was the harshest territory I had ever seen.

The Architecture of Humans

I realise I was never wired to say 'no' when my hippy aunt Merle is levelling me with two beer-bottle-green eyes, asking for an egg donation. I say 'yes', retreating to 'maybe', and Merle's face brightens with a joy I have just relinquished the right to tamper with. Merle has turned up in London at the pub where I am working part-time, striding over in a flashy printed dress and clacking beads and looking West African after so many years there, even though her skin is freckly porcelain with broken red lines. She says, 'Fern, you're the only one I can count on!' Merle only calls when you can hear she's on a bus to Abidjan, on a windblown beachfront, in the teary corner of a bar. She slams over the counter and pulls me into her embrace.

I fly out. This is the first time I've been back to Ghana since I was a child. Merle is a sax player who teaches music at an international school here. She's had affairs with politicians and wears headscarves around her flossy red hair. We give each other swamping hugs. In common, we have the steel pin of her sister, my mother, a woman who refracts all light and touch. Merle is my mother Fabienne's younger, startling sibling, whose life is a cavalcade of summer returns and resumed kitchen bickering and flip-flops at the airport; a cradle of tropicana that makes Fabienne shake her head. The egg donation is a colossal secret. Merle already has one child, her mixed-race daughter Victoria, conceived eleven years ago with a francophone guy in her band. Victoria is prim and tubby, which hits you afresh every time Merle repeats she can't understand where Victoria comes from, and she feels that I am hers.

Ghana is hotter than I remember and Merle doesn't have air conditioning. I sleep on the bed in Victoria's narrow room; my cousin sleeps on a rolled-out mattress on the floor. When it is time to get ready for school, Victoria sits up sleepily and looks at me in fright. She takes her clothes into the bathroom and locks the door. She comes out in her uniform with buttons about to burst all the way down her middle.

In the kitchen there are shouts, and a slap that cuts off Victoria's whines. I think about these insoluble markers along my cousin's childhood, wishing I'd guessed Merle would be such a crappy mum. When Victoria leaves with the driver in Merle's boxy olive-green Lada, I wait ten minutes before I walk into the kitchen. Merle is putting mugs and half-burnt toast out on the porch and the screen door whacks each time she enters. Noise doesn't seem to bother her. Today she has taken the morning off school and we are going to the clinic for my first tests.

'Sleep okay?' she says.

'I'm not used to the heat yet. I'll get used to it.'

'Do you want a fan? Sorry, I never thought.'

'Yeah, maybe. It was hot.'

She pours me some filter coffee and pushes across a can of creamed milk and a stainless-steel pot of sugar.

'Here's a spoon for that,' Merle says. 'Do you want eggs?'

'No, thanks. No eggs.'

We both smile.

'I'm not really sure what you eat, Fern. You just tell me. You just tell me everything.' She sits back, drinking her coffee, her broad shoulders scattered with freckles. She's wearing a sarong that pushes down her boobs, which were uplifted blossoms once. Each summer when Merle came back I learned things about my womanhood that my mother never told me. Merle went braless and her spine dug deep into her back and her rump kicked out and I understood what men wanted from a woman's body just by looking at her. Now she is 43 and she's been trying for this baby for over a year. She told me she's done everything. Local herbal doctors, tests in a big clinic in Abidjan, a check-up with a Swedish gynaecologist friend. I'm not exactly sure what's going to happen next. I've taken eight weeks off university, supposedly to work on my thesis, and given up the pub job. Merle paid for my ticket. I don't ask Merle how her boyfriend feels about this, but I know that once they take my eggs, they'll put them with his sperm in a petri dish. Merle told me on the phone they'll implant her with a long needle, and hopefully the embryo will stick. Her uterus was good, she said to me: *if bloody Victoria could cling to my uterus wall, then any baby can.*

Merle's yard is mostly dirt. There is a tan dog. She has house-help, a young girl with dark rings under her eyes. The girl walks behind the house with a chewing stick at the side of her mouth and a worn towel wrapped around her.

The clinic is a short way out of the city along the coast road. I don't remember ever coming to this end of town. The blocks are a cram of rundown and new, and the clinic is on the lower floor of a refurbished colonial building. There is a painted sign in front expressing some doubt:

Doctor Henry Danquah, Questions of Fertility

Inside, an older nurse sitting at the desk observes our entrance. She has glazed black hair and full cheeks. The nurse greets Merle and her smile moves over me. I am the promised one. The bearer of eggs. It is icy cold in here and there are bars on the windows and a terrazzo floor of shattered marble. As we sit waiting for the doctor I think of Victoria as a tiny emblem, descending Merle's lightless fallopian tubes, now probably blocked or stuffed from disuse. Merle puts her hand on my knee and I feel we are unlawful. This is not about fertility, this is about creation. We are here to mix up a being that does not yet exist.

I want her hand off me. I smell her breath.

'Are you okay there?' she asks.

'Sure.'

We hear chairs shifting behind the doctor's door. Before there were no voices, and now we hear threads of conversation.

'We'll meet up with Kwaku when we're done,' Merle says. 'We'll pass by the building site on the way home. He's waiting for us there.'

'Building site?' I ask.

'It's my dream house. You'll see. It's our other big secret. It's where this baby's life will begin.'

A stocky pregnant woman ambles out of the doctor's surgery and we are called inside.

Merle is elated. She's brought a special cool box to chill the vials of hormones for my injections, and organises my syringes into a separate plastic container which she rolls up in a canvas tote bag that I know is dear to her. She tucks both of these on the floor behind our seats as though they are precious cargo, not to be stolen or touched. She drives into the stream of traffic, talking, asking me when was the last time I had sex and what drugs I think might still be in my system. I tell her René and I had dawn sex before I flew out, and he doesn't really like what this is all about. She wants to know if René might turn up here on a whim and expect to get laid. I tell her he won't. I tell her we took stuff at the festival we went to last weekend and she bites her lip.

'I'm sure it's okay,' she says. 'It's not as though Kwaku isn't smoking dope.'

Last night on the porch Merle told me about the first time she and Kwaku went to bed. Merle said he dropped his jeans and she saw his thighs. His thighs! And she was smitten. It makes me think of René who is French and burly and quite reluctant to undress. I don't want to meet Kwaku, who is somewhere between my age and Merle's. It feels awkward now, being the conduit between the two lovers. I thought I would feel happily involved – and Merle did put an unnecessary cheque in my account – but I feel like a piece of plumbing, my ovaries a pair of helpful pods. I wonder what Kwaku thinks about the child they couldn't manufacture through sex, now being partially extracted from my body which is 20 years younger than Merle's speckled limbs. I wonder if I will feel attracted to him, and what I would do with this hard fact if I am.

'You just wait till you see the place,' she says. 'We're right on the water's edge. It took an age to get all the permits and then James – that's our architect – had to go back to London for two months. But we're up and running now. I mean, it won't look like that to you, but the basics are all done. Kwaku's always out there taking care of things. God, Fern, I must have *Witless Woman in Love* stamped on my forehead.'

'No, you don't,' I say. 'I can't see it anywhere.'

Merle smiles. 'We were hoping the first rooms would be ready for you to stay when you got here. You'd be closer to the clinic to have your ultra-sounds and check-ups. But it didn't happen. There aren't really any pipes out here so we had to build a big septic tank and bring electricity down from the village. Neither of us has built a house before, and James does get a bit up Kwaku's nose. James spent years abroad, only came back here when his mother died. He tends to treat Kwaku like a bush boy.'

We branch off and take a withered road towards the coast. We pass a couple of villages grafted onto the dust, both with colonial villas whose columns and scrolls are sketched with rich orange. I see two barrels of water tied either side of a donkey whose eyes are trained on the ground, and a jet-black cannon sitting on a white concrete pedestal. The cannon and the pedestal have been recently repainted. I wonder what type of thinking makes an ex-colonised people want to parade this trophy. It must be some sort of gravitational pull, an echo of subservience. I think of my mother Fabienne, who would have stood under the sun reminding the man with the paintbrush that his people had been blasted, chained and trafficked by the owners of the tilted iron cannon with its pyramid of gleaming balls.

But not Merle. Merle's russet hair whips with delight and I hear the glass vials clinking under my seat and she takes the next potholes carefully.

My hand flattens on my belly as though this is the starting point, this furrowed patch of terrain. But there is nothing in there. Just a set of young woman's organs, possibly a slick of René's sperm, we didn't use a condom before I left. (I'm not telling Merle this.) On the phone, she never said a thing about her dream house.

'Kwaku grew up out here,' Merle says. 'He's the one who got us the property. There's a polo club further on where the Lebanese hang out. Our band did a month of Fridays there and Kwaku had a job on the grounds.'

'Instant attraction?' I ask.

'Are you joking? I had my eye on a Lebanese guy with digs in Knightsbridge. This is the last thing that was meant to happen. Kwaku turned up every time we played and just stared at me.'

A final dusty hill then the sea spreads out ahead, the beachfront concealed by a forest of coconut palms. Out on a rock shelf is a construction of cast concrete beams like an empty shoebox.

There is only one word in my mind right now. It is *folly*.

—

In the evening I give myself my first hormone injection. I load the syringe, pull down my trousers and shoot it into a roll of flesh I gather on my abdomen. Victoria lies on the bed watching me. Merle was surly at dinner and spooned reheated rice and stew onto our plates. She has just driven out to meet Kwaku in a bar. Victoria has plugged in the fan and the air frees itself over both of us, but the metal basket makes a tinny noise I know will drive me crazy in the night. Victoria turns over onto her tummy and ignores me. I disinfect the pinprick and wonder how many pinpricks it will take to produce a viable cluster of eggs. The doctor wants to do an ultrasound in a couple of days.

René kept asking me if the setup was legal, or monitored, or even safe for my health. He thinks I am doing this because nothing I have ever done in my life has produced a consequence.

René said he wouldn't give these people a kitten.

Victoria is not asleep. I'd like to ask her what she thinks about Kwaku, who wasn't at the dramatic building site this afternoon, who called up Merle in the middle of our tight-lipped meal. Victoria is wearing pyjamas I suspect my mother has sent her from home. Her hair spills onto the pillow, the wall above her is blank.

I boil up some citronella stalks and strain the scented water into one of Merle's mugs.

—

Merle looks in on me in the morning. She's parcelled Victoria into the car and sits down on the bed. I feel shitty; my intestines feel like there is

146

water running through them.

'How did the injection go, darling?' Merle says.

'Fine. It was okay.'

'Kwaku's here. He's not up yet but he'll make you breakfast. I have to fly.' She kisses my forehead. 'Got to look after you. You're our little incubator.'

I stay in bed as long as I can, until my bowels are knotted and I am bursting with piss. I can't hear Kwaku in the kitchen. I sit down on the loo, expel everything then quickly shower. Light-headed, I think of digging myself into René's arms. We have agreed to call once a week, no emails. By the time I call him on Friday I will have had five injections of hormones in my belly, and at least two ultrasounds; perhaps there will be a batch of microscopic eggs trapped in the wavy turbines of my ovarian follicles. René is going back to Paris next weekend. He said he needed to catch up with a few people. I worry that means an ex-girlfriend called Sabine.

In Victoria's room I fold up my clothes in my suitcase on the floor, roll away the mattress, and stand in front of my cousin's crooked wardrobe with its chipped brown paint. I hear nothing from Merle's bedroom. But Merle's door is ajar and I see the long, rippled extension of Kwaku's spine on the sheets. His shoulders are turned inward and arms collected beneath his chest, the back of his shaven skull is square. Seeing this faceless outstretched body makes me struggle with Kwaku already. I wonder if Merle has ever gazed upon him like this. Of course she has. A woman always watches her man cruising through sleep. For a moment I imagine stretching along that back and inhaling the column of his neck.

He comes out when I am sipping tea on Merle's porch. He looks embarrassed, eyes narrow with sleep. I see he doesn't want to spend time alone with me either. We make small talk about how early they traipse off for school, about how he tried to get to the site yesterday but was held up in Ada, a town on the river towards Togo. He apologises for that. The young house-help crosses the yard with a tub of wet clothing, chewing stick in her mouth. She shouts something to Kwaku in Twi which makes him frown. I see the smile doesn't leave her face as she rounds the house.

For some reason, I am certain this woman can intuit our baby plan. She would have heard Merle and Kwaku over and over at night: the lovemaking turned into laceration and shouts.

I wonder how Merle put it to him: *My niece Fern is coming out from London, they'll bump up her egg production, remove her eggs and mix them with your seed when you jerk off at the clinic one morning, then vroom!, they'll plant little embryos inside of me. That's our child, Kwaku, that's what we'll do for our lovebaby. See?*

Kwaku balls his hands between his knees. He looks about the yard as though there are things to be done. He shovels sugar into his coffee. You can't tell me Kwaku's carnal aims included producing a baby with her. Not this lean, restless youth Merle could engulf with her limbs, who could go out there and impregnate a whole nubile village. It's possible that we could talk about Merle's dream house, though I'm worried my consternation will come out fast. And I'm even more afraid of seeing through to Kwaku's unsteady feelings. I watch his fingers roving over each other. They have very lengthy joints. I can't believe this man and I are providing the raw material to create a child. Would it be ours, in anything but the language of souls? Should it be?

Kwaku lifts himself out of the rattan chair and runs a palm over his head. His eyeballs are slightly protruding; I'm hoping Merle's new child won't have these. Kwaku says he has an 'errand' to run. It sounds like a line from an American film. He walks off the porch and across the yard, up to the gate which he hooks shut. I hear a dog barking along the road.

—

Though I said I would, I cannot get used to the heat during the night. I lie awake, listening to Victoria half-snoring and the night birds outside. Kwaku rarely comes to the house. Merle says he likes to keep an eye on the building site. But when he does pass by I hear them talking in the dark and I know her urging him to stay goes unheeded. I listen to them make love and it makes me miss René, who on the phone has a flat, defiant voice. René asks nothing of the procedure. In three weeks I have produced a worthy clutch of eggs according to the doctor's ultrasound screen, a harvest I cannot decipher within the topography of my abdomen. Merle is enthralled but I see a tiny galaxy of consequences. Dates are fixed for the egg extraction and embryo transfer. Merle takes me out a few nights before, to a windswept bar in the grounds of a luxury hotel. We meet a friend of hers called Tina, from Barbados, who arrives dressed in parrots and flowers. Tina has a local husband and runs a guesthouse on the coast, but Merle warns me in the car Tina knows nothing of our arrangement so I should keep my mouth zipped. We drink non-alcoholic cocktails. Tina is an easy talker until she points out that Merle's architect, James, was once held in a cell overnight for beating up his wife. I see Merle's eyes scramble. Merle says she knew about it, but it's obvious she's been stung. Tina tries to recover the conversation, before her daughter calls from downtown with car problems. She hurries off through the floodlit garden and we are left alone.

'I'm sorry, I don't know why I asked her to come,' Merle says to me. 'Fucking nosy.'

'Yeah, she was. She had a parrot thing going.'

'Yeah,' she says. 'Thanks Fern, love. You must be bored silly out here.'

'Pretty close to it.'

'I don't think it's going to work.'

'Say again?'

'Oh, fuck it. The transfer. This baby,' Merle says, staring at Tina's abandoned glass. 'You know, Tina's right about James. He took ten thousand pounds and disappeared. I had to pay people – thugs, dammit – to get him back here. He'd gone and set himself up in Hackney with a girlfriend. He's an overeducated prat.'

'I hear you.'

'He sold off a lot of our building supplies too. Now Kwaku keeps an eye on him. He's back with his wife at McCarthy Hill. She took him back in.'

That first week we drove along the sandy trail with the car panting,

Merle's incomplete villa revealing its nave and struts between the palms. It was further back from the sea edge than I'd thought, but its static structures already looked like ruins. We walked out onto the platform where the glass window panes should have been, above rocks where the sea fluxed. We imagined sipping tea and watching the sky draw away. Our dreams were elegant. We walked upstairs to the empty first floor where four bedrooms and a studio would be installed. My aunt stood on the cement, hair in red strands like a mermaid on a plunging clipper.

—

The day before my doctor's appointment Victoria isn't feeling well and won't get up to go to school. Merle comes in, tries to shake her whining daughter, who she concedes has a temperature. I tell Merle to get going, that I'll look after Victoria today.

'Stay away from her,' she says. 'You don't want to pick up anything.'

Merle storms out and the car revs off.

Victoria turns away from me on the mattress on the floor. Merle told me her father was an older, agile guitar player from Mali who returned to wherever he had come from. She said he had a big bun of Rastafarian snakes coiled on his head, and the day Victoria was born he'd had them all cut off and come to her as a dignified man she barely recognised. He had land and wives and he didn't need the music. He had wanted to bring her and the baby up north, Merle laughed. They parted ways and Victoria was fatherless. When Merle came to London in the summer she used to dress Victoria in exquisite pinafores sewn out of wax prints. The little girl would hide under the table in pub gardens; any number of people would try to entice her out. Merle would drink pint after pint and it wouldn't show for a long time.

I ask Victoria if she wants a cup of tea or some water from the fridge. She doesn't answer. In the kitchen, I boil up some water in a pan and drag a teabag through it. I pour the tea into two mugs, adding clumps of sugar and the only piece of lime I can find. When I come back into the room

Victoria is sitting up in bed, staring out of the window louvers at the dog pawing the ground.

'Are you leaving soon?' Victoria says.

'Not yet. I'm not sure when. You know why I'm here, don't you?'

'Merle's too old to make a baby, so you and Kwaku are doing it together.'

'That's not exactly true.'

I give her the cup of tea and sit down next to her on the bed.

'I saw Kwaku's thing,' she says. 'He was in the bathroom.'

I try to think of a way to decriminalise this instrument, to make it into something generic, a common tool. But I don't want to be the one to explain Kwaku's penis or Merle's frail cosmos. There must be a seam I could mine to tell her that her life is more than this airless room, and the cries she's heard for a year on the other side of the wall.

I wonder what a grown-up Victoria will say to me about the stash of eggs not far from where I am resting my hand. She'll figure it out one day, when Merle's new toddler is running around another poky house with fingerprinted walls, when she is doing homework and yelling at him to be quiet. She'll read an article somewhere and remember the nightly injections in my belly, and Kwaku's weirdness around me, and it'll all make sense.

We drink our tea. Victoria watches the dusty yard. I open my hand over where Merle's borrowed eggs are stored, waiting to be siphoned out tomorrow. One day, perhaps when Merle's new baby is a young jobless man and Victoria herself is a slim chain-smoker living in London, I will tell my cousin a story. It is the story I am not brave enough to tell her now. I will tell her that on the day she was born, a man sat down in a barbershop in Accra and had his high, crowning hair cut off. Our eyes will connect and hers will be alert. I will tell Victoria that this man watched as these woven cords dropped to the floor and he saw his bare scalp for the first time in decades. I will tell her that this man rejoiced for his newborn daughter and he felt jubilant and blessed.

151

My Family

He says, *My Family*, and the furthest reaches of your organism, regions that have dwelled in peace within your being as an undiscovered terrain, are incinerated by light.

He says, *My Family*, and you are awash outside a citadel where the walls run into the sky and these are walls that would repel you with a charge, send you smashing across a room.

He says, *My Family*, and you know you have reached your last bastion of hope, and there will be further chains, and no water.

He says, *My Family*, and you remember you were once chaste.

He says, *My Family*, and you imagine the song of their flesh, her cries, his body sweeping, their original compulsion, the shifted radiance, the old radiance.

He says, *My Family*, and you wonder how that pointing of his body felt within the sleeve of hers.

He says, *My Family*, and you remember feeling wishful, all intuition jammed.

The Vineyard

They were advised to remove the vineyard. The grape trunks had heavy, unruly kinks and were clothed in moss, and the vines that sprang along the wires were each summer weaker and less adorned with fruit. A fast-growing more modern plant was suggested, a hybrid that would show results within three years. It was a soft, easy decision to make given their father had passed last year, so there was no wrath in the room or fists shaken over the table, just three of the four brothers (Valerio after the car smash had remained slow and staring): Lorenzo, who was in the military and mostly concerned with controlling his rebellious daughter; Gigi, who was dully married; and the youngest, Maurizio, who as a boy had told unblinking lies but now ably managed the property with his wife Sonia, who was accepting and stifled.

The wires that ran through the grape plants were cut and coiled for further usage. Any plant with additional props had these removed and the concrete posts that rose every three paces were hoisted out of the earth: this took place on a day that Maurizio hired three additional Romanian labourers.

When all that was left standing were the rows of limbless grape trunks, Maurizio used his power saw to cut each down, as close as possible to the dirt. The following week he would bring out the digger to overturn the root systems. Then this long job would be half done. The wood gave off a stricken oily odour as he went along.

Maurizio's wife, Sonia, watched his progress from an upper vineyard where she was pruning. These *tocai* plants they always left to the end as they were drier and less prone to sickness, and it was also the most attractive part of the property to work. She stood along an arcade of cropped vines and stopped the compressor for a moment, watching her husband at work. The severed grape trunks were strewn messily in his wake, where Sonia would have told him to stack them to one side. Half the vineyard now lay felled every which way on the wet winter grass. Sonia saw how Maurizio half-knelt with the chainsaw in his lap, and she listened to the whining sound that rose and ceased as he sliced through each one then moved on to the next. She thought of the stash of new green plants in their plastic pockets of fertilised soil, waiting in the barn, how they emanated an unreal eagerness. For a moment she imagined her husband's heartbreak should these young plants fall lifeless to the ground; how he would sit at the table and she would protect him from his critical brothers.

Behind Sonia the sloping vineyard met a stone support wall that harboured snake litters in the summer, and above this a gravel road encircled the rocky hill but led nowhere. Neighbours of hers dumped rubbish there, youngsters buzzed around on motocross bikes, boys stoned cats, and puppies were abandoned.

Trionfo di Pesce

Helen and Marco are celebrating their second wedding anniversary with an outing to the new Italian fish restaurant. Marco, whose parents sailed out to Australia from Puglia, orders *trionfo di pesce*, an extravagant mixed platter. At 54, unmarried, Marco had flown to Sydney to visit his brother, when at an inner-city bus stop he met Helen, a childless librarian. Now the couple is living in West Africa until Marco's contract runs out. Opposite them sit their friends, Megan and Geoff, who have been married 34 years.

Helen and Marco have not yet mastered the art of being touchy in front of other people. Helen's hands become faltering appendages, and Marco's arms feel like unbending steel rods. So they refrain from closeness in public, although Marco touches Helen's hand when the waitress waltzes away with their order and returns with a tray of thin-stemmed glasses. Helen looks at their clutching digits.

Geoff is given the wine to taste. His quiff of ragged grey hair makes him seem head of the table.

Marco is bald.

One of Geoff and Megan's four daughters has just been involved in a drug-related incident where she fell from a first floor balcony onto a pool deck. Days ago Megan flew in from Brisbane, assured that there would be no long-term spinal damage. Megan apologises for being a bit teary, and Geoff's large arm swings around her shoulders, patting her upper sleeve.

Helen looks beyond their heads to other couples, other groups of diners, then through the window with its embellished security grill, to a local man leaning on the balcony railing outside.

At first it had felt extraordinary to be a man's wife, but she found so much conversation draining.

Marco refills everyone's glasses, remarking that the wine was a pretty good choice.

'So how does it feel then? Two years of marriage?' Megan says, nudging

Greg's round abdomen. 'They're just babes in the woods.'

Marco looks at Helen; they were still reading each other's looks.

'Wonderful,' she replies. 'He's just short of being a saint.' Helen genuinely believes this. Marco brings her a cup of tea in bed in the morning. She doesn't always like his nuzzling, but tries to. Helen is fierce-looking with long coarse grey-blonde hair and has never much been interested in men, or women. But Marco had struck her; he was only in Sydney for two weeks.

She and Marco have a dream for when they leave West Africa. A little stone terrace in Puglia, the one he'd shown her that had belonged to his grandparents, in a village by the lapping sea. They have both saved their money. They both like to fish. Helen believes that as he ages, Marco will chatter less and he will teach her Italian. That in the afternoons he will fall into a serene silence in the sunlight.

In the carpark the couples hug goodbye and Geoff's arm gathers Megan's shoulders. Helen and Marco stand side by side.

Inside the car Helen kisses him and kisses him.

They Came from the East

They came from the east in buses; becalmed men, devoid of propulsion. If you bumped into one on the Underground you would see no forgiving nod of his face, just a trigger, a finger on steel. You'd sense a pulse somewhere, a relic almost bred out of you, the garlic reach of his breath. You'd apologise, aware of the titillation of the word *mercy*, looking for a raft through the percussion of his stare. The train would move on and a brief audience would look at their feet.

These men found jobs and made themselves useful; they had been very useful. Your father who believes in contribution takes one in, saying this man had been thrown out of his windowless squat, saying that these wars had occurred on our doorstep. Saying there had been snipers and bombings and massacres and *we had watched.*

Your mother says she'll have no stranger in the house. Your father makes the back shed comfortable. One evening a man is introduced.

You shake this man's hand. You think of corpses nursed together on stinging summer days.

—

It is two years since your parents failed to persuade your brother Milo to reside in this world. One autumn night Milo never came back from the park. At home his cut-out is still everywhere, his osmotic reign in doorways, adrift on the stairs. Milo's *danse macabre* takes place every night, an ache of energy from the kitchen to the computer screen, then barefoot through the frosted, mugger-ridden common. Milo's physical health was always inviolate, merely brushed.

Your parents remain distraught. Most nights you come home to find your mother banked against your father, who is fastened around her body.

Tonight, the foreign guest steps into the kitchen from the dark garden. For a moment his back, entrapped on the glass door, braces. The man's eyes are strange and gel-like.

Boiling water rolls in a pot.

Your father releases your mother, whose tears mark his shirt. Except for Milo, who had a labourer's job and grew thick, pulsating digits, you are all musicians in this house.

—

The foreign guest is a voiceless man who observes. On a Sunday, he sits on the step outside the back shed. His not-home. You look down at him from your window, the way the war has cast this man into a script of fenced-off yards and the undulations of a new city.

You step back when his eyes shoot up to your eyes.

You are a tenor. You return to your exercise. But as you sing you realise the house is empty and the back door is not locked. You listen for creaks on the stairs.

You begin a more complex vocalise – Rachmaninoff's – yet beneath the ascension you hear a firm knock. You stand there, chin rising, score gliding to the floor. Your armpits prickle. You think that terror is the intrinsic, bowel-trembling note aligning all beings. You think of nocturnal rapping on apartment doors and men being dragged off, ankles bumping down stairs.

You start again, expelling the notes, riding the upward carriage of the music. But hear a capable voice mirroring your own. You stop, the singing stops. You have heard the largeness of the foreigner's voice on the other side of the door; its airy lift, portions of its unschooled embracing. This is a travesty.

You are furious. Are you being mocked?

—

Your father says that the foreigner calls himself Peter. Peter has found a job on a building site a few suburbs away. He catches the train in the morning, at night he walks home. Your mother has not warmed to him. She has followed the war trials on the news. She says, 'What if?' But she cooks for him, sets a place for him at the table. Peter washes the dishes and your mother goes outside to smoke a cigarette. Then she drives into the city to rehearse. Other evenings your mother and father watch a film in the front room with the door ajar. You enter and they are entangled on the couch. They stretch out with fronts together, fingers in hair.

Peter reads a tabloid newspaper on the cleared table under the kitchen light.

You go into Milo's room which remains a lair, a loophole. Sit at Milo's desk staring at the dead cells of the computer screen. You think of young men your own age, promised safety but pushed off buses and led in single file through the woods. You think that Milo, had he been raised in Peter's country, would have worn a uniform and slaughtered men. You are not sure how this skill is devised but you know that your brother would have given captives water, pronounced their names, absorbed duty.

Shot them.

You disconnect that thought, but it stays awash in you.

—

Your father travels to Devon to see to work on your grandfather's house. Your mother is at college teaching. Peter has long departed across the suburbs on a dawn train. You have a recital tonight outdoors; your throat is dry. You swallow honey and make herbal tea. You do not possess Milo's exuberant organism. When Milo finally hanged himself in the park, the doctors wished to dissect his brain. You don't know why your parents agreed to surrender this immense portal, but then they never thought to ask you.

In slippers, you tread across to the back shed where Peter has now lived for three months. You have your mother's extra set of keys. Since your father swept up the wood-planked floor and cut a carpet piece to fit the room, no one else has been in here. Inside there is a bed, neatly made, a chest with a lamp. There is a desk and a buckled landscape hanging under glass. You begin to ransack. You strip off the bed, pull away the furniture from the walls, lift up the carpet corners and peer as far as you can see. You are looking for trophies. You remember the tooth that a Belgian soldier kept for decades, shown in his palm on a current affairs programme on TV. The tooth had been taken from Patrice Lumumba's dissolved head.

You pull out the drawer of the desk and in the cavity underneath there are two things. A gold chain, bloodied or rusted, with a crucifix. And a blurred photograph of your mother. Now you are satisfied.

You shred the photo into minute, unbearable pieces. When you look at these morsels at your feet, you realise the woman was not your mother at all.

—

The performance goes well. Afterwards you go out with the group and drink a whisky, not your usual drop. Your heartbeat has quickened; there is a girl who seems to admire you standing at your side. She looks at you with slow enquiry. She also sings. The girl drinks white wine, glass after glass, bumping into you. Your flanks graft together, you separate from the others. A voice travels around with the name of the restaurant where the group will go next, but you've told your mother you'll be home early. She's not comfortable alone with Peter in the house.

You're single, you haven't had sex in months. You can feel your loins begging, churning. You're ashamed, looking at this girl, at the force your body has compiled from nothing. A glass of whisky and a few scrapes along your thigh. You're ashamed at how you've ceded to rough thoughts. Where before, while singing, you felt a holy surge, a climb towards a communal sense of articulation, you now feel demoted, belonging to a species at its vulgar, grappling genesis.

You turn away from her, leave the group and catch the Tube home.

—

Milo used to run through the park with fierce love. It is where you go now. Your throat is hoarse again as night air roves over you. The trees are scarcely visible, then loom up with their architecture, buttresses sliding into the ground. Your mother calls, worried that you have gone out with friends. She asks you to come home, 'Please'. You don't tell her you are around the corner on the common.

You sit on a park bench. You hear druggies up on the hill and wait a while, listening to their cracks and calls. You wonder if that would be an easier way than this.

Twenty minutes later when you walk into the kitchen, you know a physical force has passed through here, you feel it jarring the air. Your mother is immobile at the back window. When she turns, you see her face has been employed in a frantic way; it looks lopsided. You ask her what has happened, what's wrong. She says, 'Where were you?' As if those lost moments have been critical. Food steams on the stove.

Peter is absent.

In the night you hear your father's keys in the front door. He bounds up the stairs and they remain enclosed together, murmuring. You hear one low cry.

—

After rain, your hands dig into the earth where you buried Peter's shredded photograph. The pieces are half-dry, stuck together. You take out the mass and put it in a bowl on the radiator in your bedroom. When the bits are dry, you rub off the dirt and spread them on your desk. You separate the lower, darker tones from the aura of daylight cast down from above. You gather pieces of the woman's olive-green sweater, locating the contours of her body. You identify her breasts, her belly, her shoulders. You discover a row of stitching around the neckline and link this up. Her neck presents itself, smooth and broad. Next to the border of her skin there is a creamy wall in the background, perhaps a cottage. You didn't notice it before. You look for her curly reddish hair, identical to your mother's, you certainly remember that. You lay out this halo and her face looks like a devoured saint, an empty reliquary. You search for her features in the pile. You separate her brows and nose, her eyes that are unlike your mother's, smaller and without beauty, her mouth, which is colourless and compressed. You flatten these overlapping pieces and are surprised. This woman is nothing like your mother. And yet in that horrible moment you had thought. You sit there, observing. She wears no expression, even though her eyes are breached by the camera's gaze. Her hands are wrapped together beneath her waist and she wears tight jeans; she is a heavy-hipped woman. To the left of the cottage there is long grass, a wooden fence, pines.

A chain disappears beneath her sweater and you know there is a crucifix resting on her skin.

You scan the photograph. You print it.

—

Your mother drops out of her production and your father takes time off work. They leave for a week in Brittany, taking their instruments. You wave them down the road that skirts the common, seeing the bench where you sat the other night. You watch the car take the bend out of the neighbourhood towards the thoroughfares leading from the city. You are standing on the footpath with a cup of cold tea.

For the past few days inertia has driven you into your bed. You know that it is your doing, whatever Peter inflicted upon your mother. You were told no details. You know there were visits to the clinic. To your parents you said nothing about ransacking the man's room, or ripping up the photograph of the woman with red hair. At night your limbs jerk you awake and you hear Milo moaning, Milo scratching the walls. You see the schoolboy who you know discovered Milo's body swinging in the park. That kid's life now has a rotten thing inside.

It is not hard to find Peter. You catch the train to the suburb where he works. You begin to wander along streets. It is windy, gritty, and you think of your parents driving through France, windshield wipers crossing to and fro, French road signs diminishing in their wake. How, in lumpy beds before the glow of dawn, they will refuel their love from these embers. You approach a building site with a skip on the roadside and white-dusted men ferrying detritus from the house, an orange funnel releasing a cloudy ziggurat of material. You glimpse Peter. At first you think he is going to do a runner, but he walks over to you calmly. You see how he is robust among other men, how his damp hair spiders over his temples. You see it in his spine now: he is a soldier, he has executed men. He has never known capitulation.

You hand him the printout of the woman's photo. He takes the corner, eyes dropping, an infinitesimal slippage. He gives you a turbulent look, folds the image into his pocket, rejoins the other labourers. You stand there watching their cohesion among the rubble.

Return from Salt Pond

All the way home she talked. Even her suffering silence was dialogue, insinuating itself along the cords of his brain, snaking with his thoughts, coaxing words from him that were unwilling and clotted. That way he often dwelt in defence, and she had become so agile. When they had nearly arrived at his mother's house at the edge of Accra, he took a short-cut behind the new formal streets of the estate, driving through a cuff of blackness under a disused railway bridge. At the exit there was a crump, or a blow, and the windscreen shattered over them. Gunning the car as flashes became ragged youths, he glanced at her face in the dark, saw its bloody supplication, saw the rock sitting in her lap like a grinning child.

Kenneth had lived abroad for years but he came back often enough to know the unsealed roads out of here. He accelerated, charging in the dust, cackles surrounding them as the night air entered the ruptured window, sailing over the silver splatter on their clothes. He could not speak. Not even an *Are you okay?* could come from him in these moments. And he knew she was just as misshapen, tossed in the same gulf.

He reached the estate with its clean kerbs and glassed-topped walls. Street lamps. He could talk to her now. Decide whether to take her to the dodgy hospital on the far side of town. Better a clinic nearby. But still Erica's mouth stayed closed. He heard a gust of her prattle from five minutes before, the reprimands as echoes on the air. He stopped the car at a junction, reaching for the moist map of her face. He pressed his lips to hers, feeling a fleck of glass between them, and her tongue was cool and unresponsive.

'Erica. Tell me you're okay,' he said to her.

She nodded. They both looked at the substantial rock that had been lobbed through the glass, now in a corona of shards on her jeans.

'Take this off me,' she said.

He wondered if they should go to the police. But then thought of the hours sitting in the hot oil-painted rooms, the officers like cartoon cops, their adhesion to cardboard colonial praxis. Then the unfolding hassles afterwards. He and Erica on trial for not being locals. What were they doing under a railway bridge at night? They were surely committing indecent acts? And finally, the row of thugs from downtown. Thugs who could find out where he lived. Thugs who could hammer a nail into his dog's head and rape his old mother. If he were more righteous, he could put time into this thing, root them out, spit on their faces. He could spend the next year sitting on a grimy court hall bench waiting his turn amidst the punks and uncles, the battered market girls and baby thefts, the crocodile tears and pragmatic stink of pardon, with a judge in a crisp wig waiting for a fatter handout.

He turned to her, lifting the thing from her lap; he opened his door and let it fall to the roadside. 'We'll go to Ibrahim's,' he said. 'We'll clean you up there.'

The rock gone, she clasped herself and began to cry. Slivers fell from her hair to the masses on the seat.

'Oh God, Erica. Look at you, baby.'

It hadn't been such a bad day, but to end it like this. The Salt Pond property had been what they were looking for. The timber of the main building was sound. The mud huts for guests were in fair shape. The trail to the beach was magical, and able to be fenced off. If their dreamy move to Ghana was ever going to be orchestrated, he felt that these could be its initial chords. He envisaged the platform construction on the hillock where the jazz bar would be located, and she had noted the nearby well-respected clinic and proximity to the busy coastal road. The divisions in their thinking hadn't been palpable immediately. She touched his arm as the agent led them from the main building through the unkempt grounds sloping to the sea, around the parched huts with their weary vegetation and carved stools. She kept turning back to him, smiling at him, her eyes wide. But as soon as the agent was gone she said some bullshit about not wanting to shift all her savings for the deposit and expecting him to cough up at least 30 per cent. It was said carefully as she sipped her second beer. There had been forethought and he felt played. Then, as they were leaving, she said she wanted to see one of the huts again. They walked down the trail to the dusky sea. Inside he pulled down her pants and fucked her quietly, the door half-closed and children running past and their two faces pushed into the coarse walls.

It was more money than he had earned in the past five years.

Kenneth curved into his oldest friend Ibrahim's street, hoping that his wife Fifi was at home to see to Erica. He wanted to throw off the shock by discussing it with another man. A part of him even wanted to imagine what the youth had felt – the rock rough against his shirt as the car entered the short tunnel, lifting its mass into the night air. Then hauling back and volleying with force. Now he saw their shattered car from the outside, the faceless crash dummies and the chitter of the glass. He wanted to tell Ibrahim how the impulse had run through him – *Gun it! Gun it!* – while Erica was midway through arguing with him, undoing him. And how shit-scared he was that there might have been a dozen of them in the night.

'How you doing there, baby? We'll get you through this. Don't sweat, darling.' He put his hand on her thigh.

He beeped his horn and Ibrahim's ancient watchman slid across a metal peephole in the gate, staring at the vehicle for minutes. Kenneth heard Erica's sobs and reached his arm around her shoulders.

———

Fifi took Erica to the bathroom where she began to tweeze out the glass. He and Ibrahim sat down with two beers on the porch. He was exhausted, his shoulders were wrought and a rogue pain travelled along one side of his neck. He had a few cuts, but the glass had landed mostly on his jeans. His knuckles were scratched and he had dug a jagged piece out of his forearm. It was now sitting on the coffee table in front of him, blood-free, a piece of today's ghastly jigsaw puzzle.

'It's the fourth or fifth time I've heard about it. I'm amazed someone didn't warn you,' Ibrahim said lazily. 'It's some bunch of thieves from Tudu, they come here in the night. Things will move when they knock out some politician's son in a sweet car and steal his gadgets, you'll see. But small fry like you – bet you didn't have a hundred bucks between the pair of you.'

'Not exactly. But Erica had some dosh.'

'Then here's to you and dosh, bro,' Ibrahim said. 'Did you see that place you were talking about? Where was it? Sekondi?'

Now Kenneth wished he had never told Ibrahim about the Salt Pond place and their impossible hopes. The jazz club. The music school. The cool beach hotel. It seemed as foolish as tonight's crushed glass was coldly tangible.

'We went there. It may well be a rip-off. Ownership stuff. You can never know who you're buying from,' he said.

'Erica's interested?'

'We both are. It needs some thought.'

Kenneth knew Ibrahim was biding his time, waiting for the cracks to widen. Erica was older, she wasn't first-choice material. Divorced, she'd made a mess of her career, changing in her thirties to become a musician, failing, then returning to teaching. They'd hooked up in Guildford outside a pub between sets, both jaded exiles on a landscape of dripping buildings and shrouds of rain. Someone had read her cards that afternoon and said she'd fall in love with a dark-skinned musician. He'd thought she was bonkers, but he let her lead him to her flat. The morning after she was all honey and roses in his heavy arms and he couldn't let go of her.

'I had an almighty shag with Adua this afternoon,' said Ibrahim. 'Christ! I've still got blue balls. They're paining me! And now I've got Fifi to look forward to tonight. Dutiful spouse sex, there is nothing sweeter. Ah, my sweet cock-sucking wife! You ought to tie the knot and start having fun again.'

But as Ibrahim talked, Kenneth looked out over the neighbourhood with its stands of satellite dishes raised to the sky. He smacked a mosquito on his neck. 'Thanks for tonight, you know.'

'Don't be foolish, man,' Ibrahim said.

'Erica was pretty shaken up. It all happened out of the blue. I'm sure she thinks it was aimed at her.'

'Don't be thick. Those cunts couldn't see a thing in the dark.'

'The thing is, if they'd got inside the car, I don't know what might have happened. It doesn't bear thinking about.'

'No, it doesn't. Look, you have your woman. You can borrow Fifi's car. Take her home along the main road.'

Ibrahim was smiling at him. This was the smile Erica had said she found unsettling. She said she could feel him beneath her skin, his insatiable sexual navigation. Now Kenneth tried to hear some sound from inside but heard nothing; the women were tucked deep within Ibrahim's house of slick tiles and crooked doors. Ibrahim's fingers were running a riff along the cane armrest.

'Weren't you supposed to be playing tonight?' Ibrahim said.

'Yes. I backed out. I asked the guy who helps out at the Golden Tulip.'

'Adua says you look kinda kinky when you play. Says you get this grungy look that sends a ripple around the room.'

He snorted. 'So who's this Adua?' he asked.

'She's just back from the US. She did a journalism course at Columbia, now she wants to shake things up. Starting with me,' Ibrahim said.

Kenneth shook his head. Winding back, he thought there had been an instant when the windscreen was still intact, when there was a smear or friction on the glass, poised or stilled as they bickered. Had there been time enough for him to whip out his arm to protect her? He felt such sorrow now, such grief. For what he knew – though until this moment he had deflected the thought – was that the rock had finally shut her up. All she had spoken of the whole way home was his lack of money. How she couldn't be expected to risk her life savings. What if they split up? What if the business was a failure? He had hardened, breathed in and out, at one point wanted to see her crushed, slapped, mortified. Driving on, he had overturned these thoughts, ashamed, but discovered he found her repellent, and even the warm fuck two hours ago seemed grotesque.

He had to see her. To apologise for this. To hold her, inhale her.

'Shall we go inside?' he asked Ibrahim.

'What's your hurry, man? I can hear them upstairs. Fifi's probably empty-ing out her whole wardrobe.'

They opened two more beers. A donkey bayed from the scrub surround-ing the estate. Then a car horn sounded in the night, headlights slewed one way, then the other. 'See? They're still out there, your stupid thugs. They're most probably bored as hell and high as rafters.'

—

Kenneth drove Fifi's jeep out onto Ibrahim's road under the lights. It was a compact woman's vehicle, all wheezy and light, tyres that sang on the bitumen.

'You look better now,' he said, touching Erica's cheek. She had on a pair of Fifi's flashy designer jeans, loose on her thin thighs, and a white T-shirt with a bird on it.

'I had a good hot shower. Fifi's bathroom is like the fifth dimension,' she told him.

He laughed, thank God Fifi had opened a bottle of wine. All he wanted was to go home, commune with her. He saw them slithering on the bare floor.

'You don't want to pass by the club?' she asked.

'No. Why should we?' Now that he had spoken to Ibrahim, Kenneth wanted to tell her. He wanted her to see how he had been bold and, in his way, successful. He wanted to sluice into her, whisper that Ibrahim would lend him fifteen grand. They could buy the Salt Pond place. Next week even. It was all going to happen.

'I thought you'd feel like playing. You know, shake it off.'

'That could be a plan B,' he said, reaching for her thigh.

'I don't want to go to the house.'

'Why? I thought you'd want to wind down.'

169

'I am wound down,' she said. 'We stayed far too long at Ibrahim's. I don't think I could go home and stare at the four walls. Not after this.'

He backtracked into third gear by mistake and the car threw them forward. Originally, his compulsion had been to be out there every night, his bass creamed to his hip and whatever happened. There had been women. Foreign, local; curvy, slim. He was big and bulky and wore small round glasses and he was very dark. They would say yes to him and he would make love over and over to their bodies. But it was Erica who had locked him into the rare, amplified state that now governed him. He would raise his face during a jam, look everywhere for her in a panic discharged only by connection with her eyes, and he would crave her open thighs and the heat of her cunt.

'You don't want to talk about the Salt Pond place?' he asked her.

'I think we're done with that,' Erica replied. 'In every bloody way imaginable.'

'I don't see your point.'

'Kenneth. It seems pretty obvious to me. Someone throws a rock in your face when you're talking with the person who's never going to come to the table for your dream. To the person who doesn't realise it also takes physical commitment to show belief. To me that pretty much means it's over.'

'It's my dream too,' he said. 'And it's not over.'

'Can't you see?' she cried. 'What happened tonight was a sign. It had to be, Kenneth. These things just don't happen. A rock in my bloody lap? And you think we're going to last long enough to have children?'

Kenneth felt the twang in his neck return. He thought of Fifi on her knees, Ibrahim tugging her thick hair and holding her scalp, rolling her over afterwards as she secretly wiped her mouth. He stared at the angry face next to him.

'Whatever this was,' she said. 'It's a blockage. Someone is telling us to halt. This is not the way we are meant to be going. Or me at least.'

She turned away from him.

He shifted the gears of Fifi's stupid car, reaching fifth on a short stretch before a bumbling taxi loomed up in front of them. He accelerated around this. He glanced at her pale folded limbs, everything folded against him. At the intersection he made a U-turn back into Ibrahim's neighbourhood and then – as she sat up in alarm – veered onto the dirt road they had taken earlier to escape. The lightweight car rocked down the trail and he knew he wanted to hurt her.

'What the fuck are you doing? Stop the car!' she said.

He skidded on, headlights bouncing as the vehicle jerked their bodies. In an instant they were back where it had started. Beneath the railway bridge entering the cuff of dark. A wall of hefty rocks slid down from the disused track and he saw bottles and cans, a discarded handbag with its entrails in the dust and a woman's shoe. He cut the engine and they were alone. By now her cries had ceased and her arms had fallen and her whole body trembled.

He sat there in a fury, not believing what he had done, not understanding anything. All he understood was his desire to disprove her, to upend this woman who believed in cards and signs, to discredit and disown her. He stepped out and slammed the car door. He left her there crying and walked away.

He scuffed along a trail, a few times stalling, closing his eyes, drawn to her. She did not call out to him. As the path climbed there was silence and the night air drifted over his skin. He wiped his glasses which had fogged over. He heard Fifi's jeep revving below. It reached the street and Erica had the same problem with the gears. He stood there listening to the sound of the engine disappear.

On the road he caught a taxi to the club and when he arrived he asked for one of his old guitars from the back room. He watched the guy from the Golden Tulip play for a while, but when Seth saw him in the audience he finished the piece and lifted his guitar strap over his neck. Kenneth finished a neat whisky he thought he deserved, and stepped onstage to a round of clapping. For years he had played on and off here. There had been an uninterrupted stretch of six months when his father had been dying, when every night he had come to the club from the hospital with stricken hands. Every night he had changed the old man's soiled garments and sheets. Kenneth had a strong suspicion he would end up like him, a marooned vessel other people would have to feed and bathe. He hoped he still had time to think about these things. But tonight, as he thought about the burst of shattered glass, he realised that what he wanted more than anything was a companion to see him through. He wanted a wife. And what Erica saw as a sign that they would never stay together and produce a child now made him think of orgasm, the grappling and piercing and deliverance of sex. He wanted to explain this to her. He imagined her limber body over him and felt weak in his groin. He knew they would never make love again.

He nodded at the band and the Norwegian trumpet player introduced the number they'd planned to do next. He smirked at the tight, enfolded audience; there was a good crowd, faces he knew, old friends and unknown women he knew he could sleep with tonight and every night of the week. He waited for the dizziness he felt when he couldn't hunt down Erica with his eyes. He was surprised this was already waning.

As he began to play he imagined the group of thieves on their way back to Tudu. For a moment he thought of them as princes with wiry, anatomically precise bodies. They were warriors and these skirmishes unleashed a hurtling force. He wondered what these young men would say to each other as they crossed the city with pockets full of riches, when they swaggered back into labyrinthine neighbourhoods that stank of goats. He saw the torn foam mattresses where their bodies twitched through the grand chapters of their dreams, the maggot-ridden *kenkey* eaten in tongues of light.

Banking

A few weeks after Charlotte left her boyfriend she selected a celebratory handbag but discovered her credit card was missing from her purse. Darius had been raw, scented and occasionally violent, in a way that had marshalled her into passionate submission. She had finally seen that he was an inconsiderate bully, badly programmed as a child.

She checked online and found that 42 pounds remained in her account, and the other three thousand had been spent or withdrawn over the past few days. She was livid. This was hard-won holiday money she might have spent with Darius on Corfu, clubbing and staying at a beach hotel and drinking cocktails every night. She wouldn't have minded paying for him before, but now she was planning a trip to Norway on the fjords – alone – with her new, non-existent handbag. Did he think she was stupid?

She parked outside his block and pressed his buzzer. No answer. She pressed again, long and relentless, remembering how she used to stand burning right here, how once she had gathered a bag of rose petals from the park and cast these on his bed sheets where they had made spellbinding love.

Darius leaned out over the railing, bare-chested, his halo of wild hair cast down. That mane she used to love was now so scrappy.

'Hey, Charlotte.'

'Darius, I need to talk.'

'Can't talk.'

'I'm coming up.'

She pulled her body up the stairwell. He let her in. She had already bolted herself up tight so that his lean abdomen and those loose drawstring pants would have no effect upon her. She felt a little undone but thought she was doing fine. Darius said he would make her a cup of tea and, although there was no evidence, Charlotte knew the presence of another woman was on display. That noisy woman had been subdued by the magnified, matchless moments of intimacy when she had groaned, like Charlotte, like a cat.

'Did you take my credit card, Darius?' Charlotte called out to the kitchenette. 'The money's all gone.'

'What?'

'Give it me.'

'Don't have your credit card, Charlotte.'

He came and sat next to where she was hunched on the couch. Charlotte cupped her hot tea. Darius lolled back and his hand reached out, making warm contact with her waist. She felt the journey of his hand, the architecture of the bones, the electric impulses on their travels out from his brain, his bitten-down nails and the bustling transport of his blood.

'Don't touch me,' she said.

She splashed the tea all over him and his grimy couch.

———

Charlotte did not go to Norway. She did not buy the overpriced handbag, inappropriate for a fjord cruise anyway. Darius's cries had brought a neighbour running to the front door and rushing inside. Charlotte had never seen this woman before. Much older, with loose clothing, loose breasts, but a firm high rump that stood up challengingly. She looked past Charlotte at Darius clutching his stomach. Charlotte was now appalled by what she had done and Darius's moans had tapered off.

'Darius! What's happened to you?'

Darius pulled himself up, retrieved the empty cup Charlotte had tossed at him, told this woman he had been clumsy enough to spill his tea.

'Doreen, Charlotte. Charlotte, Doreen.'

'Hi.'

'Hi.'

Doreen marched out with her firm bottom following close behind. When the door slammed, Charlotte sat there for a full minute. Then her hand crawled over and untied Darius's trousers. She got onto her knees

174

and hiked up her dress and steered herself over his cock; gasped at its clean plunging.

Their eyes careered into each other.

⟶

After making love they slept. Leaving Darius had truly exhausted Charlotte's body. Her desire and her reason had thrashed together these last weeks; she had lost weight, and her colleagues had become concerned. But now, in the bedroom, enveloped in Darius's scent and arms and skin, Charlotte unpicked her rationale. She could easily earn the money again. They would go to Corfu and stay by the beach. She kissed his forehead with its light film of grease after his exertions, marvelling at the way he could drop into slumber the way a bird cruised off a cliff. She wanted to crawl into his dreams.

On the way back from the bathroom Charlotte saw Darius's stuffed wallet on a shelf above the bed. It was at eye height, next to another book he had never read, inviting her to rifle through and prove one of them honest, the other thoroughly unjust.

She looked over the composition of their bodies, hers nude and standing, his folded in shades of beauty. She stared at the wallet.

Darius's eyes opened.

Fighters

Delphine Blekker was a busy ambulance worker who had seen many deaths, sheer escapes from death, and not-at-all deaths in her district of Beaune. After work she would come home and lift off her heavy orange coat and hang it in the hallway, and feed her mewing cat before she scooted her out into the tangled yard. If it had been a night shift, she would shower and crawl naked into bed with Matthias, whom she would arouse as he turned and groaned. After all those needles and emergency incisions and oxygen masks making amphibians of elderly faces, Delphine delighted in the charged life of Matthias's member, its disregard for the rest of his grumpy body and the fresh tragedies she saw every night. Delphine was blonde and chesty and an ex-skier, so often, a mildly injured man – say a street fight or a fall down stairs – would interpret her coercive eyes and soothing questions as womanly interest in his person, when it was not.

The Temperature of Islands

After her heart attack Barbara returned to the island. She knew very well that should anything happen, the helicopter – if available – would take 20 minutes from the mainland. She went straight to the stoned guy on the beach who did winters in India, and bought a purple sarong.

Barbara sunbathed nude. It was heartening – *heartening!* – and her ropey body soon gleamed. Friends passed by. Georges and his poodle-headed partner, Fernande, from Lyon. They were already seamed and brown. The northern Italians with their glorious sons. A waddling Greek woman whose rear was a graceful rotund vessel, and whose breasts moved as though they were water-filled gourds.

They all asked her how it had been, this first year without Hervé? Did she have plans to move? Had the children been supportive?

Barbara replied that she, too, had a heart attack. A minor one – not at all like the one that had thrown Hervé to the ground when he was sitting at Roula's pouring back raki – but a heart attack nevertheless.

At that her friends remembered the clumsy act of Hervé's dying, the useless propping of his head, the lack of final goodbyes, and Roula's extinction of the music. Barbara watched each of them recompose after this.

But –

They wanted to say, But are you not afraid? But the helicopter? Do you not remember that drive to the heliport in the dark? The way those imbeciles had almost tipped Hervé's body onto the rocks?

In fact Barbara did. She smiled at them and rolled over and tanned her bottom.

—

Barbara dragged herself up to the heliport. This was where she had seen the life leak out of Hervé, vanish from his furious face. It was true, the paramedics had levered him unevenly so his body almost slid to the ground. One

177

young bearded man had looked at her apologetically. The other had not.

She stood at the rusty chain-wire fence that had been tossed over by the seasons. Growth burst through the concrete slabs, mostly relieved of their coloured paint. This was where she had realised Hervé was leaving her. This was where she saw that life would blaze through each of them, leaving carcasses and flickering shrines. Barbara thought of Hervé the day before, elbow on the table, trying to entice Georges to invest in the faded discotheque on the hill, or at the least hire Manolis's fishing vessel that afternoon – when Hervé knew very well that Georges would never leave Fernande alone on the beach. And then Barbara saw the two of them on their separate beds in the room, each shrouded in greying sheets, Hervé's farts uncontained.

Barbara's heart attack had happened on a train crossing Germany. With discomfort she had stood up to move down the carriage, but found herself wading in water, blind in all but the centre of her eyes, crashing into head-rests and shoulders and landing with an injured face in one man's lap. At first they had thought of terrorists, and police charged through looking for youths with knives or guns, until Barbara, whimpering, was surrendered.

Barbara rattled the chain-wire fence. She kicked the metal web. There were wells on the mountain tops with wooden planks laid over the openings, and these were held in place by abrasive stones. There was a temple of loosened rocks with a font made of a burning black substance that Hervé had said was certainly from a meteorite. There was a white church several peaks away where there were candle stubs on a stand upon a powdery square of carpet, and an icon of Saint Gabriel sweeping across a gold frame.

The Bamboo Furnace

He was sent back with a tropical bug eating through the flesh of his leg. They had tried treating the advancing wound with dry ice, but it hadn't worked. Further doctors came over from the Spanish mission where one local man had had the skin cut away from his cheek, and his jaws now worked like a moistened machine. When the limb began to putrefy, he was airlifted out to Singapore. They had to prise Sybil away from him: first from his torso, then the bedpost; there was grappling and she was dragged screaming across the floor. In Singapore they did the job. He found himself back in Brisbane, sitting opposite his sister Martine at the yellow Formica kitchen table.

Martine had tried to set up the house as best as she could. She had taken out unwanted chairs from the years when the family had run riot, and given him their parents' double bed with its isolated hollows. She had put an extra chair in the bathroom, thinking it might serve for balance, or to lean the crutches on when he was relieving himself, so they wouldn't rattle to the floor. Lionel had shrunk while in the hospitals, though she could tell that until recently he had been robust. Much had been robbed from him, and now he had been felled.

After their tea she poured two glasses of beer, watching his sun-ravaged forearms and the shaven mould of his chin. He had come to her in civilian clothing, a shirt with small arabesques. Thirty-one years ago, his cheek-bones had been concealed in a puffy boy's face, but now they seemed crafted with ceramic grace. His ears had grown into fleshy rinds below his crew cut. She was certain they had heard night sounds from bamboo forests, and babbling voices from villages of half-dressed women.

Lionel looked around the unchanged kitchen remembering what was in the drawers, knowing that Martine would keep her bills clamped by a wooden clothes peg as their mother had, with the fabric-covered shirt box full of photographs underneath. She would have followed her ways with little modulation. Martine's whole aspect had broadened, where a woman like Sybil would spend her life becoming fine-boned and minute. He had forgotten how white women aged with such symphonic slowness.

On the sideboard behind his sister's attentive curls were cedarwood framed photographs of the clan who had driven him to the port. Their faces had stayed creased with pride these long years, a vigil in serge suits as the cancers and heart failure had pulled them down one by one. He saw himself in their midst. Just six months after being ordained, a shiny-faced buck gripping the rail. He remembered how they had posed along the ramp up to the rusty ship, squeezing his hands and their tipsy embracing. How they had touched him that day! Daubing his new clothes, anointing him. He could still feel his father's hand grasping his shoulder and its repugnant demand for salvation. He had ridden the old man's pride like a show pony. His mother could not be convinced to make the trip that day: she'd known she would never lay eyes upon him again.

A week into the voyage he had caught typhus and landed in Manila a ruin, his gut and whole equilibrium off balance for years. He had suffered the boat south to the islands. Mules were ridden, he no longer remembered much. Two black-haired brothers in cassocks had left him at the outpost that would become his contracted world.

'Would you like some more beer?' Martine asked.

'Of course, yes. Thanks.'

Martine went to the fridge and Lionel envied the way she had stayed close to this earth. He could see how the shape of her life had drawn down her shoulders and made a dense slab of her back, a broad swimming bundle of her rear. Through all these years he had rarely thought of his sister or her placid tragedies.

Martine noticed how he no longer wore the silver ring they had given him at the seminary. In the past she had studied this ring on his fourth finger. Inscriptionless and rounded, a talisman that said he was bound to *them*. As children, she and Lionel had run off from a picnic and followed a trail to the river where willows swung and a boy had drowned, trapped in their roots. Lionel had gained the knowledge that their mother would produce no more babies. Martine had watched his arc of piss against a tree. They saw the upriver ferry pass homesteads on the other bank and the wash pleating murky water. A great aunt of theirs had lived in one of those homesteads. Martine knew this aunt had been rich and vibrant once; she'd seen sepia photographs of a striding woman in fur collars and button-down shoes. Lionel had told her that as soon as she died their father would buy a new motor car.

After the operation there had never been any question of Lionel going back to the seminary on the coast. Deirdre had said more than once she couldn't understand how Martine could take a stranger into her house after 31 years, even if he was her amputee brother and a priest. It was Deirdre who had made the largest inroad into her life. Deirdre's kids were her godchildren. At 18, straight after Lionel left for the Philippines, she'd started going into the city to work. Deirdre Sheldon was in her typing pool and Deirdre's sandy-haired fiancé Sten was a building contractor who'd come out from Hungary and learned the language. They would go out with Sten's friend Tito and it was jolly. Tito soon unravelled the first confines of Martine's womanhood, but then disappeared from their quartet. By that time Deirdre was already throwing up and one evening in the car Sten apologetically ran his heated, level hands over Martine's breasts, and through the gestation of each of her godchildren he had booked a room for them by the river. When Deirdre's third child – Christopher – was born, Sten had paid to extinguish the embryo in Martine's womb.

'Could there be a little food later on?' her brother asked as he closed the newspaper. 'I think my appetite may be returning.'

Martine knew how he relished peas and lamb chops.

Lionel often became aware of the tingling dampness of the wound and felt razors of fear. If the cells reignited in his body – to whom in this tight-lipped, fair-eyed country could he release his cries? The Spanish priests had understood him, with their clipped beards and their hollering offspring in the compound. One had wiped his face and heard his mutinous confession. When the cut had first begun to fester, Lionel couldn't believe the jungle had turned on him. He had seen these open wounds char the life of a man. Yet he knew what he had done. He knew it was his years of fondling Sybil under the netting, and the children he had seeded in the low sling of her belly. All but one of them had been taken back, pulseless remains Sybil had buried while he raised leaden arms to his God. Even the fifth child – he'd had no faith in the thriving creature until he recognised Martine's hardy genes.

The day the baby girl reached six months a wrinkled letter was spat out of the jungle. It told of his father's long-ago death and burial at Saint Anne's. Reading and rereading his uncle's letter, Lionel thought of the rank casket at rest within the earth, and blind worms weaving through the old man's flesh. It was a shock to discover his daughter, Candide, had been born the very evening his father had passed away. With that knowledge Lionel had gone on a bender for days. He had thrashed through the bamboo furnace beyond the village, tormented by the passage of their souls in the underworld.

Sybil, feeding the voluptuous baby, did not stir when Lionel stumbled back into the compound three days later. She knew Lionel had glanced at her through the eyes of the buried cadaver, she knew he had seen her as a sinful hussy holding his cursed child.

—

Lionel was sitting out on the veranda reading *The Courier Mail* with his head tilted back and his stump on the side table. It was the first time she had seen the tortured limb with its cranky purple sutures. Lionel brushed away a fly. She saw this was an introduction he had planned. He cast over another page of the newspaper.

'You don't think you should cover that?'

'Cover what?'

Oh Lord, and now to name it. 'Your leg, Lionel. It looks as though the wound might still be weeping.'

'Yes, perhaps you're right. There are bandages next to my bed.'

He watched the skirmish on her face. Heard her steps along the linoleum strip through the house, heard the squeaky wood strut nailing down the carpet in his room. She was searching through his drawers now. One day she would find the photograph of him with Sybil and Candide standing in front of the cooking sheds. She would sit across from him, holding the quavering photograph, and she would have to be told.

But Lionel had never been able to name what he felt for the fine-boned woman. Even as the plum babies died and he held Sybil's deflated body, he had felt a coreless alarm that was outside of his understanding.

Martine came onto the veranda with the bandages. Lionel looked at her unrolling the white cloth. Until it happened she would be his foot soldier, his unknowing Magdalene.

'Is this comfortable?'

He winked and she brought him tea.

Martine lay awake, worrying about her visitor and this coda to their lives. He floundered along the hallway but his face was a resilient bronze and his eyes, equipped with untold visions, would close their soft shutters. She knew the same blood ran through them and it was unalloyed. At night, this duality bobbed through her. Deirdre was right when she said that Martine didn't have a clue who Lionel was any more, and Martine had never considered that there might be good priests and bad. Deirdre had said flat out she wanted to meet Lionel, said she'd shake him down in an instant. But even after all these years of depleting discretion Martine never admitted Deirdre too long into her house.

⟶

She found the photograph. She came out one afternoon with the image of the Filipino woman tucked under Lionel's arm. A solid, barefoot child between them.

'Who are these people?'

'This is my common-law wife Sybil. And our daughter Candide.'

'A daughter?'

'Candide is now 14 years old. She was born the day Father died.'

'You've got to be bloody joking.'

Martine stormed back inside and stayed there an hour. She sat at the kitchen table, her shock rolling over and rising in twists.

She returned to the veranda with a dark brown bottle of beer, filled their glasses in a disorderly way.

'We thought you were pious,' she said.

Lionel looked out over the patch of ground he had sprung from, the gormless youth grown into a deplorable messiah. In the middle of the grass stood a thick-limbed frangipani tree and his eyes exalted in the blossoms.

'I am glad that you now know of them,' he said.

She picked up the photograph again. Looked at the woman wearing a gaping cotton shift. Skin like burnt amber, tight over her face. Eyes that reached out to stare. All those years her brother had lived among them, she had never pictured their individual faces. They were a submissive mass, she'd thought, chanting and weaving. And yet here was Lionel on an ill-lit day in front of sheds somewhere, and stripes of bamboo forest gushing from one side, with a woman who looked like she belonged to him, and he to her. Martine traced the line where their clothing melded and saw that Lionel's enveloping arm promised loyalty, and the treasured child bore their own family bulk and possibly Lionel's torment. She wished he had not given them names, wished they had never come here with him.

'You're just going to leave them there?'

'I don't know, currently.'

'This house is large enough.' Martine didn't know what she was saying now. She didn't want a pair of Filipinos in this house.

It struck her then that her brother had not given her a thought in decades. He had left her a woolly-headed girl over the washing tubs, steam wetting her face. The years had poured over her and her letters to him had been unwanted vials of news. A cyclone along the coast; their school burned to the ground; three friends in a car wreck. Martine looked at the stump again and wondered what implement modern doctors had used to carry out their barbarism.

Those three times Deirdre was with child, Martine's life had become gilded. Sten would collect her at the corner after work, then they would drive to the guesthouse by the river. In accented child-speak that collected along his throat, Sten said the house belonged to another Hungarian. Martine never saw anyone else but when he washed afterwards she would hear door latches or wood sighing. By the open window Sten told Martine she reminded him of someone and she felt a lyrical, feminine pleasure. When he mounted her Martine would strive to vacate herself, leaving the cast of her body on the sheets, allowing him to heave into this lost woman.

Deirdre had met Sten at the Eastern European Club when he was just off the ship, and two years later she finished his obtuse sentences and told Martine in the kitchen she wished to God she had married an Australian. After Christopher's birth Deirdre had her tubes tied, so there was no need for Sten to take Martine to the river any more. Besides, for months after the abortion, Martine felt unfit. She would drive across the suburbs to Deirdre's and take boisterous Christopher into her arms, shedding gulps. Sten no longer addressed her and seemed ashamed those afternoons had ever occurred.

—

They sat drinking whisky under the awning after rain showers. Martine had returned the photograph to his drawer, but Lionel knew that Sybil and Candide now stood in silence behind his chair. He could see Martine observing their trio. Barefoot, Martine scratched bites on her long sturdy legs with stray blonde hairs. Her calves were a splatter of scabs. They stared out over the back garden with its radiant yellow frangipani blossoms and beds of tossed, wet flowers. Beyond the fence there were rowdy neighbours who kept a crop of car hulks in the unkempt grass. At times the youngest son would rap tools on metal with a deranged ferocity. A bank of Norfolk Island pines released needles into both gardens. Lionel hadn't thought of their lives ahead except to assume that staying with Martine would be bland and safe. It was critical now that he understood motion, and how he would newly walk. His cropped nerves and arteries had barely learned that the leg was no longer there to be nourished. His removed foot: how its absent articulation pulsated at night.

Each dense day that passed Lionel could feel the humid jungle slipping behind him. Sybil had always known that he would be reclaimed. She had spoken these words in corrosive bells over his sunbeaten hide, her tiny body clamped upon his. As Candide grew tall Lionel had seen the Irish grit that lay under her face, beneath the fine Asian planes. He knew the young woman would lumber through the village with her straining features to stare at fading photographs in the community church. She would see her father in his worn vestments; she would imagine her parents rutting in the leaky shack. Nothing could shame Lionel more than Candide's harrowed being. Martine had suggested bringing the pair of them out here, but he could never have them where they would become shadowy, disregarded chattels.

When Martine went to the shops he limped over and took up the framed pictures of the young priest. His eyes studied that fair, fatty face. He recalled reverberations of prayer in his skull, yet as soon as they departed his belief had yielded to the sea's rocking template and the explosions of his bowels. None of them had had an inkling where they were sending him. Into what morass. Into what inferno. He was simply left there, banished, all those years extricated from him. He recalled the first infants he had buried in rice sacks, the men slung into pits. The villagers had always known that he was no more than a quaking servant before the great beams of the forest. Sybil, a young widow designated for the white priest by the village, had crawled into his bed one night.

'I'd like to understand,' Lionel said as they had drinks on the veranda. 'Why I was sent away from here.'

'Why you were sent away?' replied Martine.

'It was Father's idea, mostly.'

'You seemed so almighty then,' she said. 'That is what we thought of you.'

'If I think back, I felt no particular calling. And I was sent to the most degraded outpost.'

'Even so, I don't know why it had to come to that, Lionel. A woman and a child.'

'You know I nearly died on that passage,' he told her.

'We were not informed. We prayed for you.'

Martine remembered she had cried a river when he left. Then there were Deirdre and Sten and Tito. Her own ghastliness had begun.

'And now it seems I have returned like a man from battle. And what war was this?'

'Lionel, they are all dead now. All of them.'

'Yes.'

'I believe I have done worse,' she said loosely.

He found his eyes had gone to her cotton-clad thighs. Martine assumed a rare, billowing nakedness in his thoughts that he shunned.

'You might wish to confess.'

'To you? I could never.'

But he would always be detained by this point. 'What crime did you commit?' he asked. 'Tell me.' As Lionel stared, he saw her face become a colourless enamel.

'I aborted a child.'

Lionel's eyes blazed. 'The father was married.'

'Yes.'

'Then we are not equal.'

He stood up on one leg, hand bulging upon the armrest, and slapped her face. Fell back into his chair and pinched his eyes.

'Please go inside,' Lionel said.

⟜

He apologised to her. He said it was the alcohol, and the sense of wrong-doing that had burst through him. His words drifted through her head, they entered and flew about. But after Sten's years of silence Lionel's slap had not been an injury. She had walked up to her room and sat down on the bed, palm to the burning cheek. In circles, she heard their words on the veranda, *I aborted a child. Then we are not equal.* She saw Lionel's torso rise over her as the decades snapped and the atrocious truth crawled back into her being with its bloody fist. All these years she had heard Deirdre complain about her kids as these joyful children ran around the wooden house on stilts and swung from trees; all these years she had watched Sten go to the toolshed underneath as soon as she arrived. And Lionel hadn't even had to ask twice because she had wanted to feel her soul scalded. Her admission had been waiting for him.

She gave Lionel his tea. She cooked his bacon. She glanced at the stump on the side table. It looked dry, it was healing. Lionel's odyssey was perhaps coming to a close.

They sat in the heat of the morning. He handed her the newspaper and she read it through. There was a murder in the north. A woman's body parts had been found along an estuary. A ship had run aground on the sandbar off Stradbroke Island. The neighbourhood was soundless except for cars up on Wellers Hill Road. She brought more tea, then a beer for them both. In the afternoon she said she'd like to drive him into the city for a look around and he agreed.

—

The car wove through suburban streets of more wooden homes on stilts, cages of shade beneath; gardens with electric flowers. Further bushland had been colonised and there were new thoroughfares busier than before, and bricked buildings on corners with loud signs she didn't care to point out. He attempted a walk along the block near the Town Hall, but after a few hundred yards his armpits with the crutches driven into them were soaked, and she could smell his sweat. His stump swung between the crutches and his healthy leg, a pendulum attracting stares. The sun beat on their faces and the cafeteria she had wanted to visit was still far off. They returned to the car. He threw his head back on the seat and was silent.

'Shall we go to the river? To the place we used to?'

He nodded. Martine drove through traffic over the new bridge, finding the municipal park which had been cleared of undergrowth after some riverbank murder. The homesteads fronted up on the other side along the brown water, iron fretwork and corrugated roofs soon to be bulldozed away.

But as she pulled on the handbrake Lionel shook his head and said he wouldn't be getting down. He gazed at the river. Martine stepped out and walked a few paces; the air was loamy. She turned back to her brother's face in the windscreen and the sky with its thunderous contours pushed upon the car.

Lionel smelled the eddying water. He saw a mudslide interring a school hut, a father dragging out a child by the leg. He saw a woman pouring water into a son's eyes, the boy's face illuminated.

Martine came around to him and said, 'Do you remember great aunt Joan who lived on the other side of the river?'

'I do.'

'You told me that Father bought a new car with her money. That he'd been waiting for her to pass away.'

'I recall.'

He looked at Martine's arms crossed over her dress. He found he did not regret slapping her cheek, for in her culpable eyes he had seen two paradigms of consent. Through Martine and the years cast between them, and the idols both had coveted and smashed, Lionel would understand whether he had ever been a priest.

She drove him home, handed him his crutches lying on the back seat of the car, followed his exhausted catapulting down the side path by the fishbone ferns. She unpinned her hat in the hallway.

—

Martine brought him a mould-spotted letter with stamps from the Philippines. Lionel recognised his daughter Candide's handwriting. Martine left him alone on the veranda, launching back through the house where she went into Lionel's room and took the photograph of his family into her hands. She wondered if she could induce some supply of sentiment towards the Filipino woman and her daughter, but no new emotion presented itself. Lionel's wife looked out from her wishful, triangular face as though she could foresee Martine sitting disrupted on her lover's bed. The woman's shoulder and black hair were eased into Lionel's shirt, a coastline against his shores. Martine trembled to think of the wedding of landscapes.

Lionel read through Candide's poor, devastating English. Sybil had taken ill. He hurtled through the tenses he had taught his daughter in the shack. *She is very bad sick…Close to die…* But almost immediately he understood that Sybil had been restored to good health; that this was just an aggrieved call sent out by his daughter. The page fell to his incomplete thigh. For years that he groped towards now, on nights that were summits, another man had propelled his body. But after the heft of fornication this man would desert him. Then Lionel would see Sybil's slight hands flitting over utensils, her bottom and the purse between her legs. He would call out to her to cover her body, while she would just as easily come over and nestle into him.

Lionel shouted all the way through the house to Martine's room where she lay turned to the wall. The youth next door was hitting metal against metal among the derelict cars, and this as well as the memory of his rugged wanting had made him enraged. Martine's bare feet thudded outside ready to hear of some crisis.

'Everything is as it should be?'

'Your neighbours.'

'Yes, that's the young son.'

'It should be stopped.'

'It will stop soon enough.'

Martine glanced at the nub of his leg dressed in scribbled pages, a distant frontier. Over and over she saw the word *She… she…* The metallic noise stopped, resumed. Then ceased. A back door swung shut.

She brought out refreshments but saw that Lionel would not confide in her and drag her to his depths.

'You used to have your music,' he said.

'I sold the piano.'

'They are difficult to keep in tune.'

Martine stood, hands loose at her sides. She reached for her pruning scissors and went to cut flowers.

In the evening she heard Lionel showering as she held the telephone receiver to her ear. It was Deirdre, marching through the conversation. But Martine heard protective tones in her own voice.

'He's in shock. He's hardly present.'

'He hasn't said anything?' Deirdre's voice came through a warp.

'No.'

'Do you think there was a woman? For goodness' sake, he was in the jungle for 30 years. There must have been a woman.'

'There was no woman.'

'So, the man is a saint? I don't believe for a minute…'

'He is not a saint.'

Deirdre wished to visit them and Martine was terrified her statuesque Holden would roll up their drive. She told Deirdre they were leaving on a trip to Bribie Island, for a week or so, as Lionel's wound required the sea air. But Deirdre had already tired of the conversation and was lamenting her husband Sten's fanciful yearning for a boat.

Lionel looked for his face in the steamed mirror, wiped away cloud, saw eyes and bones. If the disease were to return he would welcome its advance. He would beg Martine to bury him as a pagan with coins on his eyes.

Sitting outside, Martine listened to his clopping through the house. She sipped her whisky, legs outstretched, ankles crossed. The smell of frangipani was a low sweet stench. All along the neighbourhood a line of Norfolk Island pines had been planted and these now thrust beyond the roofs. They were brooding, dark-willed trees that other householders had taken to with saws. Lionel appeared in the doorway. He lay down the crutches, lowered himself into the chair, propped his stump on the table. He poured whisky into his glass.

'This is where our lives began,' he said.

'Yes.'

Martine looked at the glowing tree in the middle of the garden, the beds of gerberas and hibiscus and zinnias muted by the night, their sorrowful Eden.

Slaughter of the Innocents

This is how it goes down. You're at your parents' place out of town in Quinto. Your father leaves the apartment. He leaves the front door unlocked but you don't give a shit because you know what he's done and what he'll do next. You're standing in your knickers holding the dog while your mum is stretched out in her knickers and bra too. You're getting ready to watch TV cos the heat has fucked around with you all day.

That's when they come pounding through the door and you know he's behind this. He was high when he left; he collected all the bottles, dropping them in a carrier bag with your mum screaming *Laisse-les! Laisse-les!* and there they are still sitting on the kitchen floor.

They are six. You smell aggression but you know better than to say a word cos they gave Sandro's sister an anal check when she back-answered in Verona. The creeps told Sandro to take off the scarf wrapping his face and she got dragged away kicking when she said *What the fuck?* Sandro said the bitch's fingers went fucking *deep*.

They turn on lights and dip their heads into all the rooms and want your identity cards which your mum has to rummage for in her bag. She's half-naked standing up pulling out receipts, her boobs jigging in a sort of rage and her pocked thighs and slack arse, and they just stare over her nudity and piled dirty hair.

Now they look at *you*. You are clutching the dog. They have insignias on their shirts which are made of a thicker material, not cotton. This is your last week home here before you trek back to Milan where you are close to moneyless, where you've done some porn stuff with a guy called Luciano whose cock is cartoon-huge.

The dog leaps to the floor and you cover your breasts but for one brown nipple peeping from your arm crook and this is what six pairs of eyes are tonguing and biting hard.

They are saying neighbours called them up cos there were odd lights but this is bullshit; there are no thieves out here. Each one of them has a stitched leather holster nursing a gun. There's a T-shirt rolled in a ball on the couch so you slide it over your tits, and your mum who was a flawless Tunisian girl with a blessed childhood holds a cushion to her belly. You hate your father more than you love your own life and your skin feels flayed and you know these are the breed of men who can fuck a woman with a bottle or watch on.

They do just that, barely containing their combustion, before they march onto the landing, down the stairs and you hear boots crunching gravel in the courtyard. It's all you can do to hold yourself from running to the window and shouting down *Pigs!*

Hours later your dad returns and your mother is still crying in bursts.

My Thoughts Concerning Letizia

I was told that Letizia was an appropriate type, she was what we wished for. Given you won't supply images I've had to furnish your words. Which can only be called ratty given the level of visual technology at hand. Is Letizia athletic? You mentioned she did some sport – was it volleyball or tennis – I wish you would illuminate. In case you're wondering it's because different muscles are highlighted and given traction – this is something that appears on the screen. This is the arthouse end of a competitive industry, I thought you realised. This is not personal. You will never lose your place. Is that what this is about?

So is there any chance you can get some shots to me? By midday? Or send me her email so I can ask for her portfolio myself? Baby, it's not enough to know that she has an S-shaped body and her shoulders are thrown back, and her breasts are dark-tipped cones. Or that her neck is a little short and she has knock knees that can be hidden initially by a tight skirt. That could all be good material – you've done your homework baby – but her hair, for example, I'm not clear on this. You said it was cropped. Cropped? What does this – for filming purposes – mean? Has it been cut savagely? Will she need a wig? I'm also not reading you with regard to skin tone. You said she was half-of-this and half-of-that, but you know yourself that these mixtures can turn out any range of gold to black. What does that mean in terms of lights?

Right now I'm trying to imagine how she moves. You know we require a walking shot along the balcony of the motel. Does she walk well? Does she know how to incorporate her ass into the architecture of her body without seeming like a tramp?

Will you be kind enough to answer me? I'm being kind here. Nothing's at risk. Is it because I refused to rein you in that night, and perhaps it hurt? Okay I made a couple of comments, okay I said what I felt in the moment. But that was encapsulated, it's gone. Baby, just send me the shots. I know you've been working on your own photos – your work is getting stronger all the time and I admire you for it. Look, I've only got the room another day and the guys are on my back, they want their equipment.

Is there something I'm not getting here? Is she so alluring you've taken her for yourself? Well, that's okay baby, that's fine baby too. We can write that into the script. You can show me what you've created together and I'll watch, I'll collaborate with you on this. We could film tonight at the motel – any time is good – I'll be waiting for you in the bar downstairs, the guy with the hair transplant and the caipirinha (joking). That's if you have the decency to turn up.

But just fill me in baby. Jesus, I had a feeling it would turn out like this. You and Letizia. It's that name, it spoke to me from the start. Does she know who I am? Don't even dream of thinking you bitches will get away from me.

On Being Eaten Alive

Two years ago I had a dalliance with a prominent person. A tall, esteemed, white, award-winning author. Obviously I can't name any names. Shall we call him J perhaps?

I queued up to have J's book signed for a girlfriend whose daughter broke her arm that afternoon. Last in the line, dying for a pee, I was contemplating doing a runner and signing the thing myself. At university I had adored J's books but thought he'd become pompous in later life. I had no intention of reading the novel I held in my hands. As the woman in front talked, I imagined her sitting astride J's lap and licking his nostrils. J would be into that sort of thing, I thought, and this kept a patient smile on my face. But then I reached bursting point and rushed off to the toilets.

On the stairway back up to street level, I met J meandering down alone. Initially he looked through me. Then he warmed.

'I'm sorry,' he said. 'You had a book for me to sign.'

Having sat through J's self-absorbed talk, and then watched every crinkle in his face as he listened to the gushing woman, I was bereft of awe.

'Oh, I left it somewhere. I really had to get to the loo.'

J belly-laughed and asked me out for a drink.

—

I didn't fall for him immediately. I am used to a very different sort of man. J was certain of every word that came from his mouth and sometimes seemed to be playing word games with himself, or trying to speak in cadences or chords. In my own life I had decided on music rather than writing (footnote: I am a jazz singer), so J's forays into my world felt clunky. His taste in music was firmly Phil Collins. Sometimes, I had to recall him speaking to an audience of bobbing heads, all eyes feasting upon him, to reboot my fascination.

In bed J was lusty and overt. He would eat me for hours, absolutely entranced and tireless. My orgasms were rich heavens that I could barely clamber down from back into the world. Neither of us had said any words of attachment, and when we made love we did not stare into one another's eyes. But we were kind and chatted daily on the phone (J didn't like texts), even when he was abroad on his book tour he would call and wish me goodnight.

—

The girlfriend whose daughter's arm had been broken that day (who had since bought her own copy of the book, read it and felt unnerved) was at my place one evening and we were getting trashed in my kitchen. J was in New York. Earlier I had sent him my first erotic photo, taken with my phone tilted against a pile of books as I fingered myself on my bed. J was ecstatic. He even called to thank me, just before he had a big interview in a Manhattan hotel. He said he would call me again afterwards, and I told him my friend was here and I'd try not to be too trashed. Then faintly, almost as an aside, he said, *I love you.*

My girlfriend was just divorced and mopey so the drinks went down fast. She was dating madly online and received text messages every five minutes. She showed me a photo of the primary guy she was seeing, a beautiful Brazilian with a shock of mad hair. *Danger*, I thought, but that's not what I said to her.

By the end of the night all I wanted was for my girlfriend to go home so I could sit around, naked perhaps, and wait for J's phone call. I rang her a taxi and she staggered outside, leaving her car parked in my street. I brushed my teeth and sat nude on my bedcovers, opening my legs and taking invasive photographs of my body which I peered at under the bed lamp.

J did not call.

—

The thing that had unnerved my girlfriend about J's book – this came to me as my mood grew muddier the next morning – was that there had been a new note of intimacy in his work. Charged with being lofty, J had written a love story, one that was teasingly erotic at times. I knew the book had been written before me but I was curious. What if he'd lost the catalyst behind his work, and now sought it through others, and through what everybody wants to read about – sex?

My girlfriend came around in the afternoon to collect her car but she was cranky and still looked a mess. She had to pick up her daughter from hockey, and she and her son had had a fight. She was older than me by eight years and always told me never to have kids. She'd forgotten who she'd loaned J's book to, and what would I care anyhow?

When J flew back to London I expected him to call me up with apologies and announce his need for repose in my arms. I thought of his head parked between my thighs and grew horny. I thought of his cock which I hadn't really liked but had grown used to, even the yelps of his orgasm next to the groans of my own. I thought of the three words whispered from the lobby of a fancy Manhattan hotel.

—

I managed to speak to J once before he changed his number. I caught him when he was in Edinburgh, waiting for a car to pick him up for the Festival, so I guess he answered the phone by mistake. He said, *Ah, I see*, when I said I missed him. He said that he'd call as soon as he came back to town. As I said goodbye, there was relief in his voice.

A while later I heard J in a radio interview saying he was about to 'hunker down' to write a new novel. (He actually used the words 'hunker down'. This is when I realised I had been miles away from falling in love.) The journalist asked – in view of the success of his current novel – a love story for those who hadn't yet read – would he continue to mine this field?

J thought not. In a minor cadence, he mused. 'A thing akin to love,' he said. 'Almost music. Perhaps jazz.'

I knew a lanky Dutch guy called Yannick who played double bass. He was foreign, thus oblivious to J's prominence. I also knew that J wasn't seeing anyone else and that he really had 'hunkered down' to write his new novel. I had Yannick run into him a few times on the footpath near his house, then recognise him at the local coffee parlour. Yannick dropped the word 'jazz' in their talk, mentioned that he played double bass, and J was in the front seat at Yannick's next concert.

—

The night of the concert I caught a bus to J's house. I walked up the footpath and slid across the latch of his front gate. I had never been given keys, but I knew the pot plant out the back under which they were hidden. They were not there. I looked under a range of sculpted objects and plant pots but found nothing. I stood before J's back door with its framed glass pane revealing food relics on the broad wooden table where I had once provided the author a carnal meal. The door was ajar a half-inch.

I went straight upstairs to J's office. Not to wreak havoc, but to look over the birthplace of this new novel, the novel that people would read and praise in 18 months. I looked at the icons J had set up; they were different from the ones that were here a month ago. Sheet music for percussion that I doubted he could read; a print of an older black woman singing in the street, angry-faced. Some arty porn, including stuff that was close to the images I had sent him myself. Next to the open laptop sat a cold cup of J's idea of coffee, but I was not unkind enough to splash it over the keys. Tempted, but no. Through one of our confessionals J had told me that masturbation was a counterweight to his work. He said he needed its cleansing torque. He said that sometimes he would be midway through a reading, and a turn in the text would signify moments when he had been euphoric, when the drag of the words had been given new unthinking vigour, a window fisted through.

I curled up on J's bed. I wanted to do nothing but leave some residue of my body – even a drift of dead cells here on his bedcover, an iron coil of hair – that would pass into the premises of his thoughts. I pulled off my jeans and touched myself. I rocked hard. I left my cries in the air, in every recess of that room, and I slept.

Wandering downstairs afterwards I met J in the hallway, pulling arms out of the flaps of some sort of all-weather jacket. I glided past him and he was transfixed.

Tokyo Frieze

Tanja and Kurt's story absorbed none of the usual shocks and fractures that beset a union. They lived on different continents, in different time zones and contrasting seasons. The few friends who knew what lay behind this panel in their lives believed their rapport to be unrealistically sound, like a creature never saddled or ridden.

It had gone on for ten years now. Meetings in Rome; a week in Bucharest; a few days in Fez; another week outside of Helsinki. Tanja's children were grown and didn't care when she was absent. Kurt had invented a daft seam of conferences and research projects branching from his company work, which his wife might have plucked apart in moments, but did not. He would look over his sons before he left for the airport, visualising a poison tributary through all of them, seeing Tanja as a foreigner upon whom he should never have laid his hands.

If compressing this guilt was difficult, it was even harder to hem off the great pasture of time they might have shared, into counted hours in a hotel room. They often said they suffered the tyranny of these volumes, absolving them through the same anonymity that accused them a thousand times. There was relief and trepidation in their first hugs. A homecoming, a bearing of gifts. Would it be the same? Would love still reside within him/her? Touch was symphonic, placid, brows were smoothed, a nipple mouthed, the unveiled sexual organs already engorged and moist. Sometimes the lovemaking was rushed and instantly completed, while there were other instances imprinted upon both their minds when they had been almost motionless, a maw appearing between them that each had wanted to enter whole, blind to whatever currency had brought them there and a place where both had wanted to die. This had been said. They always spoke freely; he with his accent and she with hers. Perhaps because of the zigzag through languages they were emboldened when addressing each other's eyes.

Tanja and Kurt met in Tokyo in the cherry blossom season but never left their room for the first three days. Kurt had been ill. It was an unresolved affliction, and though he hadn't told Tanja, she had guessed. They were on the 27th floor above Ginza, a harbour of lights. Kurt had said he wished to avoid all the promise in the air, the nectar and straying blossoms, as well as the tourists. Tanja gazed at him, outside it began to rain. Kurt turned on Japanese baseball, and later Tanja read a Murakami story aloud, which left the room airless as the characters joined their thoughts. Tanja walked naked to the kettle and while she waited Kurt watched her form touched by the city light, cusps illuminated on her buttocks and the shadow welling behind, the shiny trail of his spilling traced on her thigh. She made two mugs of green tea. As she walked back to him the light caught on her breasts in the way of Caravaggio, or Georges de la Tour, and Kurt felt his abdomen rustle and every ligament he possessed distend. He declared that he loved her in his language. She placed his tea by his side and nursed his head. Kurt's skin was sheer and worn.

Tanja wanted to slide within the bones of his body.

That evening Tanja wanted to go to a jazz club. She told Kurt she wanted to drink a cocktail and perhaps go dancing. Kurt had outgrown gatherings of people and often played the old man with her. Once, in a club in Athens, he had watched her dance with a youth whose beard became a scrubby collar down his neck. This man had grasped Tanja from behind as Kurt leant on a wall with a sense of this clutch – for he knew the format and cushions of her body. The youth had come home with them. Kurt had watched him possess Tanja, then the pair of them had ridden her until her eyes rolled and she stiffened and howled.

Kurt said he wasn't going anywhere. Tanja showered and zipped up jeans, boots, swung her hair around and combed her ravishing eyebrows upward. Her work took her to intricate places often and alone, and her energy was quixotic and rangy, he knew that in real life they would outpace each other or lag. *Come with me. No. Just take care. I adore you. I do.*

Tanja caught a taxi outside of the hotel to the Roppongi Hill area, to a bar she used to frequent when she was a young woman living in Tokyo with a Japanese man. She had not told Kurt this. Kurt had come in the later chapters of her life. As she sat in the taxi she remembered being within the taut skin of that young woman, how it had felt, what she had eaten, where she had walked in her platform shoes, being lost and then guided along streets by a middle-aged woman or a schoolgirl in a pleated skirt. Once, the Japanese man had brought home a friend from Osaka and the three of them had drunk Tennessee whisky and then fucked together. It had been the first time Tanja had found herself pinned between two men. She remembered blood that took a week to pass and the men kissing, hands clasping heads, how alarming that beauty had been and it had flooded through her.

She entered the bar and saw it had barely changed. She'd thought it might have been upgraded given the area, but it was quiet and shabby with the same fish tank behind the bar and blue lights. A tattooed woman served drinks with her hair dyed blond, a black arc cutting through it. She ordered a whisky and sat on a stool by the bar. When younger she had felt porous, hyper-human, tied to a common energy or saturation. But now she knew she was bound within the body enclosing her and went no further. Her history was a stream of dioramas like this.

As she sat there a couple of men walked inside. She expected one of them to be her old boyfriend, whom she'd walked out on, into snow.

In all of these years she and Kurt had shared so little of each other. She knew he had three sons and a loving wife who was broad and short with thin sandy hair. He said she'd fallen pregnant the first time they had fumbled together. Tanja had imagined a much younger Kurt spreadeagled in a student dorm, genitals depleted, a *father*. Kurt knew the names of Tanja's daughters and when there had been ghastliness at home he had locked her in his arms. Then they would exult in their possession of one another, and he would break down all the feuds within her.

She knew that Kurt, in Ginza, stood at the glazed window of the hotel room, the city dropping below him.

One of the men who had come in ordered her a fresh drink while she sat there, and it arrived on a frilled pink mat. Soon after the other led her onto the dim platform where couples had begun to dance.

Hôtel de Californie

They left in separate cars, each with his driver. They took different routes out of the hilly town, one back up to Koforidua where he was working with the plant, the other back to the smouldering city on a winding single lane road. From here the West African coast was a blur of grainy colour, a discontinuation. He breathed easier now that it was over. In another place it would never have been done like this, so furtive and fucked up. Two men in a hotel room on a quiet afternoon, girls swaying past with buckets on their heads.

He glanced at the driver whose eyes were muted screens. The young man had dozed in the car park the whole time, bare feet tossed out of the passenger window.

Now he breathed in deeply, sweating more. When they were inside his skin had been dry and silken, an endless terrain. He had bitten the other's lip, drawn blood, licked the wound, felt unquestioned. He wondered what the other man was thinking now as his pickup negotiated curves, sped beneath boughs reaching over the frayed road, women in chop bars glimpsing his profile. He had watched his lover dress: printed boxers stitched once or twice, jeans from the second-hand market, a Lacoste shirt washed many times.

Clothed again, they had simply stood in the room, organised nothing further.

He glanced again at the driver, a northerner who had sharp, wide features. Probably it had been unwise to bring him up here today, but he had no way of knowing the roads out of town, the exact location of the hotel, and the pluck of his seasoned vehicle. What if the jeep had petered out on the ascent, or the engine failed to turn over in the parking lot afterwards? How to explain this out-of-town excursion to colleagues at work, or rely on local goodwill?

The jeep drifted down to the coast, tall grass and stunted trees whipping past. At the city edge there was a roadblock where a group of soldiers sprawled under a broad tree. They were thrown back on benches, khaki trousers tucked into polished boots, slick berets on shaven heads, hands holding rifles. One of them stood to wave the car through the busted gate. He had a thick blue belt snug around his waist, temples giving off flints of light.

At the house he showered. His lover's smell was raw over him and now he wished he had washed at the hotel and not brought the strong odour of their skins inside the vehicle. Had the driver seen the other man saunter up to the reception, carrying the folders as he had suggested? He pulled on a pair of shorts. He sat on the bed, looking at the wood grain of the parquet floor.

—

The driver said an envelope had arrived at the office when the secretaries had all gone. It had his name on it in slanted capital letters. Uncertain, wavering letters. It made him think of a classroom with 60 beaming kids, windowless frames over a dusty clearing, hours of football under the sun. His lover had told him that had been the sum of his schooling here.

HÔTEL DE CALIFORNIE
SATURDAY 4PM

He looked hard at the driver, made sure he didn't show him the page. 'Who gave you this?'

'A woman,' the driver said, hands clasped.

He could have folded over with relief. That afternoon he sent the driver home and stayed in the office, working on for hours. The sun fell and the cleaners mopped. In the evening he walked outside and joined the flux of shadows moving along the trafficked road to the fast-food shops at the junction. Open gutters gaped beside him; girls tittered in his wake but mostly he was ignored, his fair skin a velour of perspiration. At the junction he fell onto a plastic chair by the street and ordered a beer, guzzled it. A smooth girl caught his eye and he smiled at her. She came over to flaunt her rich figure, draping herself over him.

'Sista,' he said, touching her fine plaits. 'Tell me, where is the Hôtel de Californie?'

She told him and he drew a map in his mind.

'You want to take me there?'

'No.'

He bought her a beer, he was finished with her. There were other things to work out. Where to go from here. How to steal him away, luxuriate in him. Perhaps to employ him?

It was punishable by law in this country.

As people coursed past he was surprised to see his driver walking along, his arm around a young woman, both wearing light smiles. He shied back in his seat, half-covered his *obroni* face, watched their backs recede. His lack of safety disarmed him, his exposure.

He was sleepless in the night. He turned off the air conditioning, opened the window louvers. He saw the night watchman shuffle to the front gate and lower himself onto the bench under the strip light, open a Bible and begin to read. Now his skin flushed with sweat. He went to the kitchen for water, pushed his face under the tap, felt the cold stream fill his nostrils and eyes. He stretched on the tiles, rolled his shoulders. Thought of his lover in a prefab house in the hills, a woman by his side, a baby in a cot at the end of the bed.

—

The jeep refused to start. He sat sweating at the wheel, turning the key on and off, hearing a clicking coming from somewhere in the engine. He lifted up the bonnet, clueless. It was three o'clock and he was early; he'd been certain he would lose his way in the warren downtown. But a taxi? He needed the shelter of his own vehicle in that dubious zone. A quick getaway and no wandering in the streets. He swore, skin blistering all over. Fuck.

He called and the driver sounded drowsy, put out. But he knew the young man was obedient. The driver said he could catch the *trotro*, he'd be at the house in a half hour.

He kicked a cactus in a pot, which toppled over in a pile of soil and roots. He bent down, gathered up dirt and pebbles in his hand, righted the plant. He walked to the end of the yard, saw that children were watching him through the patchy hedge.

The driver pushed open the gate and walked over to the jeep. He peered under the bonnet. Picked up a rock, hit the two bolts on the battery, gave them a really good whack. Told his boss to try the ignition again.

The engine turned over and the jeep started.

They reached the Hôtel de Californie at 4.20pm. He was nervy now, he could sense that it was all going pear-shaped. *He won't be here. This is the wrong place. This is a hoax.* He thought of being discovered, being thrown into a cell, strung up, pummelled. He almost asked the driver to reverse out of the car park.

But then he saw a face leaning over a balcony, forearms on the railing, smoking calmly. Oh, the rush. He grabbed the briefcase he had thrown in the back, left the driver a roll of bills.

———

The driver gave him another envelope. He read his name in slanted capitals again.

It had been a while now. The last time there had been a knock on the hotel room door, someone trying the locked handle. Everything had been suspended – all fondling, all love – in that moment. They both stared at the agitating curve of metal. He'd felt a current travel through the body of the other man, saw him draw back destroyed, haunted, their coupling a noxious stain upon the baby and wife. They had solemnly resumed love-making. He had watched the other man dress and leave, a different shirt this time, treasured and washed. He'd opened up his laptop and covered his face.

He stood before the driver and opened the envelope.

NUNGUA BEACH
HOUSE 37
SATURDAY 4PM

How on earth to find it? Why couldn't he just have him at his own place? A beer on the veranda, a snack inside. Then the discovery of his rooms, the air tightening as their mouths locked together.

'Who gave you this?'

'A boy, sir,' the driver said.

Was this a game or a trap? Was someone watching him? He worked late into the evening. He addressed a backlog of emails. Emails from old university friends, emails from ex-colleagues back in Europe, from a some-time lover in Berlin, from his sister travelling through Australia. He told her about him.

I've met this guy. He's not free but it's really something. It's going to be another agony thing, I can tell you. I feel like a dog on a chain, on a stake hammered into the ground. There is so much beauty in this place and I can't run from it. Hot, tropical beauty. Huge thunderclouds and red dirt that steams under your feet. I've read the book you gave me. I really loved it, you know.

He sat back. It wasn't true. He hadn't even opened her book. But it would make her happy. He wished he had a photo of him, even a shot on his phone. Something to stare into, something to examine with intimate recollection. A metal bucket clattered outside in the hall and he listened to the slow sweeps of the mop.

—

This time when they set out he was calmer. He'd told the driver he was buying some glass beads to take home to his sister, that one of the girls in the office was sending him to a guy at the beach who brought them from upcountry. They gave him the house number, did he know where it was? He didn't show him the paper, just told him the address. The driver thought for a minute, then nodded. They drove out of the city along the coastal road. Today he had a feeling it would be fundamental, eclipsing. He had wanted to bring some sort of gift but couldn't think what a man would give to another man here, in this country. In the end he brought his sister's book, but knew the other would never read it.

210

They passed a group of soldiers on the roadside. There was no real checkpoint, just an open-backed military jeep parked in the sun, five men holding guns sitting in the back, heads leaning on the struts of the vehicle. Down an incline to the sea were the hillocks where former ministers had been dragged out at dawn and executed after a *coup d'état*. It had happened years ago and the place bore no new growth, just sand and weeds, the ocean a blue cloth hanging beyond them.

He looked over that scarred cemetery of souls. To think of the thrashing waves as the firing squad took aim, crosswinds entering a pasty mouth, then a bloodless falling.

Deep inside Nungua they pulled up in front of a tin-roofed house with a narrow veranda. His lover was sitting outside with a young woman in a patterned dress and headscarf. She was wearing purple plastic sandals. Two half-empty bottles of Fanta sat on the table between them. The girl had high cheekbones pressed to the top of her face; her skin was glossy.

At first he pulled back, recognition flooring him, and the woman was something he did not comprehend.

Then his lover on the veranda waved at him. He raised his hand back behind the windscreen. He told the driver to wait in the bar on the corner and stepped out into the salty neighbourhood of laughing mammies and loud Tupac playing and kids trailing wire contraptions on wheels. The pair watched him. The jeep took off and the woman led the men inside, placed the Fanta bottles in the kitchen sink, locked the back door behind her.

⟝

They were holding each other on the bed when the woman's voice rang out. They kissed. They crawled apart and began to dress. This time he did not watch the other man pull on his worn clothes, but sat there, elbowing into his T-shirt, inhaling traces of their entangled skins. They embraced. He was given a fresh Fanta from the fridge while his lover finished one of the warm bottles that had been left there.

He walked alone down the street and came to the bar on the corner.

It was empty. For a moment his innards seized and he nearly stumbled on the ridge of the gutter. He felt obscenely visible, his crimes written in colossal scrolls on his person. He ordered a beer and threw it back, grateful for the chemical swilling; he looked for options in the degraded sky. Then the jeep pulled over and the driver was most apologetic, saying he'd been to a timber yard.

He climbed in, said he preferred the windows open, realised he didn't have a single bead to show for the afternoon.

—

Now the soldiers turned to stare as their vehicle crawled past in the tired file back from the beaches. One soldier pointed to his white face as they inched by, and urged them off the road. The soldiers were always looking for easy money. The driver swung over untroubled, jerking on the handbrake, glancing at his boss for what would happen next. But he was already grinding his jaw, thinking of colleagues he could call if they were hassled too hard. Papers were fished out; they were all in order. His documents were pored over with a theatrical intensity that set him on edge.

A soldier in a badly-fitting uniform commanded the driver to step down. The driver looked across, swept with worry. His panic increased. But he could only think of his lover being harangued by these young bastards, the ripples he had tongued along this man's beautiful throat, the unguarded facial expressions he had received as gifts. He tried to step down and follow the driver, but was stopped by a second soldier standing by the window shaking his head.

'What's going on here?' His voice nearly failed him. 'What's the problem?'

They marched the driver down the incline into a pit in the land, beyond the stream of traffic. As he watched his head began to spin and the faintness spread in tingles to his hands and legs. Again, he pushed on the door; again the stern soldier shook his head. The man turned laughing to the group fixed in a circle of olive-green shirts and blue tassels on muscular shoulders, berets on foreheads, guns dangling.

The driver was pushed to his knees.

'Stop this!' he cried from the vehicle.

The driver raised his hands, long fingers with bony joints. On the kneeling man's face he could read no expression, hear no sound through this horrible act.

One soldier playfully raised a gun.

He sat there watching the scene, compelled. He thought of a gun raised to his lover's temple and this shocking vision wet him through: he would rather feel the cold steel in his own mouth. He pulled out a fan of cash from the glove compartment and waved it at the soldier's flanks. Begged him.

The soldiers fell away laughing, ribbing each other, guns thwacked against lean spines. The driver stood and dusted himself.

—

They drove back to the steaming city, which was soon awash with stormy gusts and red-swilling streets. The driver accepted his apology for this random singling out. As the car crawled on he looked at the young man's angular face and wondered what thoughts he had summoned in those unlawful moments. But the driver held the steering wheel and his face was indecipherable. He turned away, staring out of the window at the splattered shacks. He now saw the lovemaking earlier as fragrant with doom, prologue to the staged execution. The two contexts overlapped and he saw the beach road with its bloody memories as a poisoned conduit through the afternoon. As the rain pelted down, and the city passed in grimy prisms with half-dressed children caught in doorways, he saw their fervent bodies on the soaked bed and knew he would never risk seeing the man he craved again.

—

In those weeks he worked long hours and went home directly. He wrote jaunty emails to friends, contacted a woman who had wanted to marry him, who sent him photographs of her twins. He looked up house prices in his old city and considered doing an online language course in Chinese. His sister wrote to him: *I'm so glad you liked the book. It was great, wasn't it? Thanks for the photos. The house looks rather swish, at least you're not sweating all day. What about a shot of this famous man you've met? A wife (and kid?) this time? Something tells me you are barking up a very thorny tree. I'm so glad to have left everything and more behind. Here the deserts are crazy with flowers...*

But in the night he dreamed of being raped in a cell and woke up floundering, uncertain of his senses. Another time he saw himself surrounded by soldiers, prone on the sand, anticipating ecstasy. It repulsed him.

When two months had passed he knew there would be no more envelopes or hotel names written in slanted letters. He remained calm. After work the driver took him to the tennis courts, where he met a young waiter who slipped him his telephone number as he paid for a round of drinks. He watched this man's alluring spine and the clipped back of his skull disappearing into the kitchens. That night he called him up and gave him his address.

Pia Tortora

When he travels with his father, Cam is reminded of the wheelchair-bound American Jew who was shot and thrown off the *Achille Lauro* in the '80s, into the Mediterranean Sea. Earlier, the steward helped his father out of his chair and coaxed him up the steps of the aircraft. Vicious-eyed, his father had been thankless. Cam has looked up the cruise ship hijacking, read that the irate American hostage had triggered something in his young inept executioners: singled out, he had been taken on deck and shot twice. A Portuguese waiter had been forced to haul his body overboard, and the man's wheelchair had followed him into the sea.

Mid-flight, Cam looks over the icy mountains of Western Europe. He thinks of warriors seizing villages, pointing filthy digits at those they would rape or enslave, a history of selection. That bright afternoon on the ship's deck, he thinks his father, too, would have railed at the young terrorists, reminding them of the wrath of their own fathers. Cam imagines the shock of the killers as life left the American paraplegic; he can see his father's body dropping through the air.

Next to him, the old man stares at the strip of emergency measures affixed to the seat in front.

In London another steward wheels them through the airport where they meet Dominic, Cam's son, banked against the railing where passengers flood into the main hall. Dominic is an effigy in a black T-shirt, grown immense. He embraces Cam, bends to kiss his grandfather's cheeks, allows the old man's hands to mould themselves around his. They are in London for Dominic's graduation tomorrow, which Cam feels as a marker in his own life. When the young man turns, Cam sees the flesh amassed across his upper back, and the haunches of an overweight woman. Cam suspects drugs, too much dope, or the same inertia that nestles within his wife's psyche. Dominic is half a head taller than Cam, he smells unwashed.

Dominic delivers them to the hotel desk then says he has to meet a friend and backs off, heading out to the street. Cam watches his bulk cross the window, as alien to him as any of the people pushing past.

—

Three months ago, Cam's wife booked their hotel rooms for the trip. But even then Cam would have wagered on her absence. His wife has chosen well. They are in a Hyde Park hotel overlooking a bus-jammed avenue, the building surges over treetops. Cam hands over his credit card to be swiped and says that the third member of the party is not with them, and could their rooms be on the same floor? However this cannot be altered as the hotel is full. Cam considers sleeping in his father's room on an extra bed but cannot abide the idea of shitting or pissing with his father beyond the wall. Besides, his father says he wants to be able to wheel to the window. What else is there for him to do here? Cam knows that he is mobile enough to look after himself.

Upstairs his view is a wider stage, hazy with light. He throws his bag on the rack. The room smells of fixtures and laundered fabric. He pauses at the window, watching a woman charge across the grass in the park below. He texts his son to arrange a meeting at the flat in an hour. He could call his wife, though there is little chance she would answer. Cam turns away to the bathroom but the woman below still tugs his eye. Is she being chased? He watches her sprinting further and further along the green plain, until she dips under a fringe of trees and he will never know.

Down on the street he walks by the rim of the park to the Underground station. There is something wafting across from the greenery, adrift above the street. It showers over him and he feels warm air on his neck. He'd never thought of London as a sensual city, coming from baroque, whimsical Rome, but he feels a shiver of horny youth. New breath coming from an unknown mouth. The scent of underarms, fingertips. Rome, for all her girlish sculptures and fervent overtures, makes him feel ancient, living in the mouth of death. At night, when his wife sleeps, he looks at porn. He likes slender, breastless women with dyed black hair. Lately, when

Cam has travelled across Europe for work, an otherness propels through him, carrying gusts of the lives he might have lived, while a clawing starts through the territories of his body. He feels the plateau of his age and the pressing of his soul for release. He thinks, if his soul has inhabited other men, he knows that one of them has been lawless. The porn makes him relaxed. There are certain women he would recognise if they passed him in the street. He would wish to speak with them, that is all.

He has been to Dominic's flat once at the outset, when there was only a cheap desk and a pile of books, but he hasn't been over there in a good eight or nine months. Three years ago he assembled the Ikea bed and improved the lighting, led his son down to the student kitchen where he showed him how to prepare a *soffritto* for pasta sauce. Dominic was less weighty then, worried about his choice of course; he stuttered a little. Cam was shocked when Dominic said he was afraid of getting beaten up by thugs. Cam said, *It won't happen to you.* But it had, not a month afterwards. The boy had been knocked to the ground, kicked, his phone and wallet taken. Dominic lives in a shared house now, and Cam supposes he has mastered cooking, hopes he has savoured sex. Cam hasn't asked if there is a girlfriend. But he thinks back to the clammy man in the black T-shirt he embraced this morning, with his odour of fried food and folded skin. There is no girlfriend. His son is a child of the flat, groaning underworld of the internet.

Dominic opens the door. He stands there a moment too long, filling the doorway, a little unsteady, or perhaps Cam imagines this. Who could have known the boy would grow so huge? Dominic's eyes are bloodshot and half-closed. He is stoned.

'Come in,' he says.

In the kitchen, Dominic lights a cigarette and lets the lighter drop to the counter. Cam watches him smoke, hands in pockets. They drink cans of foamy beer. Cam's thoughts flounder. How is this done? He tries to untangle his parental will from his sense of insult and realises this is too large, the scale of this. He wants to abdicate, he wants to pace back along the street to the train station and pretend he never came here, never stood in this foul kitchen drinking Slovakian beer, staring at his fat son staring back at him.

In Dominic's plunging eyes, he sees his son understands this.

Dominic's mobile phone rings and he steps outside through the half-rotten door to take the call. As he walks up and down the path Cam watches, insulating his emotion, slowing it such that it ticks inside of him, an atomic energy. When his son enters again he is calm.

'Let's have a look at your room then,' Cam says.

They march upstairs where the situation is full-blown. A screen sits on the desk, a game console and headphones, all else has been elbowed away or tumbled onto the floor. Towels, bedding, food wrappers and containers; clothing in mounds along with unopened letters and curling books. Cam thought as much. He thinks of the combat between fathers and sons, displayed here as surely as shouts and punches.

They stare at each other. Then Cam shunts up the window and the stale smell escapes. He swings around in a fury. His hand falls upon a shoe on the desk, which he picks up and launches through the window. He begins throwing his son's belongings wide into the garden. Books, clothing, shoes are flying. Cam sees the controlled fist and mangled grin on Dominic's face. His son had wanted this trial, even though he swears at him.

Dominic watches his junk sail out into the weeds.

—

When he is just abreast of the hotel, he notices a woman staring. For an instant the air muddles him; it is evening-scented now, and the mass gathered over the park sheds upon him.

'Camillo – ' the woman says. It's his given name, used by a handful of people in his neighbourhood.

'Pia?'

He crosses the street, jolted. This is London. This is Pia. Pia Tortora. Arms wide, light kisses. So far from the Rome days when their social circles had interwoven.

'What are you doing here?'

'My son is graduating from university tomorrow. We're staying in the hotel.'

Pia stills before him, a magnet for his eyes. Her skin, buttery once, has collections of stains, she is swept with them; too much sun, years of tobacco. Their paths crossed one summer on the islands. Cam grows bashful as that time flares in his memory and ignites. They both glance aside.

'You look well,' Pia says.

Cam has never gone back to those days. It was when he and his girlfriend were estranged, and then that winter he had married her. He sees Pia's fine hair plugged into her scalp. Did they ever have children?

'My husband – Gerard – is no longer alive. You may not have heard this.'

Cam, who was picturing Gerard's face, now feels a wilting in the gut.

'I'm truly sorry,' he replies.

'It happened not far from here,' she says, her head motioning down the road. 'A heart attack. There were problems that should have been taken more seriously. But Gerard thought the doctors were being overzealous.'

Still shocked, Cam can't engage Pia's eyes. She is glad to be telling her story afresh. On either side of her, people are waiting for buses. Cam imagines a man with a shaven, burnished head propped against the spearheaded fence, he hears the sirens crashing through.

'This must be rather recent,' Cam says.

'It's been a year now, or just over that. I usually come here on Mondays. That was the day it happened. I catch the Tube up here, then walk through the park back home.'

Early on, their socialising lapsed when Gerard had outmanoeuvred Cam at work, leapfrogging ahead abroad. At work Gerard had been bloody-minded. And Cam's wife had felt she was disliked. Cam follows Pia's eyes into the park, noticing a pair of sneakers strung over electricity wires.

'I'm truly sorry, Pia,' he says again. 'Are you alone now?'

'My daughter is studying in Montreal. We don't get along very well. It's really so pleasant to see you, Camillo. How is your wife?'

Cam knows he has time for a drink with her in the hotel lobby across the road, but does he want to? The theatre with Dominic has all but emptied him. He wants to remove his shoes, throw his body onto the bed, shave again and shower. Before him, he has an evening with his father.

'You are still married?' Pia says.

Cam nods. He wonders if she has had some sort of surgery. He pushes it back but the past returns in grainy, mute frames. On the island, he and Gerard scaled the volcano with a group of hikers. They spent the night in sleeping bags on the summit as the lava roared and rats scampered over their feet. The whole time Cam had thought of Pia's tits swaying as she unrolled the cane mat she took to the beach, or their displacement over her ribs as she read. For those first days the three of them had cooked and ate and slumbered with the warmth of siblings.

Cam touches Pia's forearm. 'Listen, why don't we catch up later on?' He tells her he has to get back to his father upstairs, taking her telephone number which he knows he will delete the moment he passes through the doors. Cam has a habit of ruling people out. And Pia, there is nothing he wishes to renew with her. As they stand there and Pia's eyes begin to dance into his, he feels aversion, and the sense that she has stolen from him. Tomorrow Cam's buoyancy will not return and he will hear the defibrillator pads smacking Gerard's chest.

'Camillo, may I hug you?' Pia says.

Her arms rise to him and their torsos connect, necks linking. He encloses this woman, alarmed that his senses recall her smell and skin with quaking fondness. Cam's lips open on her hair. The three of them had become brazen playthings of the island, he had always left it at that. Pia feels stronger than he would have assumed, stronger than a woman who visits an unmarked shrine every week.

—

'Who was that woman you were talking to?'

It comes as a relief to see his father slumped in his wheelchair, his red-rimmed eyes landing upon him. The old man's stomach rumbles.

'Pia Tortora. I knew her years ago in Rome. Her husband has died of a heart attack. It happened very close to this spot, it seems.'

His father ignores this. Most of his friends have passed away. Cam remembers those who congregated until the end at the local bar, the marbled skin clinging to their skulls. Sometimes, his father will speak of the early ones who died long before their bodies became wrecks. There was a chap called Guido, piniored between two train carriages, whom his father spoke to while he was dying. His father says that in the last moments Guido's voice came from somewhere above, that he had taken flight from his crushed frame. His father has towed his own body for years now.

'I'd like a good meal,' his father says. 'None of that English rubbish.'

They leave the hotel and the evening air is warm. Cam ties a sweater around his father's shoulders which the man pulls off. It is a fawn colour, it lies in his lap. Dominic says he can't join them for dinner, that he'll lunch with them after the ceremony at the university. Cam will collect him in a taxi tomorrow morning. He never asked if Dominic had his garments ready. After his dramatic jettisoning of Dominic's belongings out of the window, Cam had just told him not to turn up stoned.

There is an Italian place among a group of restaurants. It is empty, there is a struggle to introduce the wheelchair into the room. The waiter is disinclined to help and the cook is leaning on a counter lodged in the back wall. Behind him, the bright lighting of the kitchen is framed.

'Could you help me move some of these chairs?' Cam says to the waiter who unfolds his arms.

The young man is slight and bandy-legged, the skin polished over his face. His hair is gelled in spikes around the exposed scalp atop his head and his eyebrows are plucked into arches. It's a common look in Italy, but over here the man seems androgynous and feline. Cam looks around at the hanging Chianti bottles and sepia photographs of Vesuvius.

'Are you sure you want to eat here?' he asks his father.

Cam would just as soon eat at the hotel but his father is already combing the menu.

They return to the hotel and his father banishes Cam from his suite. He says he needs to use the bathroom. Cam smells urine. He tells his father it is okay and he wants to help. He doesn't mention the word 'urine' because he knows his father abhors any language of the body. His father admonishes him for choosing such an unpleasant restaurant. Upstairs in his room, Cam sits on the bed and finishes a beer.

He turns on his computer. He resists. In the bathroom he splashes his face. Cam thinks of Pia Tortora in her flat across the park. He has deleted her number. He takes the lift down to the hotel bar, where he orders a whisky. He calls Dominic and the boy answers. He's in a pub, a chaotic backdrop until he steps outside. Then Cam is not sure what to say to him after his wild gestures this afternoon. Dominic laughs, but the laugh is meant for a friend, not Cam who stands there waiting until his son's wheezing giggles have ended.

'Well, tomorrow then,' Dominic says and rings off.

Cam is straddling a stool, watching a rugby match played out under driving rain, when he becomes aware of a shape and scent behind him. It is Pia Tortora. She stands there in a black blouson dress drawn at the neck and waist, a dark plum motif scattered over the fabric. He notices the cloth first, how the pattern represents some kinder variation of the swastika. He has seen this geometric form before. Pia looks more relaxed than this afternoon. In this light he can see the direction that her skin has been tugged and stitched back.

'I was quite certain you weren't going to call me so I decided to take my chances and turn up. Am I right?' Pia asks.

'Yes,' he replies. 'You are right.'

She orders a whisky and sits next to him. 'Gerard would have been very happy to see you again. You haven't thought very much about us, have you, over the years?'

'Quite honestly, no.'

'There's no need to worry, Camillo. I haven't come to transport you back to our devilish past,' she says. 'You're just a link to Gerard, whom I do miss. Tell me, did we not corrupt you that time on the island? Not even a little?'

'I don't believe so.' Cam shies away to the drenched rugby.

Pia rattles her drink. Beyond the street, the park is blackness. He thinks he should have called the laundry downstairs, or at least taken his father's clothing down there in a plastic bag. The old man's piss, it is rancid.

'How did you get here?' he asks.

'Taxi,' she replies. 'Where's your son? He must be around the same age as Chiara.'

Cam's arm swings over the unoccupied bar stool next to him.

Pia laughs. 'And why is your wife not with you?'

'My wife? My wife no longer travels.' Cam looks at Pia's face and realises she will be the first person to whom he tells the truth. 'My wife hasn't left our apartment in months,' he says.

Cam tells Pia about his wife quitting her job at the journal and her self-imposed exile from the outside world. About her fears of bomb blasts in the train stations, and black-masked terrorists breaking into offices. A colleague of hers was gunned down in Paris.

His eyes return to the rugby; Pia's stray into her drink.

'It's easy to become afraid these days,' she says after a while.

Cam watches the players fly on top of one another, grateful her reply goes no further. The pattern on her dress vibrates on the outskirts of his vision.

'You know, Camillo, I still enjoy thinking of Gerard,' she continues. 'Gerard was enchanted by you.'

'Please. I'd prefer not to revisit any of that,' Cam says, his gaze pulling away from the screen and falling down her front.

'Are you looking at my breasts?' she asks.

'Yes, I am looking at your breasts.'

'My breasts are good. I've had work done.'

'Have you come here for me to invite you upstairs?' Cam says. 'You want that, don't you?'

'Yes.'

'I think not,' he replies. 'I am married, Pia. It's still a marriage of sorts.'

Pia finishes her drink. The barman glides before them and Cam nods, but Pia's hand draws across the air. She watches the young man reach for the whisky and the liquid slinking in the bottle.

'Camillo,' she says. 'I think I misinterpreted what happened on the pavement this afternoon. Is that so?'

She looks at him, her face groomed and tawny, her eyes are dark cul-de-sacs. She says, 'I'm going to walk to the door now, and not turn back. Are you okay with that? Camillo?'

'I am,' he replies, while thinking he would have her on her knees with her bosoms rocking. 'I think it's for the best.'

The barman glances at their frank faces. Pia pulls up the strap of her bag. She leans in. 'Let me tell you this,' she says. 'There's no good reason to, but I will. For many years Gerard used to bring home young men. They all resembled you. The length of their thighs and torsos, more than the size of their members. You know he had a professional interest in proportion.'

Pia steps down from the stool, kisses him on both cheeks. Again, her scent produces an undoing and he feels his armpits sting and dampen. Pia moves back and looks towards the doors as if to confirm her course.

'The boys became younger and younger,' she says. 'While we became older and older. Until one day Gerard said there would be no more men and we would no longer sleep together, and we did not. We called that day *The End of Camillo*.'

—

At first light Cam stands at the window in his pyjamas. He finds relief in the reappearance of the cityscape. He wants to project himself out there, needs to get walking. He has been waiting for the natural light to dismantle his thoughts. All through the night hours the mass of memory, cut free, extruded through his being, has blown up as visions in this room. Cam remembers Gerard's phone call when he was shattered in Rome after the breakup. The ferry trip from Naples. He sees the house that belonged to someone in Gerard's family. The building's solitary prominence on the hillside as you walked up from the bay. The volcano looming behind, an immortal trembling.

It takes Cam a long time to furnish this setting with their beings. He remembers the pair of them barely dressed, emerging on the balcony and calling down, a display of genitalia even in those initial moments. Pia's bare arms washing peaches in the wide flat sink. The arabesque floor tiles and ceramic plates hooked to the walls. Finally, he admits Gerard, his rich, bronzed torso coated with sun-bleached hair.

Outside the light rises into blooms in the sky. Cam fixes himself a horrid instant coffee that burns his mouth. He watches traffic circling the park. He decides he will walk in the direction of Dominic's house, then catch a cab the rest of the way when his thoughts have cleared. Bring him back here for a decent breakfast with his grandfather. The three of them, together at least, to get the day started. Cam regrets going downstairs to the bar last night, but no more than he regrets refuting her. He had known all along that Pia would show.

He remembers Gerard's first challenge, *Kiss my wife*. The rest emits a squall inside of him. But he makes himself travel to the end, to the last night when the three of them had slept melded together, to the final morning when their bodies had interlocked on the tiles.

When his memories complete their course Cam reaches the same vantage point, he feels the same soft expulsion as the day they waved him down the trail. He sees himself board the ferry back to Naples. He sees the wedding dress and the young precarious bride, the inanimate cosmos he had chosen.

The Sneeze

Suzanne Dessange has been feeling testy. The thought of what Gaetano has just done with her credit card account. Vaporised it, in a word. Shifting what used to be joint to a slim flow into her muddy domestic account and saying, *what does I need to nourish the banks for?* She roars along Chaussée de Vleurgat and feels an angry, head-throwing-back sneeze coming on, fissures through her nostrils along the hot catchment behind her eyes. She slams into the rear of a Fiat Panda and sees three people stumble out as she wipes snot from her cheek. Fuck. A North African man. A fully pregnant woman. A boy with a block of iron-coloured hair.

She steps out onto the footpath. Says in French, 'What were you doing stopping here? What do you think this is?'

Before realising the woman is braced against a parked car, holding her belly, the sobbing boy hammered into her hip. The father explains that a vehicle came flying out from the right and he had to give way. Suzanne swears at the idiotic Belgian road rules.

She asks if the woman is injured.

The woman's face is dragged downward, steeped in pallor. The little boy's hands are fanned out, one clasping her thigh, the other the seat of her jeans. Why do women let their sons touch them like this? She nods several times, looking to the husband who stares at the beaten rear of their car, which Suzanne's Gaetano-sponsored insurance will pay for. The woman takes a few steps along the footpath and straightens her back, the son still stuck to her. Both the father and Suzanne watch her steps, her swollen feet spilling out of her sandals. The right thing would be to take them to the hospital. Suzanne offers to do this, as she checks her own undamaged vehicle. It's a large Audi she won't be able to run for much longer. She sees shopping bags in the back of the family's Fiat, spinach leaves sitting brightly. She clutches her handbag, feels prickling along the canals of her nose.

'Shall we fill out the forms?' she says.

She is certain something will be amiss. No insurance, no licence, dud working visas. She retrieves the documents from her car. When she opens the forms on the roof of the Fiat she turns aside and sees the man's eyes are full of water. Suzanne passes him the pen and he writes with difficulty, sometimes wiping his face. His hands, she notices, are of a stone-like beauty, hewn or carved with many shallow creases. The woman now holds the boy on a hip, his face in her neck. She wears a loose shirt which has a jagged, diagonal design; her breasts are prominent pouches.

Suzanne takes back her pen, fills out her declaration and signs. She hands the man his copy, hears herself again offering to take them to the hospital. Now they stand facing each other on the footpath and the man's eyes are dry. He takes a step away from her. Suzanne is tall and knows that people often step back because she is looking over their heads. The man's wife removes the clinging child and settles him in the car, then eases her body into the front seat. For the first time, Suzanne hears the woman speak to her husband in a high-pitched Arabic spatter of sounds. The dented car pulls into the traffic.

Suzanne goes back to her vehicle, turns off the hazard lights and drives into an empty parking space. She blows her nose and feels lightheaded. She had been going out to lunch. When her phone rings, she sees it is her sister Paule, who has been calling ever since Gaetano left. Suzanne does not answer. She sits there breathing, watching another North African woman pushing a stroller. When this woman passes, Suzanne turns on the ignition. She drives through the city and on to the forest.

It is a clear, ink-filled day with all colour saturated and distinct. Trees embrace over her car. She looks at her rings on the steering wheel and the toneless skin of her hands. She is not wearing varnish and her nails are weak and split. When she was a child, these hands had sat in her lap, had played scales and mastered a Liszt duet. She used to scratch her sister's bare back in fights. Suzanne has not taken a warm, living thing into her hands in months. She has not touched flesh. The avenues twist further into the forest. Lean men are jogging past. She feels a tickling in her nose again and holds a tissue to her face, and the stinging impulse fractures behind her eyes. She blinks away the hot light, she thinks of insertion, cavity. She sees a man whose back and bottom look like Gaetano's and she slows the car, staring at this man's buttocks.

She accelerates down the avenue.

Further on there is a grand dilapidated museum she has not visited since she was a schoolgirl. She follows signs to the parking area. She puts her handbag strap over her shoulder and strides along the façade. The stone-work feels vivid and heated even though the day is cool. Suzanne looks up over the building, then down to the lake where swans squat on the grass or dock together some way offshore. She walks up the steps and into the museum. She buys a ticket.

She wanders from collection to collection, from the taxidermied mammals with their wet obsidian eyes, to the disturbing pygmies installed behind glass panes. She moves through the Congolese masks and sculpted stools, headrests and bowls, seeing where hands have moved with fond-ness over wood. After a while the objects feel voiceless and mournful, and she has seen enough. She is alone in the room. She walks over to a row of sepia colonial photographs.

In the gift shop she buys a bracelet of coral and brass beads and sits down for a coffee. Her eyes follow two brown-skinned girls rinsing cups. She goes outside, towards the fluttering lake now bereft of swans. For a long while she sits on a bench by the water, the swollen day upon her. Among the photographs there had been a village girl, a grinning naked young woman whose teeth were filed into white points. Suzanne's eyes had travelled over the girl's body like a dense caryatid, full of weight, the skin mapped with scarification textured as wallpaper, a string of beads around her hips, across her sex. Who had she been, this young woman? Standing laughing against a drawn sheet, before a European man with his hooded camera, a man in pitiless boots. One hand on her hip, the other arm bent behind her head with a shadow of hair in the armpit, her breasts in glowing points. Watching her, Suzanne's heart had thudded in her chest. She had never seen such quivering life.

Suzanne sits up straight on the bench, a thousand needles along her thighs and a gust of fingertips over her face.

Do thou, O Dica, set garlands upon thy lovely hair,
weaving sprigs of dill with thy delicate hands;
for those who wear fair blossoms may surely stand first,
even in the presence of Goddesses who look without favour
upon those who come ungarlanded.

The Woman Who Previously Worked for the Louvre

It took them two years to find the house and in those two years their rapport nearly overturned. Arnaud, who kept the studio in Marseilles, began working closely with a set designer who drove over from Nice early every morning in a white van. Marianne developed rheumatoid arthritis in both hands, and these became unseemly paws wrapped in flaming skin.

When the house initially presented itself, they were not aware that it coincided with the many conditions they had listed with the young agent, who rolled her eyes every time she saw Marianne's number appear on her phone. A bulky house in a cul-de-sac, it stood on a rough sloping block at a distance from a village. It was recently built and charmless. Marianne checked the address the woman had given them, as the woman had been called away to tend an ill child. Arnaud, a patient southerner, looked at the oleander trees rubbing against a mouldy yellow wall.

'She can't be serious. Who would live out here?'

Marianne, since her illness began, had come to believe that other people's lives were less complex, while worrying that her own life would go unrecognised. For so many years she had grappled with creative projects that had flatlined, leaving her urges gathered on a precipice. Rarely had she felt the true satisfaction of a work in flight and acclaimed at the same time. So many things came down to timing.

On the other hand, Arnaud, to whom she had returned after 15 months with a Dutch saxophonist, had always worked with lucid, committed rashness. His ideas fell open on a sketch pad, then, with the help of his assistants, were transposed into scale models. Over months these structures grew into theatre sets that were the bold embodiment of his art. He was restless and silent at each stage of this voluptuous trajectory. In Addis Ababa, Marianne had watched Arnaud attach a paintbrush to a long wooden rod with a length of wire, and spend the hours colouring wood-framed set canvases in poor light. It was the most lyrical scene of her life.

But they were considering their retirement now. Arnaud would collect a meaningful pension from the state for his many collaborations. Marianne, who had taught begrudgingly at a Paris high school, could only expect a pittance. Arnaud shook out one of the many filterless Celtiques cigarettes that kept him alive as much as killed him.

'What a foolish woman!' Marianne said again, starting to trot back to the car.

But Arnaud paused at the gate for a very sound reason. There was a sticker with the emblem of the Louvre Museum next to the metal letter-box. He had heard of a woman who lived out here, somewhere in the south, a woman who restored paintings for the great museum. He'd been told there was a slot at the back of a house through which more than one monumental Delacroix had passed. A house where Courbet and Manet had been examined and, without supervision, repaired.

The light inside could only have been astonishing.

'Wait, Marianne,' he said. 'Wait up, my flower.'

Marianne turned around. Arnaud's hair, always stringy, fell to one side. In all seasons he wore a navy mandarin jacket whenever he ventured beyond the high-ceilinged studio they still owned in Rue Paradis, even into the cobbled courtyard where he toed out his cigarettes. Arnaud asked her for the keys they had been given, and she followed him through the gate.

Inside the garden walls shrubs lunged at them. The house had been vacant for four years. The woman who lived there was Belgian and she had sold up, no reason was given. Marianne, who had never trimmed a plant in her life, felt a rush of interest in the greenery, sensing its embrace.

'Don't touch those,' said Arnaud as she fondled the bank of oleander. 'Not good.'

Marianne had raw swollen hands anyway.

Arnaud skirted the side of the building, and Marianne asked what he was looking for. Couldn't they just go through the front door? He told her about this legendary woman, and how he was certain this was the house where she had lived, that there had to be an entry passage where the great paintings were slotted through.

And there it was. In the middle of the southern-facing back wall, an elongated vertical sliver had been cut through the stucco, in between an arrangement of windows. It looked like a device for warfare perhaps, and was full of cobwebs and dry leaves. Arnaud picked up a fallen branch on the ground and poked inside. Of course it was sealed off.

From where she was standing Marianne saw the village clutching a nearby hill, in serene morning light. She knew this particular village quite well, as they had lodged there with some Armenian colleagues of Arnaud, for the pre-production phase of a project he later told her had been stifling, though no one could have guessed. The only woman in the house, she had gone for walks in the afternoons when she grew tired of their smoky philosophising. She remembered there was a trail all the way over to this side of the valley, then back to the square where the church bell had just begun its faint ringing. She felt a drag in her belly, a wanting to pee but a sexual spasm as well; she'd grown confused about the unreliable signals that climbed up from there.

Arnaud was hauling himself up the back stairs to the shallow porch crossing the building halfway. It looked like there was room for a table and chairs, and that an awning had been torn off by wind. His hands were cupped against the glass.

Marianne stood on the ground firmly, inhaling lavender and thyme. She was certain she would say *no* initially; there was a colossal amount of work to do, and much expense. It would be ridiculous to live so far from friends, from the city they knew and loved, but what did friends and a city really mean to one? Who among their friends could help them understand the interval that lay between them and their deaths?

Arnaud found the back door key in the batch and they entered. They'd been given no idea of the floor plan so what they found inside was a surprise. Apart from the narrow kitchen space at the head of the stairs, the main floor was a cavernous space. There was a sitting area evident by the windows overlooking the landscape, but behind this the studio immediately expanded into a glowing vault that lifted all the way to the roof. Extensive sky lighting had been installed, though one window was unhappily smashed, while to the rear a balustrade at the first floor level showed a series of bedroom and bathroom doors.

Arnaud walked up to the fissure in the wall which began at knee height and travelled upward. This was where the paintings had been passed through to the Belgian restorer, who had unveiled them here, beneath this mantle of light. Arnaud had long been inspired by the immense tableaux of the classicists with their heavy-shouldered women brandishing flags, or their bulbous post-rape bodies crumpled with foreshortening.

Taxidermy

Ernesto said if they ever did it again they were going to leave instructions to stuff the dog. It was spoken lightly and we were already half-drunk. I looked down at the lithe Weimaraner collapsed on its mat in the corner, whose amber eyes soaked up the lot of us. *No! You wouldn't dare!* Ray's eyes coasted to the office building opposite. The façade was chequered brick, the unrestored 1930's style still wearing pocks from the War. A man was speaking to a woman sitting at a tilted draughtsman's desk.

Ray managed a laugh, then his voice came in a lower register, plugged in his throat. 'We took 30 sleeping pills that time, didn't we? Wasn't it 30 or so? But we woke up. The doctor said it would have killed a horse.'

The pair of them laughed loudly, their Friday afternoon in-joke. The window was open and the man and woman in the office looked our way. Ray removed some chopped pineapple from the freezer and Ernesto handed him a bottle of tequila, the one with the worm inside. I watched their bodies intersecting, Ernesto's brown limbs and my brother's scrawny biceps and finely-haired forearms I used to tweak as a kid. He was wearing the shirt from the performance of *Priscilla* I brought over years ago.

A cock
in a frock
on a rock.

I was passed Ray's version of a Tequila Sunrise. I wandered out to change my dress. Afterwards, the restaurant had hard lights and the huge, unwieldy bike they'd stolen for me must have belonged to a post-Aryan giantess.

—

I read Hemingway that week. In the morning I read in bed and listened to the aboveground trains plunge in and out of the city. I thought of all the party people rousing themselves, and all of the blood-red livers squeezing out toxins. I thought of cell regeneration and Suicide Tuesday ahead.

Out in the dining room Ernesto was preparing Ray's breakfast. I once heard Ernesto introduce himself as *a housewife and a slut.* Ray might have hated the role-playing, but his job required a spiffy suit and a slightly moronic way of dragging back his sandy locks. Ray had an undeniable history of suits. I had seen Ray in a crisp junior tux hired from Grace Brothers, performing Gershwin's *Rhapsody in Blue* on a spanking baby grand.

Ernesto had left a silk housegown on the bed which I pulled over my bra and knickers. I wondered if lovers had worn it, and rinsed themselves as I had in the bidet in their guest bathroom full of Japanese porn. Seeing it like this, it seemed all too simple. Enviable. The S-Bahn cutting through the city below with its metallic fretwork, the gasping aural whir. The onion-topped tower in Alexanderplatz pricking an Agfa-blue sky. Ernesto's intoxicating wide smile. I could hardly see the patchiness, let alone the sophisticated malady they both now shared. I saw a horizon of efficient, codified bliss.

Ernesto was wearing a pair of baggy shorts and pulling out the woven leather lead. The dog had dislodged from its place and now marked time at the front door, claws submerged in a Persian rug.

'There's coffee for you. And some fresh sunflower bread if you like. I'll be back shortly. Time for a walk,' said the remarkable man my brother called his pallbearer.

I settled down to eat, familiar with Ernesto's calls to duty. For years I had thought it was Ray who commanded this boy-grown-to-man, but it was Ernesto who provided for Ray's soul. Without him Ray was structure-less. Again, I saw that Ray had out-coded me. His rules were more subtle and he moved with grace. I tore into Ernesto's heavy bread.

By the time he and the dog returned I was showered and dressed, relishing the last chapters of *Fiesta*. Ernesto commented upon the weather, as he always did, with peculiar conviction. Was it merely the shift through languages? The silky dog lapped fresh water from a ceramic bowl and folded down on its mat, the morning sun highlighting the denseness of its pelt.

I found myself wondering about taxidermy – what a ghastly profession – and what talents would be required to give mass to the cavities of the dead.

'You're not really going to have the dog stuffed?' I asked.

Ernesto laughed and gave the dog a command in German. The dog spread its jaws and tightened its lips in a grimace.

'This is your brother. You cannot see how the dog is laughing?'

I couldn't help recognising Ray's devilry at work and then a sadness approached me on a collision course. I drank another cup of coffee. I noticed Ernesto was holding a faded postcard of the royal Princes, no doubt sent as a joke. Then I remembered I had sent it myself, a week ago.

'Look, Celeste. We received your card.' He held it up. He had neat zones of perspiration under the sleeves of his shabby tight T-shirt and I could see his calling card on show. *Housewife and slut. Handyman and Dog-walker.*

—

Each time I came across to Berlin Ernesto would become my cultural custodian and we always ventured out with zest. With Ernesto, I had seen Queen Nefertiti's bust and the disappointing Ishtar Gate like a blue, chipped bathroom. Despite the volume of shimmering air and an impressive sense of hallowedness, Nefertiti had failed to stir me. The bust appeared parched – even a desultory knock-off – and her spirit evasive. I tried to cross the millennia towards her smooth stucco skin and cold limestone, or even understand the awkward egg-white eye sockets. Instead, I thought of Maria Callas in Pasolini's *Medea*, delivering a dry wink.

I was keen to see the Helmut Newton exhibition. Ernesto said there were other photographers, but Newton's work – so easy to like, so easy to despise – was the main event. We headed out of the station and entered a scrubbed 1930's building, whose dramatic stairway was crowned by a line of Newton's high-shouldered nudes. As we rose Ernesto said he felt assaulted, then stared at each model with a fixation that made me confused. His eyes nearly grazed each woman's bullet-shaped breasts.

Inside, Newton's array of works was less menacing. The Hollywood landscapes showed faceless women lounging on fissured cement, their bodies arid composites pored over by the Californian light. There were other women stashed away in hotel rooms that were studied dioramas, waiting for lovers who might ward off their malaise. While artful, the sense of relentless construction and the disorder of the set remained at hand. The photos were pinpricks, literal shutter blinks, the work of tempers and twisted cables and the hustling of the light. I became curious about the aftermath – *Now you can relax, Deborah!* – or what came before, when the model's legs were gently kinked apart, or the famous actress encouraged to roll her tongue; when a breast was made more palpable with a spray of fine mist, or a puckered nipple given time to distend.

I moved away from Ernesto. In another salon there was work by an American photographer who had grown up in a white trash country state. Everything he mapped – opioid usage, fights and car wrecks – was in the process of happening. What had occurred two seconds ago was still written on some guy's face at the back. Or you knew the woman in front was going to hit the wall. I felt the *crump*, I could hear the shouts and, inside of her, the crystalline warmth of the trip, then waking three hours later with the doorframe against a cheek. I looked back at Ernesto in the airier main salon as he viewed the works with lavish comprehension. Then back to this cluttered collection with its purple blacks and fatty whites. Here the nudity was an ugly grovelling thing about to be used up. In a car banked in a field, on a slit divan with the tissue leaking.

I sat in front of the video blurb without seeing anything. I shut down.

After lunch we caught a train out of the city for the short trip to the Potsdam Gardens we'd missed the year before. This time around it was sunny and I knew my skin was going to burn. As we were funnelled out into the light we passed fast-food shops with huge knotted pastries, a travel agency with a poster for the Maldives. I told Ernesto I didn't feel like hiring a bicycle. We caught a bus that dropped us close to the park gates and he showed me where several of the palace buildings had been shorn to the ground in a bombing swoop at the end of the War. Shaky

Prussian façades were propped against the sky.

As soon as we passed through the gates birdsong began and the deep breathing of the trees eased over us. Ernesto told me that Frederick the Great had established the extensive park as his Versailles-inspired folly, away from the rigours of government and a rejected wife in Berlin. He wanted me to see Sanssouci, the King's tra-la-la rococo outhouse atop a terrace of grapevines, which he had designed himself. We set out along the boulevard flanked by splendid trees. Local families trailed along, while tourists with backpacks hiked with more resolve. I imagined the neighs and plopping of the horses, the way their harnesses would have been absurdly intricate. I thought back to when these trees had been spindly and the views gaping, when the air of the merchant city must have travelled over the boundary walls with its stench of birth and death. How beastly for the monarch with his blueprints for immortality.

Slowed by the heat, we marched up the tiered path to the palace itself. It was a yellow domed single-story building – *Old Fritz's ranch,* Ernesto joked – with moulded cornices softening the arched windows over the vista. I hadn't expected the warmonger's leisure base to be so thrifty, or poignant. From the top, we peered over the grounds with their pockets of swaying verdant growth and the sunny esplanades frilled with fountains and sculptures. The light nibbled statues sprinkled through the grape-vines. At the end of each terrace a black-green yew tree was shaped into a slender pyramid.

'Come with me, come this way.'

Ernesto led me down a shaded side path and up another hill to a sand-wich bar. We ordered iced coffee and it came in tall glasses with a dollop of ice-cream. We sat down on iron chairs under a broad tree and dunked our spoons into the frothy drink. Not the for the first time I wondered what Ernesto said about me to Ray at the end of our long days together, but everything about Ernesto seemed to be logged into a single dimen-sion of goodwill. I glanced at his heavy brows and his mystical brown eyes. Profession: nothing. I remembered the first time Ray brought him through my front door in London. It was weeks after Ray's marriage had come to its close, when I still had a wrathful Michelle sobbing on the phone.

'Your skin is burning today,' Ernesto said gently.

'Yes, I believe it is,' I replied. Through an odd window Ernesto always extended his nurturing to me.

'Would you prefer to see the New Palace or the Chinese Pavilion next?'

'I really don't know. What do you think?'

'Well, the New Palace is rather ferocious. It's full-on imitation baroque, when King Frederick remembered he had an empire to keep in line. Whereas the Chinese Pavilion was built for his vegetable garden. It's obscene, very whimsical. It might raise a smile from you.'

I hadn't realised. Had I been wearing my severe face all day?

He found a path under the trees that led to the Chinese Pavilion. Following batty European trends of the time, it was an unchecked mimicry of what might be considered Oriental. Beneath the pagoda eaves there was a ring of human-sized gilded figures encircling the sage-green walls, each one carrying out a nonsensical activity and wearing a lacquered Eurasian face. Ernesto removed his espadrilles, enjoying the soft grass, and we took different paths around the building. I made out a wily old man holding a monkey and wearing a rice paddy hat, dunked in the King's viscous gold. But then a park official ushered me off the grass and I walked back to the gravel path, awaiting Ernesto.

'You didn't much like that, did you? But what a laugh. Now I have one more small palace to show you. It is my favourite.'

He paced off and I followed him. He diverged from the path towards a grassy hill with a delicate, cylindrical building high up in the light. Already I knew my neck was burnt and tomorrow there would be a red stripe there, with welts on my forearms and calves. I watched Ernesto moving ahead. His swift legs were those of a hiker.

At the crown of the hill was a two-storey villa called Belvedere, fashioned in golden sandstone that absorbed the day's warmth. From the rear, a curved external staircase wended up to the first level where a ring of panelled windows oversaw the landscape. Statues stood around the rim of the roof in the Palladian style, heightening the elegance of the structure.

Ernesto and I reached the windows of the bottom storey, where a single octagonal room had been stripped bare. Inside, upon wooden schoolroom-type stands, were photographs of the same building when it had been struck by bombs in 1945, along with several of the palaces. I wondered what meticulous mind had fitted the golden carousel together again and, after the violation and erasure of millions by another warmonger, *why*? It was a concrete cadaver climbing up from the ground.

—

Ray came home in the foulest mood. We were flaked out on divans in the living room, sipping Bloody Marys Ernesto had prepared, awaiting his arrival from work. He came in, threw off his jacket, showing a business shirt doused in sweat, threw down his laptop bag. He looked angrily at us and went into the kitchen. I heard the dog release a strained whine and saw Ernesto scan the brass relics on a colonial sugar chest. He hauled himself up and trod out to the kitchen.

I anticipated voices or the slamming of the refrigerator door, even the smashing of a plate. I know Ray, he is hardly blessed with self-control. But I heard nothing. My leg muscles flinched. My burnt knees and shins continue to combust, as did the grilled skin on my neck and forearms. Far below, audible through the window sash Ernesto had opened an inch, an evening train scored along the tracks.

I didn't expect them to come out any time soon. The indentation of Ernesto's bum remained on Ray's white sofa. I finished my drink and left the glass on a coaster on the chest. I walked through the shuttered doors to the library where I slept, grabbed the silk housegown and went into the guest bathroom.

I ran a cool bath, throwing in some cedar powder from a Muji bottle I found in a cabinet. When the water was high enough I slid in, kinking my head on the edge so I could check out the erotic artwork they had brought back from Tokyo. The drawings were as compressed as comic strips, with thick streams of calligraphy in the background. In each frame a coy female sat in a pool of gorgeous silks, as a heavy-headed lover parted his garments to reveal an enlarged flushed penis pushing through crimped hair. In one drawing the act of penetration generated strings of liquid.

I dozed, occasionally stirring the water so that the cedar smell was released. Otherwise I marvelled at the artist's decision to place a yellow teapot and a blue bowl of rice to one side, under a window showing shreds of snow. Or how another lover stretched his hand to give a coin to a grinning beggar, the flat woman scripted beneath him. I thought of how dirty our faces grow in climax, how quickly the skin chills.

Ernesto knocked on my bedroom door when I was browsing for a new book. I had finished *Fiesta*. I wanted a different author. Ernesto came in and I was surprised when he gave me a rundown of many of the novels present. Housewife, slut, reader of English classics? He caught my surprise and looked hurt.

'Ray's totally off the rails this evening. I've sent him to bed. Why don't you come out with me to take the dog for a walk? Now that you've relaxed a little.'

'Sure,' I said.

When I came out the dog was at the front door, its long legs fraught with anticipation. It made no sound. How could anyone but Ray teach an animal to laugh? Ernesto opened the door and the dog hurtled to the stairwell. Out on the street he pulled on the lead for the first two blocks then turned around to us gracefully, rosy tongue dripping.

'I have to be careful around here,' Ernesto said. 'There's a guy in one of the bars that he doesn't like. He took a nip at him once.'

We walked under the railway bridge, then through an open pedestrian area filled with aluminium chairs and people enjoying drinks in the evening. We headed towards the river where the last tourist boats floated by with megaphones and tanned ladies wearing hats. Stone walls kept the river in check and several beautifully restored buildings rose on the other side. Every so often the wall halted and mossy steps descended to the wash. Ernesto let the dog off in a park and he jerked about sniffing trees and grass clumps before heading to the water. We followed. We reached the river in time to see the dog lunge in, jaws clenched like a woman trying not to wet her hair.

'What's wrong with Ray today?' I asked Ernesto.

'It's his antidepressants. They make him angry. The last type he was on made him sleep endlessly. I spent half of last year waiting for him to wake up. I've given him something to calm down. He'll be fine when we get back.'

Ray's ex-wife Michelle told me he had thrown her to ground. Ray never knew she had wanted to press charges. I talked her out of it. Before, Michelle and I were close.

'How's his job going?'

'The job? Perhaps we could pass by his office tomorrow. Although the building doesn't treat him well in the summer. They've transferred and it's like a hothouse. Poor Ray comes home all petered out. But he's off tomorrow afternoon. I expect we'll go to the lake.'

I couldn't ask him about the other things – the illness they shared, the stuffing of the dog, the 30 sleeping pills. When we were drunk again I would do that. I had to.

The dog charged out of the water like a rubbery seal, thunking up the stairs, violently shaking before us. The water, stinky as it was, was a relief.

But Ernesto was wrong about Ray that night. Ray wouldn't leave his room and the pair of us went out alone. First to a Vietnamese restaurant, then to a trans show called *Chantal and the House of Shame*, in a downstairs bar near Alexanderplatz. They put stamps on the undersides of our arms. Ernesto gave me a pill and washed his down with vodka and a can of Red Bull. I didn't see him much after that. There were booths out the back. After midnight Chantal came out in a long tartan skirt with a couple of punks on guitars. She was high or drunk and during the third song she crashed over one of the speakers and fell into the crowd.

I opened the French doors onto the balcony. Ray kept his ferns out here, plus a stack of tiles and plaster acanthus leaves he collected from the antiques market. A train passed, grinding the metal with a gassy friction. Down on the footpath below, people were heads and shoulders, sometimes a swinging bag or a peculiar gait. The silver cobbled road followed the weave of the train track.

Ernesto and Ray came home together. There were both in shorts and sweaty-looking. They'd been to the gym. Ernesto asked if I felt okay after last night and Ray asked if I had found a new book to read. We moved into the kitchen and Ray opened the freezer, pulling out his box of frozen chopped fruit, his box of tricks. Across the courtyard, the woman worked in the office alone.

Ernesto opened a cupboard full of spirits and pushed bottles back and forth until he found a blue bottle of Bombay Sapphire Gin. He watched Ray throwing fruit into the blender then pulled down some handblown glasses. Ray poured in a slug of gin. I looked at the grey dog lying in the corner, gazing at his masters.

'What happened to you last night?' Ernesto said. 'I came out and you weren't dancing anymore. I'm glad I gave you a set of keys.'

Though I rubbed hard with nail polish remover, the stamp from the club had sunken into my skin and barely faded. On the way home there had been a bunch of skinheads under the bridge. Laughter and frightening German words. I'd walked the long way home in the half-light.

'Oh, I lost track of it all. And Chantal took a dive into the audience.'

'Yes, she's not usually so trashed.'

Ray looked at him obliquely and it was a look that I couldn't understand. Between us, some sort of misreading had become inoperable. I had lost the path to him, and Ray's interest in me had to sluice through Ernesto.

They had a small convertible Fiat parked under the railway bridge in a weedy lot with a chain-wire gate. Ray was a tireless driver whose overconfidence had caused a string of crashes. I watched his satisfaction as the roof folded back in a black concertina. This was the car they'd bought from Ernesto's sister and it still had Italian plates. Ernesto opened his door and I climbed into the back seat.

But whatever Ray was on was still making a mess of his face. Today the lines were harsh and his skin had a hollow tone as though its irrigation were poor. The car swung over the cobbles making a ruck-ruck-ruck sound and we left the onion-topped tower of Alexanderplatz in our wake. We swooped over the bridge through Schlossplatz then over the second arm of the river. Ray changed lanes recklessly through the office blocks, skidding past the Holocaust Memorial until he rounded the tail of the Brandenburg Gates and took the road through the Tiergarten.

Here walkers trailed along twin fronts of massive linden trees, pushing prams, carrying balloons, chatting arm in arm. Inside the paths wound over and around each other and I knew there was a sun-drenched patch where Ray and Ernesto's crowd lazed on their Thai sarongs reading after work, or entertaining their adored dogs. Halfway down the stretch we swerved around Hitler's marker, a golden angel atop a tall, staunch column. She spread her arms and wings, casting her spells over his maligned descendants.

Out of town Ray drove faster as the road widened and the traffic thinned. A couple of times he crossed lanes badly, cutting off another driver who honked his horn. Ernesto didn't flinch. I almost grabbed Ray's shoulder and once a plea escaped me. *Ray! Will you watch out!* The stuffed dog scenario came to mind and I glimpsed a metal wreck and body parts on the emergency lane, with men trying the jimmy the mulch apart. It might have been Ray's stormy circumvention of what was coming to him, but I closed my eyes and counted down to the turn-off.

We parked in a cleared section above the lake. During the War plump, golden-locked children had come to frolic on the pontoons, while their fathers shed their uniforms and stepped into bathing trunks. The big men swept into the navy water, hoisting their children's torn souls into the glittering air with its faint odour of smoke. How could these giggling children ratify the grisly turn of the continent? We gathered our bags and tramped along steps cut into the land. The lake's dampness rose on the air. We reached the bathing area with its long concrete path linking stretches of pebbled beach, each one possessing a bathing facility the War had left untouched. We walked to the last section where there were several groups of couples and every so often a lone reader basking naked in the sunlight.

Ray's eyes roved over the shoreline and his shoulders began to relax. He shook his hair and waved at me to follow him. Incorrigible Ernest went off to the showers and I watched Ray choose a spot and throw down his towel. He pulled off his T-shirt and unbuttoned his shorts. I sat down a little way from him.

'You don't mind if I go straight in, do you? I'm dying for a swim. This week has been hell at work.'

His boxers dropped to the ground and he walked calmly to the water's edge, not a twinge of self-consciousness. His buttocks clenched as the water rose over his thighs. He took a dive and began swimming.

I rolled over my belly and felt the stones prodding my breasts and thighs. I listened to Ray's slow strokes on the water. I knew this would be my last visit here, my last visit to see Ray forever. We all knew this. I tasted the gin lining the back of my throat and wondered what it had been like to wake up after the punnet of sleeping pills. To see the glazed afternoon as it had been before. To look over and see Ernesto's sticky eyes and the vomit on the bed.

The sun bore down hard on my burnt skin. I sat up and saw how far Ray had gone. His arm was hooked around an orange buoy and he was talking to another man paddling up to him. I didn't realise it was Ernesto until they began to kiss. It was a long, tender kiss with Ray holding the other man's head with his free hand, massaging his scalp as though he were soothing the thoughts within. They held each other tightly, chest to chest, arms enfolded, until the kiss subsided.

I watched them as they came back. Ray was an able swimmer, though he slowed to match Ernesto's pace. When the water was thigh-high they both stood up, water running out of Ray's thick hair. They looked at each other's bodies for a moment before Ernesto removed a strand of seaweed from Ray's waist. They marched through the water towards me.

Back on the sand Ernesto threw himself on his belly in the sun and I watched the water dissolve on his skin. Ray pulled out a hardback copy of *Don Quixote*. The book was a favourite of his.

'I saw Kristof at the showers,' Ernesto said.

'Oh, really? Is he back then?'

'It seems so. He said the trip went very well.'

'We ought to plan next January before it gets too late, you know. Celeste, how about joining us?'

As they chatted I began to remove my clothing. I felt embarrassed, even as Ray squinted at his book. The sun slanted directly upon us. I watched two other men tussling near the orange buoy and they seemed gingerly crafted, not unlike the words Ray had just spoken to me. They also drew together to embrace. I looked back at my brother's pale body as I walked into the water. The stones were slippery, the waves full of reeds.

The Cliffs of Bandiagara

A woman, her son, her boyfriend and a trader drive north to Mali to interview a musician for an English magazine. The woman is a freelance journalist, the man a photographer. She does not know that the musician is sick and leaving for a concert in Denmark in a matter of days. The interview has been arranged, or half-arranged, by a man in London whose French is not good, who thinks he has spoken to the right person in Bamako. The land is flat and soundless with her history manifest in adobe mosques crumbling along the bloodied slave routes, and painted *Boulangerie* signs in villages where commendable baguettes are sold. The road is a silver spear. The days are dense contracts between these four people.

Between the messy, unscripted towns there are baobabs. Once, the boy makes them stop the car on the side of the road. The engine tickers. The boy has a new front tooth that has come down crooked, which his mother intends to have fixed. The boy leaps onto the dust and declares he is running to the tree, the *bow-oh-bab* tree, that one there, and he begins to elbow the dry air and his sneakers produce orange puffs. The woman had known there would be moments with the boy.

'Let him go,' the man says, stretching his legs and focussing his camera on the tree's distant barrel and arms. The man comes from a coastal West African city, he has been her lover for five months.

The boy grows smaller and smaller, a wafting on the scrub, almost bodiless. The woman watches. The boy once popped his tongue into her mouth, but she knows it was copied from some guy she was seeing. Because it pleased her, this mix of animal and man, she told no one. She wonders, when her son turns back to the group by the jeep, what he feels when his eyes fall upon her: slim, in jeans, wearing a short T-shirt. Will he recall this scene when he is a man, staring back at some woman he's decided to love?

The trader, who is named Cissé, remains in the car. He is dressed in a clean shift and cradles his head. At least once a day Cissé claims he has malaria.

247

Cissé has them stop outside a city he says he knows well. It is Sikasso; they have just driven for miles and miles over rucks of sand. He says they should first buy their baguettes *ici*, pointing to a stall where a girl lies on her arm asleep. The photographer does not like to follow Cissé's recommendations. He is not convinced the trader will be of any use to them on this journey, and dislikes the singsong of Cissé's French. Instead the woman, who once lived in Paris, sees the irony of perfect baguettes under her arm and grimy notes with a northern figurehead flattened on the counter. She lifts herself back into the jeep and gives a heel of bread to the boy.

Cissé leads them to a place where he says there is excellent sheep meat. They are installed on benches in a hot back room and given four bottles of Coke that sit in pools. The green walls are smeared with handprints to shoulder height. The prints are vigorous, a record of past feasts.

A platter of mutton bones piled high is served by a man in a grubby shirt.

In the neighbourhood the blond boy is chased by other children and his flat hair is touched. He begs Cissé to tell him how to say, *Don't touch me. Please.* Cissé, who is a vulgar man, more vulgar than his companions know, tells him to repeat this in local language: *My mother, she is horny.*

———

In the morning a dog attacks Cisse on his way back from the mosque. The reddish animal lunges out from behind a shed, sinking canines into his tendons and tearing the surface flesh. It is only just dawn and the sellers are on the move along the roads. A busty girl comes up and he does not understand her dialect, so they speak in French. Cissé is petrified, his temples are wet. The girl shoos away the growling dog and brings Cissé to her room where she raises his torn ankle and pours warm salted water over it, then stinging alcohol. She is young and her kindness makes Cissé wish for his wife. He hobbles back to the hotel where the others are asleep. He walks through the compound. He asks a woman bent over sweeping for some tea, but the woman scowls.

Inside the room the boy lies in a netted cot that is just longer than his outstretched body. He sleeps on his back, motionless. The couple made love in the dark of morning and now lie in repose. The photographer awakens. He covers their bodies and stares up into the netting. He wants to put his fingers inside of the woman next to him but he does not want her consciousness alive or her body animated. He lies still. His cock is soft and he cups it in his hand. There was a woman from his city a few years ago who had fallen pregnant with his child. It happened just when his love for her had begun to blaze. Each day he had photographed every region of her body. Her manly shoulders and short humpy breasts, the knuckles of her spine as she crouched to wash her sex, fingering herself as she squatted. But the young woman came home one afternoon and said she'd had an abortion. Said they were living in a bubble. She left him for an American journalist who was later shot. What he was told was this: the man had arranged an interview with an opposition leader in a nearby country and drove up to the politician's house. A police officer put his pistol through the window and discharged.

If he concentrates he can still cry for her. He used to believe that the photographs of her body were his most intimate images, but his work has improved and now he sees that his obsession made her hidden to him, and these photos were bereft of craft. In one she has a white cloth knotted around her neck. She has a boxy forehead and she turns away, her body twists; she does not belong to him. She stands before a half-built house on the salt flats out of town. It was not the story he had seen or wished to tell, but it had emerged. He has learned that much of his work is subterranean, that he must lie in wait. Recently, he was told that she has given birth to a daughter.

The singer that his new girlfriend is to interview was groomed by one of the icons of Malian music, a man who lived for decades within the embrace of the West. At 60, he grew tired of concerts in Bercy and the clamour of people and the breasts of white women. He dreamed of irrigating the barren fields around his village with channelled well water; he heard the sound of gushing water in every moment. The old man severed his record contract and returned home to his wives, and his absence left a vacuum that was filled by the young disciple. This man, in the music world, quickly became known for his immense talent and rudeness. Many journalists, given fraudulent directions, have failed to negotiate the dusty warren of Bamako's backstreets.

—

After breakfast she leads him to the shower recess where a trickle falls over their necks. He rises to her, they grapple and laugh, he pierces her and knows the shower taps are grazing her back, but she likes the pain; he has seen this. He dislikes her biting, he prefers fluid lovemaking.

The child watches them return to the room half-dressed. She tells him to brush his teeth. He is disgusted that the child enters the bathroom where they have just fucked, then his disgust separates from him. It's her child. His children will never be subjected to this. In fact, their affair is instructing him how to correct his life in advance. Looking ahead he suspects they will last a few more months before the sex is spent and the boy becomes paramount to her. When the boy goes out into the sunlight, he savages her lips.

Outside they see the boy is speaking with a man on a bicycle who is wearing a wooden mask. The mask is elongated, chalky white with sea-blue dots; inverted triangular incisions for eyes and two hare ears curling forward. Standing astride the bicycle, the man holds the mask to his face, tilting down to the boy's captivation. He talks in muffled phrases. The woman paces over to the man who can only be a seller. She does not know that the cyclist is the brother of the busty girl who bathed Cissé's ankle that morning. Cissé, by way of thanks, had told the girl he was travelling with a white woman when he saw a pile of artefacts on the floor. He had given her the name of the hotel.

'You want buy? *Tu veux acheter?*' the hare man is saying to the boy.

His mother holds his shoulders, pulls him back. The large-headed man frightens her with his turbulent voice. Cissé watches from a stool in an alcove. The photographer thinks that perhaps there is a shot if the woman and child would move away. The hare man on a bicycle as a mythical outlaw. He sees that his woman is braless, accessible; she has told him she can be no other way. Now he sees Cissé staring at her small evident breasts. The hotel manager flies out and chases the cyclist back onto the street.

The woman drives. They reach the outskirts of the town and head forth along a sealed road into the scrub. There are fewer baobabs and ruins in this area, and they have brought bottles of bright orange Fanta and grilled peanuts in newspaper cones. After an hour she stops the car on the side of the road. There is waist-high grass and she goes off to pee, unzipping her jeans as she walks away from the jeep. She is gone a while and her lover grows edgy, thinking of snakes. He looks out but she has crouched down and he can't see her. It is not concern that he feels, but exasperation with her flights. She emerges from the grass calling his name, tells him to bring his camera. Leads him along the trampled column she has made through the growth. At a distance from the car she pulls off her T-shirt and throws herself down in the grass, topless in her jeans.

'Photograph me,' she says. 'Photograph me.'

He captures her arms on the scratchy pressed halo, her plum nipples and the contortions of her face. Her skin is a shimmering, colourless garment. He brings her torso into focus, thinking of her organs overlapping in shades of plum and red. She wants him to straddle her but he will not. She pulls him to her and their faces are ill-aligned, bitter.

In the car, the boy empties a Fanta bottle and hands it to Cissé, who throws it wide into the grass. The boy asks Cissé why he wears a dress like a woman.

—

Bamako rises like a defeated cloud before them. The heat repels them, traffic pushes them to and fro. Cissé, who claimed he lived here as an adolescent, tells him to swing right. 'No, swing left! *À gauche! Ici!*' The photographer drives now; his lover is solemn at the window and the boy asleep. Scant directions were sent by the London office but Cissé says they are all wrong, says that the musician she is to interview lives at the opposite end of town from where they are headed. The photographer mentions the quartier of his colleague Sami, married to a French air hostess, where they have been invited to stay. Cissé's hands fly out again – *'À gauche! À gauche!'* – and it is clear that he is clueless. The woman shakes her head. Cissé finally sits back, smiling out of the window at the clutter of bars and dwindled Pan-African monuments along the boulevards. The boy wakes, climbs over the front seat, settles into his mother's arms.

Sami's house is a cool bungalow with concrete support struts throughout the main room. The front veranda has been screened off and writhes with contented plants. They are seated out here. Sami's house-girl serves them duty-free pastis from France before bringing out a round of local beer. Cissé's hands fidget between his legs. He drinks a bottle of Sprite. The photographer knows Sami from a major exhibition, held in Bamako, where both of their images were praised. Sami runs a gallery that he would like to support. The woman feels her lover is distant from her now, even inconsiderate; she sees he is relieved to be in different company. He laughs hard at Sami's jokes. He asks of Sami's wife, the French air hostess Kitty, who is doing the Paris-Rio route this week.

She takes her son to the bathroom so she can look through the house.

She sees the couple are childless. She sees that Kitty has a love of antique beads, which are arranged on coffee tables; that she collects the indigo-stained cloth they weave here; that she admires the blocky Dogon horsemen who ride across their porous constellations. Kitty, too, has perhaps read of the reaches of the Dogon universe, their preternatural knowledge of the galaxies above. There is a framed photo of a European woman with a fringe that brushes the top of her sunglasses. There are prints of Sami's work on the walls. They are tight, incised portraits of Malians. She wonders if Kitty is fleshy and broad, a vivid juxtaposition to Sami's work. She wonders how it would be to spend most of the day in the air, groundless.

Her son is hungry. In the kitchen she asks the young girl for *une banane*, absurdly happy she has produced a riff of French without thought. Her son peels the banana and eats it. The girl's hand moves over his blond straight hair. The boy says the words Cissé told him and her hand jerks back.

In the evening a woman named Maryam comes to Sami's house. She is a local singer and she knows the musician the journalist has come to interview. She knows him well. She knows his compound, it is on the other side of Bamako and it is very difficult to find. But she will show them. Do they know he has a concert in Denmark this week?

Maryam's hair is shaped into two splendid coils that entwine at the back of her head. The boy wants to touch these elaborate, necking snakes. He kneels on the couch beside her, his hands reaching through the air. Maryam arches her neck in his direction.

The photographer has spent the afternoon speaking of his current project with Sami. It is a political work with an Algerian colleague, which will document the offspring of the generals executed during the coup in his country. Now he is fascinated by the tilting of Maryam's body. The asymmetry of her face and shoulders and one breast below the other, its form compressed. He wants to study the itinerary of Maryam's movements. He feels a transaction is already in place. He feels this sense of exchange with the best of his subjects.

Maryam sang last night until the early hours in a low-ceilinged bar in central Bamako where she has followers. Maryam is tired of speech, though she enjoys the white starfish of the boy's hands straying over her neck and upper arms, they are cool.

When Kitty is abroad Maryam stays with Sami. Her hair lotion and face cream and brassieres and lacy thongs are in a locked cabinet in the maid's room. A few dresses are at the back of the house-girl's wardrobe. Maryam wants to make love with Sami before her body falls to the bed and her throat is gripped by the heavy hand that troubles her dreams. Sami's tongue will render her blind and lifeless. Maryam lifts herself. She walks barefoot to Sami's bedroom and closes the door.

Sami's gardener has taken their bags from the jeep and placed them at the foot of a double bed in a converted garage at the side of the property. The room is narrow and a ceiling fan makes low swoops. Sami announces that Kitty's brother is an anthropologist, Philippe, who had worked in the north when it was safe, and they should disregard *ses affaires*. When Sami bids them goodnight the woman tugs off her clothes and walks naked to the attached outhouse, where her lover hears the smattering of water on tiles. She does not call him. He and the boy look at each other. The boy stares into his eyes in the absorbent way of children. The man lies down on the bed.

The boy throws his pillow to the floor. He cradles himself on top of the sheets and turns to the wall.

When the woman comes out still dripping the man is already dreaming: he has seen her vanish into blades of grass; he has left the metallic vehicle behind and the calls of the others.

She opens his trousers and makes him erect, bounds on and off him, brings him into her gut, spears herself with him.

He is ashamed. Her fury does not break, even when he has burst inside of her. He thinks of her body stained with tears and dust. For the first time he sees an image of her that he wants to make. Then, when their bellies are still joined, he feels the indentation of her touch reaching through his skin, making a passage within him. She has felt it too. She looks into him. He wants to fly beyond himself and watch their grace from the other end of the room. He wants to roll her thin body in dirt and hear the words fall from his mouth, *I will cherish you.*

—

After prayers Cissé follows a busy road leading to a boulevard that crosses the city. The wound from the dog bite sends arrows up his leg as he walks. He raises his shift and looks at the jagged skin. A woman passes, a tier of folded cloth on her head. She clucks her tongue as she rolls by. Cissé releases the shift onto the ground. He does not yet feel fever. Cissé's life began in the river country to the west. Though he told them he knew the city well he has never lived here. Delivered by an older brother to his uncle's compound in Bamako, it was thought that Cissé would gather fare money from passers-by, for one of the uncle's many buses that roped through the town. But on Cissé's first night the uncle made use of the boy in a violent way, then whipped his buttocks with his belt. Cissé was 12 years old when he ran away to the south.

Cissé cannot remember the face of his mother.

He reaches the main boulevard where minibuses fly past and cars stream at speed across all the lanes. People in the buses sit hunched forward and he sees a goat in a woman's arms. When he had run away to the south the vehicle had lurched before a piglet squealing over the road, then careered into a ditch where it lay upended. A large wailing woman had pinned Cissé beneath her. This woman pushed his bones together until he was an airless shape. At night he still wakes with the pressure of this woman upon him.

A ticket boy hanging out of a minibus waves bills in his face and urges him to get on. Calls him a stupid shepherd when he just stands there.

He sits down. The bars and shops all along here are French. He drinks another Sprite and it is warmer than the one they gave him at the house. He eats a croissant which tastes of oily salt. He throws it down and asks the girl to get him a sweet cake.

At first Cissé thought that the white woman was interested in him as a man. He had worn a checked shirt under his shift, purchased from the Indian stalls. He had sprayed on perfume when he brought his wares to her house. The boy played outside but she disregarded his wild running.

When she asked him if he could be their guide on this trip he said, 'Of course, Bamako, *je la connais.*'

Cissé had told them he had family to stay with in Bamako. But he will never go back to his uncle's house here. When a beggar comes up he asks him where he can buy something that will ease the pain in his foot. Something fast, something cheap. The fever has started in his spine. He follows this man into the back streets.

She awakes thinking they should never have come here together. She looks at Sami's slow fan turning. Their skins do not touch. She knows he wants to photograph Maryam's superb rolling body. She has been there when it has flared in him, the desire to approach subjects for his work. Once, two women in a slum bar drunkenly began to kiss. He bought them beers and asked the women if he could snap them. It was arousing, a courting. They were young with bright white teeth. She had watched his dance around them as tongues flickered, as cheeks and breasts were touched. She had asked him if he'd had a hard-on. He'd said his work never made him hard. He said it wasn't that at all.

She didn't believe this. Watching these two women with their bold dresses and market sandals had made her slippery wet.

He had produced an astounding sepia image of two dissolving profiles. The magnificence of closed eyelids; granular planes beneath the promontories of cheeks. The connection of a kiss. She could never have foreseen this vision.

She regrets flailing on the grass yesterday, begging him to photograph her. She is so desperate to enter the canon of his work. Flattened on the burning grass, the sunlight a vicious bath on her torso, she had thought she was granting him an image. But as she lay there she realised she had no understanding of what he sought, of how it became disinterred. He had clicked a few times, even bent to her, but his eyes had refuted her and grown annoyed. He had not even wanted her sex. Today she will ruin those negatives.

She rubs her spit onto his fingers and pushes them inside of her, feels them enliven.

As they fuck she thinks of Maryam's nude body. She thinks of Kitty's photograph turned to the wall. She thinks of Maryam's purple vulva. She climaxes in a gradual, head-kicking way, feels herself spurt onto him; he licks her face and she feels choked.

She thinks that Cissé hasn't turned up, even though he said he would come after morning prayers.

The boy wakes when her lover goes off to shower and she wonders if, in the future, she can make amends for the way she has half-forgotten his father and has had a series of men. She still thinks there is a window where she can. The boy does not pull across the netting and come to her. He lies staring upward, little legs bent and hair she cannot bear to cut straying on the pillow.

The boy tells her that Cissé was bitten by a dog.

—

Sami provides them with a young man who will lead them through the city to where the musician lives. The interview is today. The photographer looks for Maryam down the hall where Sami's bedroom is located. But the bedroom door is closed. Sami wears an indigo blue shirt with ironing creases and embroidered filigree on the pockets. The photographer imagines this is a shirt that Maryam has given him recently. Sami does not speak of Maryam and their conversation resumes where it had left off before Maryam arrived at the house. Sami says he is working with a subject today, a woman who was kidnapped as a girl by the Tuaregs in the north, and held for nine years on the rim of the Sahara. He says he met this woman selling dried fish, that there was a captive isolation in her eyes. The photographer is listening, he has often seen these sentiments within his subjects' eyes; his passion lies in the extrication of this.

The woman interrupts the two men talking and says that if Cissé doesn't turn up they will go without him, and good luck to him. She will manage with her stilted French. Her equipment bag is at the door with her microphone and her battery is charged.

The boy is grumpy and will not eat his food.

The woman's parts are swollen and burning and her lover extends his hand with long fingers and bitten-down nails across the table. He rests it on her forearm. The textures of their two skins meet.

257

Maryam appears in the hallway. Her hair is unmoved, the same weighted sculpture as it was last night, and she has little yellow balls of sleep in the corners of her eyes. Her body sways under her kaftan and she comes to the table and folds herself next to the boy, asks him if she can share his breakfast. Her breath is thick and stale. She and the boy eat up mango slices, then divide a roll of fleecy white bread with groundnut paste. Maryam asks the boy if she can touch his hair and he says, 'Yes.'

At the gate, Cissé is leaning against a mango tree in the shade.

—

The photographer drives out onto a main road. The woman and her son are beside him. Sami's guide sits in the back seat with Cissé. It feels strange to be driving again after being static in the house. Sami has said that they can return there to sleep, but the photographer does not like to turn back, ever. He feels uncomfortable about the violence of their rapport this morning in Sami's converted garage. It feels like his come is still seeping out of him, as though there is a leak he cannot stop into his jeans, onto the seat. He touches his balls and his pants are dry. He wants to tell her, *We don't have to be like this.*

He remembers in the beginning she asked him to enter her when she was bleeding and this disgusted him, though he had done it, then watched his red member subsiding on her stained belly. He wants to tell her, *This can stop. We can have something other than this.*

The photographer looks into the mirror and asks Cissé how his family was. Cissé replies that they were well and happy to see him. From a polythene shopping bag he draws a hand towel and passes it to the woman in the front seat.

'From my mother,' Cissé says to her.

The woman thanks him. Then she turns around and says, 'Were you bitten by a dog? My son woke up saying you were bitten by a dog. Is that true?'

Cissé sinks back, laughs. He knows they would take him to some clinic and leave him there. Then the injections would start. The nurses, they would worry him.

'No, madam, that is not true.'

She tells him she doesn't need his help for the interview.

The dust of the city rises into the sky. There are monuments that look like bones scraped together, and many beaten-up cars. The minibuses scissor between them. There is a river of heads along the footpath.

When they have been driving for an hour Sami's helper indicates a mud-bricked wall where the road narrows, each side banked with orange sand. For the last thirty minutes they have passed along many streets like this. The man steps down from the jeep and walks away. The wall has an opening onto a courtyard where they see three women sitting on plastic chairs, a girl bent over sweeping, a stunted tree.

—

They follow the musician's youngest wife into the broad house, along hallways and past rooms where they hear murmuring or glimpse sleeping children spreadeagled on the floor. There is a pounding somewhere, a long wooden pestle driving cassava and yam into a pulp, massaged around a mortar by swift hands. The journalist knows this much. She smells sauce boiling away, thinks it is made with dried fish or smoky crushed prawns. With the bitterness of leaves, baobab leaves perhaps. She checks the boy is following them. The photographer's equipment bag whistles against his thigh. The walls are bare and powdery, an impermanent substance. Her nipples contract with the slight chill, she feels it cross her shoulders. On the sleeve of the CD they gave her, the whites of the musician's eyes have been unrealistically enhanced.

The musician is hooked up to a drip in one of the dim back rooms. He lies on a mattress on the floor and does not respond when his wife calls him. She raises her voice. The man snuffles and lifts himself onto an elbow.

The room smells of illness, even shit. Apart from the mattress and drip stand, there is a chest of drawers piled with papers and rubbish, a mound of clothes on the cement floor and a bucket. The musician wears a turban and his black shirt ripples into his skin. He looks at them. The photographer wants to pull out his camera.

The musician's wife tells them that her husband has typhus and they should not go too close. She says he is catching the plane to Denmark this evening and clucks her tongue. He has a big concert in two days. She says she has to cook now and the boy should come with her outside. The journalist tells the boy to go with her.

The couple take respectful steps further into the room and settle their bags on the floor. The journalist introduces herself. The photographer kneels to his bag, changes a lens. The metal rims slide together.

She cannot decide whether she should crouch or stand to take her notes. She sits cross-legged on the floor, opening her notepad, running over the points she has made and the brief her editor gave her, months back. She has been warned not to mention the old guy, the mentor. They are at loggerheads now. She prepares her microphone and recorder.

The photographer wants to capture the stench of sickness. He sees maps of inky colour. The man's mouth opens and it is a tender rose cage.

The woman is distracted by the way the photographer has begun to move. She studies the musician, looking for the image that she will see printed, framed on a wall, far from here. She has worked with photographers before, but it usually comes after the interview, when the subject is fatigued and barriers have fallen. She wants to tell the photographer to pull back, to give her some space, but he has seen something and she no longer exists, none of them do, it is just the light flare on a chemical-laced scroll, the unalterable narrative of exposure.

She says her lover's name. Asks him to leave the room and let her do her work.

The musician watches their discomfort.

She changes position, sitting back on her haunches. There are chinks of midday light scattered close to the wall beneath the half-closed shutters. The musician rolls a joint, lights up and inhales a couple of times, tugging on the tube so that the drip stand shivers. He holds out the smoking thing towards her. She rises on her knees and takes it.

She sits back, pulls up her spine, inhales.

—

The photographer hears the boy's voice out in the courtyard between buildings. He is thinking of Maryam and her body smeared by the night of lovemaking. Maryam's stale smell runs along his nerves. Like his lover in the past, he wants to photograph her crouched, rinsing her body, an intimate ellipse.

Cissé sits in the shade on one of the plastic chairs, given to him by a woman with lavish gold earrings. He has a chewing stick in his mouth. The musician's youngest wife settles the boy by her side as she squats on a stool over her pots. The boy asks where her children are, so that he can play. He asks her over and over again. Cissé guesses that she is childless or has recently lost a child. He knows the musician makes her work hard for him, harder than his senior wives. He thinks the musician has given her an illness that the doctor said has damaged her womb.

The young wife slaps the face of the white child.

The photographer hears the boy crying out in the daylight. He throws his bag over his shoulder and hurries on. He sees the boy nursing his cheek and the young woman storms into the kitchen rooms.

The boy hugs him hard and a knot rises in the photographer's throat. He was abandoned in a boarding school in England when he was four. In the summer his mother, who was a diplomat, never arrived. He was farmed out to older couples who devised games, who lived in silent houses.

'Come with me,' the photographer says to him.

In a corner of the blue-painted veranda the photographer deposits his bag and notices an overturned calabash and a four-legged cooking stool. He places them before the intersecting blue planes; they are cooled by the reflected light. He sets up his Hasselblad, inching around the composition until the tension peaks between objects. He shows the boy the viewfinder, makes him listen to the collapse of the shutter.

He asks the boy to go to the stool. The grooved calabash sits overturned by his dirty knees and his cascade of blond hair falls sweaty around his face. There are shadowy rings under the child's eyes he has never noticed. The boy sits with hands locked.

He tells the boy more about the camera, given to him by a German photographer before he returned to Berlin. The man had been called Henning. He remembers this man had one night invited him to a beach bar, and they had taken their beer bottles onto the sand. There the German had pulled him to his body and kissed him as he fought. A strong, straight-backed man, he had released his shoulders and walked off into the darkness.

The boy jumps up and pins a gecko to the wall.

He looks down at the box of the camera, rubs his thumb over one of the sides. He does not feel the photographs he took of the musician are worthy. There was no quickening, no communion. He thinks that to photograph his lover he will have to hurt her. Then revive her, resuscitate her. He feels love in his groin, a passion.

The boy shows him the gecko in his palm. He pulls up his shirt and entices the gecko onto his tummy. It adheres there, pulsing. 'Snap me! Snap me!' he says. The boy calls over to Cissé to see. Cissé's chair is tilted against a wall but he is watching. He throws up a hand that fans the air.

The journalist comes out of the doorway into the courtyard. Cissé sees the other women look across at her as an unkempt idol from Europe, they know the musician will go there and fuck women like this.

She locates her son and her lover on the veranda. She pauses, observes the man kneeling, the boy holding up his shirt. All along she tried to get the musician to talk, while the man released meagre answers. The musician has suggested they follow him to the airport and finish up the interview in the VIP room inside. She isn't sure, but perhaps she heard the boy cry out before.

'What are you doing to him?' she says to the photographer.

The boy sees her and begins to whimper. She rushes to him and his embrace feels awful, an endless pledge. He will not tell her what the matter is.

'I think you can put that away now,' she says, indicating the camera between her lover's legs.

The young wife slips outside and tends to her pots. She gives the journalist an extraordinary smile and says they are welcome to eat. She says her baobab leaf stew is the best in the quartier. She invites them to sit down and commence washing their hands. Cissé wanders over.

As they eat in a wordless group the musician passes through the compound and the journalist sees the majestic man at his full height. He is dressed in smart jeans and a printed shirt, wears black wraparound sunglasses and carries nothing. The wives on the plastic chairs watch him move. He speaks to no one. They hear a jeep revving outside the walls.

At the airport they have no access to the private lot where they can see the musician's jeep is parked. The journalist shows her press card, which is looked over and handed back. None of the guards will tell them where the famous man has gone. The interview is suspended and they buy iced yoghurt sachets from a seller on the street.

—

The escarpment of Bandiagara rises above the Sahel plains, pocked with the pillbox granaries of the Dogon people. Here, the god Amma gave life to the brown clay of the earth and produced twins called Nommo, hermaphrodite fish-like beings. To establish gender, the twins were circumcised. The foreskin of the male became a black and white lizard; from the excised clitoris and labia minora of the female, the first scorpion was born.

That night they drive across this highland. They've been told it is reasonably safe now. They have visited Mopti, a Venice on the banks of the Niger. They stood before the adobe mosque with her crest of vertical fingers. Here, the journalist is stared at in a different way. Her boldness wavers and she wants to cover herself.

They have little money left and the photographer's half-brother in the UK sends them a transfer. She has almost finished her travel funds for the job.

They are going to drive all night, hopefully make it to the southern border.

The photographer is at the wheel. He feels relaxed, the woman is calmer at this altitude, far away from Bamako. The landscape is a lunar surface. The road is singular, it drops and climbs over glades tessellated with glowing rocks. He would be content to stand out there in the wind, and speak of the arc of these days with her.

The woman's hand rests on her belly. She recognises changes in her breasts and skin and knows he has left his seed within her. He has told her there are twins in his family. Conceived here, in this land where twins embody the cardinal forces of the heavens. She thinks: this has to stop when we get back to the coast. She will expel these beads inside of her. And yet, perhaps she will not. Perhaps she will speak to him and they will allow these beings to unfurl.

As they drive Cissé sees two men walking, they are wearing tall wooden masks that reach into the night sky. Their robes are flattened against their bodies. It is clear that they are spirits roving the earth.

Cissé's ankle sends a charge the length of his leg, into his spine.

The photographer stops the car on an open stretch, he wants to walk with her. The couple wander ahead along the lightless road. The wind enwraps them – it is stronger than he thought – it whirs and vibrates. She turns around to look at the car tilted on the verge.

'Why? Why?' she says. 'We must go back.' She is not thinking of the sleeping boy, she is thinking that this place is too immense for them, too primordial. She wants the enclosure of the vehicle, the boy within her limbs. She would rather endure smaller things.

She remembers that the Dogon people discovered a hidden star, a blind star, using knowledge sifted down from the Egyptians, knowledge that the Westerners pored over and found a way to dismantle. And yet she knows it remains there, part of a universe beyond. They stand awhile beneath an infinite net of constellations, galaxies printed upon galaxies, a celestial harvesting.

A Woman Told Me This

A woman told me this: when her lover died she went to the church and sat in the second-to-last pew, where she knew she would attract little attention for they had been colleagues for a stretch. At the front of the church stood the man's wife with her frayed curls, and the two sons whose foibles and brushes with the law and opulent tattoos she knew as intimately as those of the children she'd never had. Did she feel robbed of a life? He had told her that she would. That one day it would seize up inside of her, the wish to uproot all he had ever planted in her, every gasp and cell and flourish of his liquid and the burning of her skin and parts. He had told her she would want to eviscerate her own bowels to be emptied of him, and remove her heart from its safe cage like a wild native, splashing it to the ground with its torn tubes. Her lover had been a dramatic, vital man who liked to toy with their deepest entwined currents, especially as he stroked her hair in bed, or his knuckles drew across her belly.

The woman told me these things, adding that the embrace of this man was the only thing she would take from this earth.

Love is an Infinite Victory

They decided to rent out the farmhouse to the daughter of their best friends. The young woman had been a charming, mischievous child always twisted around her mother's legs, and had studied agriculture before moving away to Jordan to work on irrigation projects. She and her Jordanian husband were now expecting their first child.

As best as they could, they removed mementos and personal artefacts from the rooms, using their son's upstairs study to store crates that were sealed just in case. Photo albums, treasured books, favourite kitchenware and artwork, along with both of their slim wardrobes, went into these wooden boxes. At first the husband had wanted to put them in a disused shed on the property, but they decided their effects might more likely be prone to fire, damp or theft.

They handed over the keys to the slight young woman with her swollen belly just beginning the show under her dress, and the handsome man with thick waves of black hair and erudite glasses. They felt reassured in the face of such purity, that their house would be looked after and loved.

—

They moved back to Paris where they had begun their lives together many years ago, feeling denuded and carefree as students. They had always kept this tiny apartment, and it was a good thing too. When their own son was at university he had stayed here, and it had served through the periods when their marriage had been strained, when either had gone there to breathe and revive, sometimes taking lovers there to fuck and discard, for they were bound to one another.

Free of decor, with its squeaky herringbone wooden floors and small rooms, the apartment showed no record of their lives, so they were as guests. They resumed heady, rudimentary lovemaking on the mattress their son had left there, especially through the unencumbered mornings when the city revolved and banged and wailed around them. The man found that his erections were sturdy and ongoing; the woman's parts were bathed and her breasts heaved in fiery peaks.

They were so grateful for this, crooning into necks and crevasses. They had not expected this rising.

In the afternoons the man wrote his articles and the woman strolled in the park, or all the way to the river from where she would call him, describing people or birds.

—

Halfway through the summer the young Jordanian husband called the phone that the older man had left on the kitchen counter. He and his wife were in bed together and the call was ignored. That afternoon the young man called again.

He said that his wife had lost the baby – the tiny girl had died inside of her – and they wished to leave the farmhouse. He said that his wife was broken and they could stay in that place no longer. She was coming home from the hospital tomorrow and they would return to the city. He was presently sleeping in a hotel.

He said they wanted no refund for the rent they had paid, just to be away from there. If there was a place they could leave the keys?

'Of course,' said the older man. 'I am so sorry –'

The call ended and the man resumed his work. When it was complete, he walked through the rooms of the apartment with its blank walls, and on one of the walls he placed his open palms and leaned his body weight and dropped his head. There were piles of clothing on chairs and cleaning implements grouped in a corner. He thought of the empty farmhouse with its verdant summer growth, the bird calls that rang out after dark and his wife slumbering beside him, how there were nights when there was a quickened tampering in his heart and he would go downstairs onto the terrace, feel the warm drifts from the woods like the hands that would take him.

Acknowledgments

The stories in *The Carnal Fugues* have been previously published in literary magazines and in three short story collections, *Pelt and Other Stories* (Indigo Dreams, U.K. 2014), *The Cartography of Others* (Unbound, U.K. 2018) and *Love Stories for Hectic People* (Reflex Press, U.K. 2021).

From *Pelt and Other Stories* (semi-finalist Hudson Prize, U.S.A.): 'Pelt', *Pretext*, U.K.; 'Nathalie', *The View From Here/Bookanista*, U.K.; 'The Coptic Bride', *Heat*, Australia; 'Young British Man Drowns in Alpine Lake'; 'Taxidermy', *A Tale of Three*, London/Paris/Berlin.

From *The Cartography of Others* (winner Eyelands Fiction Award, Greece; finalist People's Book Prize, UK 2020): 'Adieu, Mon Doux Rivage', finalist Short Fiction Prize, *Short Fiction* Issue 8, U.K.; 'The Wild Beasts of the Earth Will Adore Him', finalist Kingston Writing School Hilary Mantel International Short Story Competition, published in *What Lies Beneath* (Kingston University Press; U.K.); 'Three Days in Hong Kong', *Fugue II* (The Siren Press, London); 'The Book of Bruises', *Structo* Issue 14, U.K.; 'Magaly Park', (Pushcart nominated) *Gem Street: Collector's Edition* (Labello Press, Dublin); 'The Russian Girl', a version published in *The Lonely Crowd* Issue 4, Wales; 'Love and Death and Cell Division', *Ambit* Issue 222, U.K.; 'The Architecture of Humans', *Litro*; 'They Came from the East', finalist The Short Story Flash Fiction Competition, U.K.; 'Return from Salt Pond', *Two Thirds North*, Sweden; 'The Bamboo Furnace', *Southerly* Vol.75 No.3, Australia; 'The Sneeze'; 'Hôtel de Californie', *The Nottingham Review* Issue 1, U.K.; 'Pia Tortora', finalist Royal Academy/Pin Drop Short Story Award; 'The Cliffs of Bandiagara', finalist International Willesden Short Story Prize, *Willesden Herald: New Short Stories 9*, U.K.

From *Love Stories for Hectic People* (winner Best Short Story Collection, Saboteur Awards U.K. 2021): 'Genitalia', *Ambit* Issue 225, U.K.; 'Foundation Song'; 'As Simple as Water', Wigleaf Top 50, *The Collagist* (now *The Rupture*), U.S.A.; 'The Woman Whose Husband Died in a Climbing Accident', Wigleaf Top 50, *The Collagist* (now *The Rupture*), U.S.A.; 'Tabula Rasa', *Reflex Fiction*, U.K.; 'Life', *Flash Frontier*, N.Z.; 'The Mafia Boss Who Shot His Gay Son on a Beach', *Flash Fiction Magazine,* U.K.; 'A Young Man Reflects', *Literary Orphans*, U.S.A.; 'In Venice'; 'Asunder', Broadside Series, *Blue Five Notebook*, N.Z.; 'My Family', *Sonder Magazine*, U.K.; 'The Vineyard', *A Box of Stars Under the Bed*, National Flash Fiction Day Anthology, U.K.; 'Banking', *Strands Lit Sphere,* India; 'Fighters', *Sonder Magazine*, U.K.; 'The Temperature of Islands', *Lunch Ticket Review*, U.S.A.; 'Slaughter of the Innocents', *Jellyfish Review*; 'My Thoughts Concerning Letizia', *Moonpark Review*, U.S.A.; 'On Being Eaten Alive', *Fiction Pool/ The Amorist*, U.K.; 'Tokyo Frieze', *The Amorist*, U.K.; 'Trionfo di Pesce', *Jellyfish Review*; 'A Woman Told Me This', *Vestal Review*, U.S.A.; 'The Woman Who Previously Worked in the Louvre', *Connotations*, U.S.A.; 'Love is an Infinite Victory', *Ellipsis Zine/Flash Frontier*, U.K.

Thanks to my publisher Ed Wright of Puncher & Wattmann, for bringing my many stories together in such a wonderful way. Thanks to Dawn and Ronnie (Indigo Dreams, U.K.) for publishing *Pelt and Other Stories*. And to John Mitchinson (*The Cartography of Others*, Unbound U.K.) and David Borrowdale (*Love Stories for Hectic People*, Reflex Press, U.K.) where some of these stories were published.

Acknowledgment is made to the following copyright proprietors: Stephan Elliot, author of *Priscilla, Queen of the Desert*, (also to the producers of the musical and film). Edwin Marion Cox for the translation of Sappho's verse from *The Poems of Sappho: with Historical and Critical Notes, Translations and a Bibliography* (Williams and Norgate, London; Charles Scribner's Sons, 1924). Giacomo Meyerbeer for the aria 'Adieu, Mon Doux Rivage' from the opera *L'Africaine*, Act I. Epigraph quotation is from D.H. Lawrence's poem, 'Cruelty and Love'.

Eternal thanks to Hilary Mantel for her generous cover comment for *The Cartography of Others*, reproduced here. And also to Eric Akoto, Cathy Galvin, Irene Okojie, Michael Caines, Chika Unigwe, *Sabotage Reviews*. Enormous thanks to Bruce Pascoe, who published my first short story many years ago, for his wonderful cover comment for this book, and to Susan Johnson, whose writing I have long admired, for writing such wonderful words. Thanks to Michelle Elvy and Joanna Atherfold Finn for their comments and ongoing support.

Milton Keynes UK
Ingram Content Group UK Ltd.
UKHW011820131023
430526UK00001B/41